This book is dedicated to my husband;
the first person to believe in me.

Acknowledgements

Thank you first and foremost to the whole team at Choc Lit/Ruby Fiction for taking a chance on a crime thriller novel from a new author. That includes their wonderful tasting panel for putting my book forward for publication: Karen M, Hannah Mc, Hannah T, Susan D, Gillian C, Sally B, Els E, Yvonne G, Jenny K, Maureen W, Barbara P, Dimi E and Melissa B. I'm so glad you loved it!

Thanks also to my husband who has always given me the time and encouragement to write and who is the first reader of all my work, even the cringeworthy first drafts!

Chapter One

Officer Dean Matheson stands shivering against the cold night, trying not to look at the gruesome scene before him.

'Matheson? Get over here. If I have to look at this, you have to look,' says Detective Miller.

Dean moves closer to the tree the woman's body is swinging from. The strong wind has her dancing around like she's doing the jitterbug. The weather is threatening more snow and, although it's almost dawn, it's still pitch black out here in the woods. His colleagues, Officer Marty Swan and Sergeant Steve Dalkin, helpfully light up the woman's lifeless body with their flashlights. Dean wishes they wouldn't. He's going to have trouble forgetting the sight of her bulging tongue and puzzled expression next time he eats. It won't be the first meal he's been unable to eat, thanks to this job.

He makes himself look at her for a moment longer. He knows she won't be immediately recognisable to any of her family like this. If this was his wife Linda, he wouldn't want to have to remember her this way. But then Linda isn't speaking to him at the moment. He doesn't expect she'll stick around much longer now she knows about his affair, so there's little risk of him ever having to identify her if she's involved in an accident. Not that this was any accident. Discarded on its side under the woman's bare feet, he notices the stepladder she must have used to reach the branch she's hanging from.

As Miller takes notes nearby, Dean wonders where she got the ladder from and whether she carried it here herself or was given a lift by someone. Maybe she hitchhiked. There are no cars parked nearby apart from their police vehicles and an ambulance, so she certainly didn't drive herself out here. And where are her shoes? This feels odd to him.

'Are you building up the courage to ask her out on a date or do you actually intend on helping us cut her down sometime soon?'

Miller's a condescending jerk. He refers to Dean and Marty as his 'minions' but he would never talk to Steve that way because Steve's their sergeant. Dean decided a long time ago that once he's worked his way up to homicide detective he intends to treat the cops on the ground with respect. He doesn't believe in shit rolling downhill.

'You hold the flashlights then,' he says.

All three of them throw their flashlights towards Miller and use the discarded stepladder to reach the hanging woman. Dean almost slips on the ladder's steps, as they seem greasy. He reluctantly removes his thick winter gloves and stuffs them in his pockets, feeling the cold immediately. Steve uses his pocketknife to start cutting through the rope above her head while Marty reluctantly grips under her armpits. Dean holds her lifeless legs. She's wearing a skirt, exposing her bare skin. She still feels slightly warm despite the bad weather, so she can't have been here too long. There's no purse in sight and she doesn't have any pockets to carry anything that would identify her. With what he hopes is the natural instinct of a detective, Dean starts trying to piece together what happened and when.

Maple Valley isn't the smallest town in New Hampshire, but it's small enough that most residents either know each other, are related to each other, or have dated each other. Dean doesn't recognise this woman, which isn't completely unusual, but at least one of the cops showing up at a crime scene is usually quick to identify the victims in this town.

'Anybody know her?' he asks.

'Not me,' says Steve.

'Nope, me neither. She's too good looking to be one of my exes,' jokes Marty.

Dean smiles. Sometimes you need someone like Marty to lighten the mood. Especially when you're holding a dead body.

'Okay, almost there. You all got her?' asks Steve.

Before they can answer, her dead weight falls into their arms and they almost drop her. Dean wobbles on the stepladder and struggles not to fall back. He thinks how, for a slim woman, she sure weighs a lot now she's dead. Carefully, they carry her down to the blanket they had already placed over the wet grass, under the tree. Dean notices the medical examiner is patiently waiting nearby, jumping on the spot to try to keep warm in the cold wind.

'Hey, Doctor Sheila. Hope we're not interrupting date night for you?' jokes Marty.

'Oh yeah. I've got a dozen men lined up at my door,' she answers. 'Unfortunately, that's the morgue door and they're all dead.'

Dean tries not to look at her as she leans over the body. He starts making his own notes in the small pad he carries with him.

'So, who found her?' asks Sheila.

He waits to see if anyone else will answer first but she's looking at him. 'We got a call from Eric Petty who said he was driving home from vacation with his kid when some lightning flashed in the woods. It lit her up. He pulled over to check what they thought they saw and then ran back to his car and immediately phoned us.' He tries to avoid her eyes. She has great eyes. 'We've already taken his statement but that's pretty much all he said. He's pretty shaken up. I've asked him not to talk about it with anyone until we release a statement.'

Sheila looks back down at the body as she puts on some latex gloves. She crouches down on the crunchy grass and examines the woman's neck for a few minutes. She turns the woman's head to the left, then to the right. She beams a light in her eyes one at a time. Everyone remains silent as she makes her notes. Then, after taking almost twenty photographs of the unidentified woman, she's done. For now, anyway.

'Is there a suicide note?' she asks as she removes the gloves.

'Not on her,' answers Steve. 'Maybe it's at her house.'

'Okay, I'll get them to bag her up and drive her over to the morgue.' She turns to Miller. 'I'll let you know when my report's ready.'

Sheila gets in her car, an old Civic, and flashes Dean a smile that makes him want to follow her instead of going home. He tries to remind himself he's supposed to have ended their affair, but the temptation is still there. A new text message quickly brings him back to reality. Linda wants to know what time he's getting off work. He decides to ring her instead of texting and moves away from the others so they don't overhear. Marty and Steve laugh at his need for privacy and start to examine the area around the tree, for any belongings or evidence.

'Hey, it's me. We've just got finished with a suicide so I'm going to have to go to the station and help write it up before I can finish. I shouldn't be much longer.'

'So, if I call the station in about fifteen minutes you'll be there to speak to me?' she replies, clearly unhappy.

'Linda, come on! That's what I said, honey. I'm not lying.'

'How do I know that without checking on you? I can't believe anything you say to me from now on. How do you expect me to ever trust you again?' She sounds on the verge of tears, which makes him feel like shit.

'I don't know, Linda,' he whispers. 'I'm sorry, you know I am.'

Miller walks past him and laughs. 'Come on, lover boy. Sort your wife out later. You've got work to do.'

Dean gives him the finger, but not to his face.

'I've got to go. Ring me at the station to check on me, by all means. I'll see you in about an hour and I'll treat you to breakfast at the diner.' He hesitates and then adds, 'I love you.'

Linda doesn't say anything before she ends the call. As he puts his phone away and retrieves his gloves he feels like a jerk. He hates how unhappy she is and he's genuinely worried about her. But he still wants to pay Sheila a visit. He doesn't know whether this means he shouldn't be married. To distract himself he gets in the police cruiser with Steve and they drive through the howling wind, heading back to the police station.

Dean became a police officer after spending five years working as a corrections officer at the local Women's Correctional Facility. His ultimate goal has always been promotion to detective as soon as possible. Piecing together serious crimes is the part of the job he enjoys, but he doesn't get much opportunity to do that in his current role. Instead, he's too busy responding to domestics, shoplifters, burglaries, and acting more like a social worker. Knowing this is the best way to make detective, he puts up with it.

Now, sitting at his cramped desk with paperwork spilling onto the floor, he puts in extra hours to try to help piece together the story of Jane Doe, because he wants to prove himself. It was easier when Detective Jones was here. He'd throw things Dean's way so he could build up some experience in complicated and violent crimes. Plus, he was allowed to do it in work time so he got paid for it. However, since Jones retired a year ago, Miller got promoted to detective and Miller doesn't like him.

Dean watches him now, searching his desk drawers for food, and can't help shaking his head. The whole station knows Miller only got promoted because his wife's brother knows someone high up. That and the fact that he was getting too fat to be a real cop. It was getting to the point where he was letting too many suspects get away on account of not being able to run after them any more. No one wanted to be partnered with him for anything because he was a liability. Now, Miller has what he considers to be a desk job when really he should still be out in the field and not leaving the actual detective work to the officers. In the twelve months since he was promoted, Dean thinks Miller has put on at least fifty pounds. The man wheezes every time he walks around the station and the whole department agrees he makes cops look bad.

Dean shakes his head again and sighs as he thinks of the injustice of the situation. He'd give anything to have Miller's job. He retrieves some paper out of his desk drawer and writes down everything they know so far about what happened tonight: dead woman, maybe mid-twenties, shoeless, out in the wrong clothes for a storm, probably not local but with no ID, and no other obvious wounds, other than ligature wounds to the neck. That's it. Not much to go on. Like a writer with a character but no plot, he draws lines sprouting from each piece of information he has, hoping it will lead to questions and answers.

Detective Jones taught him to always start with the biggest question and work your way back from there. What Dean needs to ask first is: why did a woman hang herself from a tree in Maple Valley on a cold, stormy November night? He'd feel better if there was a suicide note. That might give them some answers, but for that he needs her home address. He thinks of his brother's suicide note. He'd left his bank card and passwords with it, being tragically thoughtful in his last moments, but it didn't answer any of their questions. Trying to avoid flashbacks to that awful time, Dean stares at his notes and decides on where to start: the woman's identity.

The other person who needs to identify the body quickly as part of their job is Sheila. At the thought of her his gut tells him it's time to go home and leave well alone, but instead he heads down to the morgue, which is in the doctor's surgery, next door.

Sheila has her back to him when he opens the door to the morgue. He can't help but check her out and wonder if she's been waiting for him. He almost leaves before she sees him but she turns and smiles. A smile that would be hard for any man to resist.

'Hi. I wondered how long it would take for you to pay her a visit, and I knew you'd beat Miller.'

'Are you down here alone?' he asks.

'Yes. Everyone else has a life. Well, except everyone in here. Come and take a look.'

Jane is resting on the slab in front of Sheila, naked apart from a thin, white sheet pulled up to just below her neck. Her tongue swelling has gone down now the rope has been removed. She's turning a pale grey colour with patches of haematoma under the skin. Even with her injuries Dean can see she was beautiful when she was alive.

'I'm sure Miller will tell you to carry out the usual DNA swabs for ID purposes, in case her family get in touch, but in the meantime, does she have anything we can use to try to identify her? A tattoo or a birthmark, maybe? Something we can release to the press?' he asks.

Sheila pulls the sheet back and points to Jane's shoulder. 'She has a cute and unusual pattern of freckles here. She has them on both shoulders, almost identical patterns and almost like a birthmark. Freckles that cute are something a lover would remember.'

Dean tries to ignore the word 'lover'. 'So, I guess we put a statement out asking if anyone's missing a young blonde woman and see what we get from that.'

'Aren't all men looking for a young blonde woman?' she asks with a laugh.

Sheila's a redhead.

'You'd be surprised.'

His radio suddenly comes to life. It's Jenny, one of the dispatchers. 'I've got your wife on the phone asking whether you're at work. What do I tell her?'

Jenny's no rookie; she knows how the game works. She knows to always check with the officer before answering questions from partners. All the cops and support staff look out for each other, because no one else knows what it's like to be in their line of work. Dean inwardly cringes and heads for the door.

'I'll speak to her,' he radios back. He looks over his shoulder at Sheila on his way out but she's already turned her back on him.

When Dean pulls up outside his house less than an hour later, all the lights are switched off, including the one on their porch. It's six o'clock and the sun is slow to rise at this time of year, so the house is in semi-darkness with just the glow from the street light providing some relief from the shadows. Linda had hung up before he'd had a chance to prove he was at work, so he left the station soon after. He knows he's screwed up his marriage, but he was going through a hard time after his brother's death. He wasn't himself. He wants to make it up to Linda, but she needs to cut him some slack. It's not like she's perfect either.

Standing outside their modest, three-bedroom home, he feels as if something isn't right. If Linda's home the interior lights should be on. At the thought of her not being there, he suddenly wants nothing more than to make everything right with her and start afresh. He closes the car door and heads up the steps. His house is never in darkness; even overnight they leave the porch light on. He reaches for the front door slowly, instinct telling him something's off. It's too still around here; even the wind has temporarily died down. He has one hand on his holster, just in case. He puts his key in the lock as quietly as possible and turns it. When the door opens, he realises he's been holding his breath.

'This is stupid. That damn suicide has me on edge,' he says under his breath.

He steps inside and reaches for the hallway light, which also lights up the lounge. 'Linda?'

There's no answer from her but Bella comes running towards him like she hasn't seen him in weeks, collar bell jingling.

'Hey, girl. Where's your mum?'

Bella purrs up at him and wraps herself around his legs. He picks her up and holds her to his chest as he walks into the kitchen and flips the lights on. He notices the note on the dining table straight away.

I'm staying with Chrissie for a couple of days. I realise this means you have free rein to invite your woman around here but I don't think I care any more. I have to figure out some stuff. I'll ring you at some point.

Dean puts Bella on the dining table, drops onto a kitchen chair and lowers his head into his hands. What a night. Not knowing what to do, he sits there for a while, re-reading the note. He doubts this will end happily, which makes him feel sick. He only lost his brother three months ago and now he might lose his wife. Reaching for the fridge, he gets out Bella's dinner pouch, beef flavoured, empties it into her pink plastic bowl and watches her eat and purr at the same time. He doesn't see anything he wants in the fridge so, when Bella's finished eating, he lets her out to roam. He decides to head to the diner to see if he can find his appetite. He doesn't want to be alone right now and Frankie's Diner offers great food and even better advice.

Chapter Two

'Deano! Where have you been all my life?' bellows the diner's exuberant Italian owner and chef as Dean walks in and takes a seat at the bright white counter.

'Right here, Frankie. Waiting for you to notice me.'

Frankie laughs and starts working on Dean's usual breakfast: pancakes with a splash of maple syrup and lots of blueberries on top, served with a glass of iced water. Dean's no longer a coffee drinker since he weaned himself off caffeine when he turned thirty, four years ago. That was something Linda made him do. She insists they do a full detox together once a year too. That's something he won't miss if she leaves him.

Rachel appears from the kitchen, smiling as usual and with her pencil tucked into her ponytail. She's the only full-time waitress at Frankie's. The others are students who work whatever hours they want to. She puts her hand on his back as she greets him. 'Hey, how are you?'

She's only slightly older than Dean but she likes to mother him when he comes in. She dated his brother, John, for a year. Long before he died. She misses him too. She and Frankie have been great listeners when Dean has been angry and confused about what happened. He's been able to talk to them when he hasn't been able to talk to Linda or his friends. Linda never really liked John. He's never been able to figure out what her problem was. His friends have been there for him in the sense that they're always offering to take him to a bar and help him drown his sorrows. He never takes them up on it but he knows they have his back.

'Well, Linda's gone to stay with her sister, so I guess I'll be having a house party tonight.'

Rachel rolls her eyes. 'You're not still cheating on her, are you? That's not going to help you get over John's death, you know. It's just going to make things worse.'

'It's already made things worse,' he says with a sigh. 'I've told her about Sheila.'

Rachel gasps and sits down next to him. 'How did she take it?'

'She's been either screaming at me or ignoring me ever since I told her.'

'What do you expect? I would be doing much worse than that! But maybe she'll come around when she realises it was your way of dealing with John's death and that you still love her. Give her a few weeks of breathing space. You might still be able to salvage things.'

Dean's not so sure. 'Maybe. I guess I thought having an affair would be healthier than turning to booze or drugs. I don't want to be one of those people I arrest on a daily basis, the ones with holes in their faces from the meth, or yellow skin from the alcohol. Being with Sheila made me forget everything, just for an hour every now and then.' He sighs. 'But, yeah, it was stupid to think sleeping with another woman was helping me. Hindsight's both a wonderful and a terrible thing.'

Frankie was listening through the opening between the kitchen and the diner. 'Women are never the solution, my friend. They are always the problem.'

Dean smiles but Rachel gives Frankie a scowl. 'If you had a woman, Frankie, you wouldn't be as fat and mouthy as you are now.'

'Hey, I like being fat and mouthy!'

Frankie brings Dean's breakfast over and Rachel goes to serve an influx of customers. It's just turned seven o'clock and the breakfast rush is starting. One of the new customers sits down next to Dean at the counter, even though there are still plenty of empty tables.

'Hi. What can I get you?' asks Rachel.

'I'll have a cappuccino and a bagel please, with strawberry jam.'

'Sure.'

As Rachel goes to sort the orders, Dean looks over at the woman who sat beside him. Her British accent caught his attention. She smiles at him. The only thing Dean can think is how hot she is. And that accent! She sounds like Kate Winslet. He wants to get her talking just to hear more of it.

'Hi. I'm Officer Matheson, or Dean.' He puts out his hand and she gives it a firm squeeze.

'I'm Beth. Very nice to meet you.'

Dean can't think of anything else to say so he carries on eating his pancakes, self-consciously.

'That would be quite a healthy breakfast if you stopped adding maple syrup,' she jokes.

He laughs. 'You sound like my wife.'

Rachel places Beth's order in front of her and heads back to the kitchen. Beth slathers her bagel in the strawberry jelly and begins eating.

'What brings a British girl to our neck of the woods?' asks Dean.

She finishes her mouthful before she speaks, but there's a bit of jelly on her top lip that she's missed. Dean tries to stop himself imagining licking it off. That kind of thinking isn't going to win Linda back.

'I've just started working at the prison.'

'The Women's Correctional?'

'That's right. I'm a psychiatrist and counsellor, but don't let that faze you!' When she laughs, she throws her head back slightly, which makes her chestnut brown hair glimmer in the slow rising sunshine that's beaming through the diner's front window.

Suddenly he's even more self-conscious. 'Well, I could give you several hours' work just on the topic of me alone!'

'No, I'm sure you police officers are all perfectly normal

and well-balanced individuals.'

She says this with a cheeky smile that tells him she's being sarcastic.

'What are you doing at the prison, helping the criminals or the victims?'

'Well, I believe some of the criminals are victims too, so I'm there to try to help stop their pattern of reoffending. I'll try to make them better New Hampshire citizens so that when they're released, they're no threat to anyone else. In fact, you could say I'm there to make your job easier.'

Dean laughs. 'Well I guess I owe you one then.'

'Not yet, let me prove myself first. I have the daunting task of trying to reduce the suicide rate of the inmates.'

The mention of suicide makes Dean think of the woman they cut down earlier. His mind starts working overtime, wondering if she could have been a prisoner who got out somehow.

'I don't suppose you're missing any women, are you?' He lowers his voice. 'We found a woman a few hours ago in the woods. Looks like a suicide.'

Beth shakes her head. 'Not that I know of, but then I wouldn't be privy to that kind of information, not yet anyway. I only started this week. I haven't even given any counselling sessions yet.'

As she talks he focuses on her eyes. They match her hair colour perfectly. He thinks she must be about thirty, maybe twenty-nine.

She hands him a card with all her details on. 'Here you go. Just in case you come across any victims who might need counselling. That might balance out my karma from working with the inmates. I've scribbled my mobile number on there, for out of hours.'

He loves how Brits say mobile instead of cell phone. He looks at her card and wonders if she pointed out her number for his sake, thinking how ironic it is to have a hot British woman flirting with him on the day he vows to win his wife back. But the thought of Linda makes him serious again. He finishes his breakfast and passes Rachel some money.

'Keep the change.'

He notices Frankie and Rachel are both staring at Beth.

'I've been on the night shift so I'm heading home for some shut-eye. See you around.'

'You can't miss me.'

He looks at her, trying to figure out if that was a come on, until Frankie explains.

'She moved in upstairs last week, so she's here every day for breakfast and dinner. She's my new best customer. Sorry, Deano, she's taken your place.'

Dean laughs and heads for the door. He notices the other males in the diner are all staring at Beth. He thinks she's going to make quite an impression in this town. As he walks to his car, he tries to ignore his excitement at having someone so hot around for the foreseeable future.

'I'm going to get Linda back,' he vows to himself, like a mantra, whilst pulling out of the diner's parking lot.

Chapter Three

Beth's first week in her new job at the prison has not gone well at all. Already, she has been spat on, screamed at and propositioned by some of the inmates as she undertook her new employee induction, which involved walking around the prison with some of the corrections officers. During her classroom induction one of the guards told Beth that the solitary cells are haunted by former inmates who died in there, obviously trying to spook the new girl. Beth just laughed, knowing it'll take a lot more than that to spook her. She knows the living do much more damage than the dead. She's also been told the prison is scheduled for closure at some point, as it's falling down around them, but until the economy gets better there's no money for a new building. During her induction tour, she could see for herself how it's no longer fit for purpose, with water running down the walls and black mould in some rooms.

When she peered through the small slit in the door of one of the solitary cells, she was spat at and cursed in several different languages. Beth's aware the inmates are testing her and will continue to do so for the whole time she works here, so she hasn't shown any reaction to anything they've said or done so far. She's not easily intimidated and, having secured the job because her certificates show she studied criminal psychology for four years back home in England, she isn't completely unprepared for the role of counsellor to a hundred and thirty-two potentially violent and psychologically damaged women. She's just glad Sue Wells, the prison warden, is enlightened enough to believe counselling might make a difference to these women's lives. That, she supposes, has something to do with the warden being a woman. Beth doesn't think any male warden would give her the time of day.

On her fifth day in the job, the same day she first meets Dean in the diner at breakfast, she's called to meet with the facility's chief security officer to discuss security and personal safety. Today is Sunday, so she's surprised to be called in for a meeting, but she's learning prisons don't follow normal weekday routines. Whilst trying to locate the correct office for her meeting, she's struck by how loud the prison is. There are alarms beeping, doors slamming and echoes of women yelling. She's used to a near silent existence, having lived mostly either alone or with other quiet people. She's finding all this noise irritating. So far, she's had to take painkillers every day to stop the headaches she's been getting from working here.

Eventually, she finds the security office near the front desk and knocks on the door whilst craning her head inside. 'Hello, I'm Beth. Can I come in?'

The man inside gets up from his chair behind the large oak desk and walks towards her, arm outstretched for a handshake.

'I'm Scott Taylor, Scottie to you. Thanks for coming and take a seat.'

She sits in front of his desk, feeling like she's been summoned to the headmaster's office. Judging his age by his face, Beth would put him in his late fifties, but his body tells a different story. He's more like a giant than a man. His uniform shirt is struggling not to tear at his biceps and shoulder muscles. His collar button looks like it wants to burst off to let out the large red neck it's straining to contain. This man clearly spends all his down time in the prison gym, which, she was informed on day one, is free for staff to use outside of inmate hours. The thought of using it herself doesn't appeal to her at all. Even less so now she knows it's used to create this kind of serious bodybuilding. She's guessing it doesn't have a sauna or a juice bar.

As Scottie takes his seat he looks very serious, like he's about to tell her she's being charged with something.

'Ever worked at a prison before, Ms Smith?'

She suddenly feels defensive and assumes he's going to patronise her because she's a woman.

'Please, call me Beth. No, I haven't. My experience is mainly with victims rather than criminals.'

'I see.' He leans back in his chair. 'Well, I'm in charge of the safety and security of every person in this prison. But you are also in charge of your own personal safety and security and for that of your work colleagues and clients. We are all in this together and the best way you can keep yourself and us safe is to listen to me and the other corrections officers, or "guards" if you like.'

She relaxes slightly when she realises he's not being condescending. He actually seems to be genuinely concerned for her.

'I'm willing to take whatever advice you have. You're the expert here, Mr Taylor.'

'Scottie. We all have to look out for each other here because if one of us makes a mistake, we're all vulnerable. Not even just the staff but the inmates too. I have inmates who are just itching to kill each other, given the opportunity. We cannot give them that opportunity because each one of these women is someone's mother, sister, daughter, grandmother and so on. Some of these women have been locked up unfairly as some will be innocent of their charges.' He looks at her for a reaction to this, but she doesn't react. 'It may shock you to know that the American judicial system is not perfect and sometimes mistakes are made. That's neither here nor there in this prison because it's our responsibility to look after everyone equally, whether guilty or innocent.'

This isn't what Beth was expecting to hear. She assumed prison staff would be more cynical and less, well, fair.

'On the other hand, just because they're women does not mean they're not guilty of what they've been charged with. We have some nasty ladies in here, no killers at the moment because they usually go elsewhere, but we have mothers who have neglected their children, child-molesters, drug dealers, drug addicts, women guilty of violent crimes and so on. No offence, but women are masterful manipulators, especially with men. They try fluttering their eyelashes at the guards, they try crying, they pretend to be pregnant … oh they try just about everything to get the guards to give them special treatment. And I do have to worry about some of my men being taken in by a pretty face and the offer of sexual favours but I'm guessing that you'll be able to see through them, what with you being a psychologist and all.'

'Psychiatrist.'

'Same difference.'

'I was wondering why there aren't as many female guards as male. I'd have thought there would be more in a woman's prison.'

'I wish there were, but we can't seem to recruit them. This job doesn't appeal to many women, and the ones it does appeal to usually don't stay as long as the men. If we had more female guards the prisoners would be easier to manage, in my opinion. Some of them are just waiting for an opportunity to settle scores with the other ladies. A lot of them knew each other before they came in as they've grown up in the same messed up trailer parks, and if one lady thinks their man has been with another lady, well, they are keen to settle the score. However, that's not to say they're all like that. Some just keep their heads down, do their rehabilitation classes and serve their time quietly. But what I'm saying is, don't be fooled by anyone. Be kind by all means but do not turn your back on anyone and do not have favourites. I've worked here for fourteen years and I still can't tell who's good and who's bad. So, we treat all of them equally. Understood?'

'I understand.' She fidgets in her seat and takes her suit jacket off. It's getting warm in here.

Scottie pushes some paper around on his desk and

continues. 'Now I have a really long safety and security procedure manual for you to spend time reading. Here.'

She takes it from him and realises he's not kidding. This document is seventy-two pages long and double-sided.

'But nothing written down on paper can really instil in you the consequences of a small lapse in concentration when you work at a prison, so I have a nice video for you to watch with me now. It's only four minutes long, so don't worry about getting bored, and there's no George Clooney to get excited about but you should still find it interesting.'

Beth smiles at his outdated idea of a heartthrob for someone her age. He turns his computer monitor around to face her and clicks 'Play'. She isn't sure what to expect and feels his eyes on her as it starts. She watches a male officer get cornered in a cell by five female inmates wearing pillowcases over their heads. The women take just seconds to violently beat him to the ground, kick his head repeatedly against the cell wall and then scarper immediately, all in different directions. This all happens within the first minute of the video. The remaining three minutes are obviously for effect because the guard is just lying on the ground, motionless.

'Why did they do that?' she asks.

Scottie turns his monitor back around to face him. 'Simply because they could, Ms Smith. Maybe they felt they had a score to settle, but poor Shane was momentarily caught alone in a vulnerable location and they took the opportunity to show us they are always waiting. And to show the other inmates that they demand respect, of course.'

Beth isn't too shocked. She had spent weeks watching documentaries about American prisons as preparation for applying for jobs in them.

'Is he all right now?'

Scottie looks like he wants to sugarcoat his delivery but then thinks better of it, as if there might be a lesson for her in all this. 'No, he's dead. Died in hospital eight days later. Never recovered from his coma. Had a great funeral though. All of the Police Department attended out of respect, and the Fire Department. It was like he was a cop.'

She takes a second to absorb all this information as she feels that's what he expects of her.

'So there ends my lecture. Please read the document, remain vigilant, enrol in our self-defence classes and speak to the guards about their experiences. But most of all, come and see me if you have any safety or security concerns at all, no matter how small. That's what they pay me for.' He gets up to show her out.

'Thanks for that, it was … enlightening.'

'You're welcome,' he says. To Beth he looks like he's trying to figure out whether she'll bring relief or trouble to the prison. Giving him her best impression of a sweet smile, she closes his office door behind her and heads off to find her way back.

Beth's office is pretty tiny. It consists of a small desk with a decrepit office chair, two small armchairs and a low square coffee table, which is where she'll hold her counselling sessions. She'd purchased a big supply of tissues at a discount price a few days ago and now places one of the open boxes on the coffee table in anticipation of her first client. Really, they're more for her than the clients. After being a sickly child, she's never without tissues and has been called a germophobe more than once. Her handbag is full of antibacterial hand washes and all sorts of pills.

At her desk, she looks at the long list of inmate names and crimes whilst eating her lunch, a vending machine sandwich supposedly filled with cheese and ham but it neither looks nor tastes how it should. She tries not to think about the kind of person who packaged it and what their hygiene standards are.

Julia Orme – robbery

Sylvia Sanchez – drug distribution
Maria Fowler – child abuse and prostitution
Charley Greer – assault/battery
Sissy Sokal – arson

And so on. The list covers twelve pages. Beth had spent her second day at the prison putting posters up around the recreation areas near the cells to advertise her free service. So far, she's had no takers, so she decides to look around the prison and meet some of her colleagues; the guards and administrative staff. She leaves half her lunch, has a few sips of Diet Coke and then closes her office door behind her, trying to remember where the staffroom is. She takes a map of the building with her, which she was given in her induction pack. Although not as big as she was expecting, the Women's Correctional Facility is still impressively confusing to get around.

After a few false turns, which lead her to the wrong floor, a woman from one of the offices she walks past directs her to the staffroom entrance where Beth uses her security pass to get in. Inside there are three men sitting in front of the old tubed television in the corner of the room, away from the microwave and drink making facilities. They were busy talking until they heard her enter. They all turn around and she spots Officer Matheson. But he's not in his uniform now; he's dressed in dark blue jeans and a casual black T-shirt. She wonders what he's doing here at the prison. From their uniforms, she can tell the other two men are guards she's not yet been introduced to, so she strides up to them as they watch her approach with some interest.

'Hello again, Officer.'

He gets up and then looks like he's not sure why. 'Hi. I told you, call me Dean.'

She turns to the two guards. 'Hi, I'm Beth Smith. I started on Wednesday. I don't think I've met you yet?'

She leans in to shake their hands and they both look slightly uncomfortable.

'Pleasure,' says the one with blond hair. 'I'm Pete Neale.'

'Nice to meet you,' says the other one. 'I'm Toad McCann.'

She raises her eyebrows and smiles at him, 'Toad? What an interesting name.' She looks him over, noticing his red hair, pale skin and watery blue eyes. Although skinny, he has a prominent beer belly.

'Careful, Toad,' Dean says, with a smile. 'She's a psychiatrist so she might analyse why you're called Toad.'

Toad seems fascinated. 'A psychiatrist? Are you here for the staff or the inmates? Because we have some messed up staff here who could use your help.'

'He means him.' Pete laughs.

'Inmates primarily, but I am happy to take self-referrals from anyone if they think they would like some counselling.' She turns to Dean. 'Did you catch up on your sleep this morning then?'

Pete and Toad share a look that suggests they think she spent the night with him. They try to stifle laughs.

Beth feels herself blush hard. 'Okay, that came out wrong! Let me explain; I first met Dean very early this morning in the diner as he was finishing his night shift. He told me he was going home to sleep.'

'Hey, you don't have to explain anything to us! What you two get up to is no business of ours,' says Toad.

Beth notices she's made Dean look uncomfortable so she goes to the kitchenette to make herself a coffee with her new work mug, something she bought so as not to have to use the communal dishes. She'd rather go without a hot drink all day than drink from someone else's mug. Dean sits back down in front of the television.

'So, how are you settling in to your new job?' he asks.

She turns back to face them with her coffee cup in both hands. 'It's been okay. I've not managed to drum up any business yet so I'm just learning the ropes and finding my way around at the moment. What are you doing here anyway? I didn't realise police spent time at the prison, especially when off the clock.'

'I used to work here.'

As they chat, Pete and Toad finish their break and leave the room.

She sits down next to Dean. 'Really, what did you do?'

'I was a guard for five years. This place taught me everything I know about criminals and victims.'

'Victims?'

'Yeah, half these women in here are victims of something. Usually of picking the wrong guy or having the wrong parents.'

'That's interesting.' She leans back. 'So, you think having bad parents automatically means someone will go on to become a criminal?'

'The stats don't lie. I'm willing to bet two thirds of the women in here were abused in some way whilst growing up. Not necessarily sexually but emotionally, physically. In all manner of ways.'

'Actually, although the statistics are shocking, not every abuse victim turns into a drug-addicted criminal. Many go on to have perfectly normal and productive lives, but that doesn't sound as good to the press so you don't hear about them. Anyway, how come you still wanted to be a police officer after working here?'

He looks like he's wondering how much to tell her.

'The aim is to make detective. Homicide detective. That's kind of why I'm here on my own time; I'm trying to figure out who our Jane Doe is and I thought maybe someone here would know something. The guards are good at keeping their ear to the ground and finding things out without directly asking anyone.'

'You mean without asking the inmates?'

'Yeah. Sometimes the inmates know of crimes before we do. Usually because it's one of their relatives involved. When I was here I worked with Pete, Toad and some of the others, so I like to catch up with them regularly to find out what's going on.'

'I thought you said this woman was a suicide?'

'That's how it looks, yes. I just thought someone in here might know who she is because I think we're going to have trouble identifying her quickly.'

She sips her coffee and watches him as he talks. She finds his New Hampshire accent alluring, and he's definitely attractive with his athletic build, blue eyes and thick black hair, which has a slight curl to the end, but she remembers he mentioned his wife this morning so she assumes he's off limits. Still, she knows it can't hurt to have a police officer as a friend. Especially one who wants to be a detective.

'That's really admirable that you'd use your spare time to further your career. How does your wife feel about it? I bet you already work long hours without the extra homework?'

His demeanour visibly changes when she mentions his wife and he practically leaps out of his chair. She thinks maybe he's divorced but still wearing his ring, or perhaps he's widowed.

He looks at his watch. 'I've got to go, I'm afraid. I've got things to do before my shift starts later.' He heads for the door but stops before letting himself out. 'You should hold a little "Introduction to Counselling" session in the rec room during lunch. That might get some of the women talking to you. I bet half the women in here don't know what counselling actually is so if you spell it out for them, it might help.'

She smiles at him. 'That's a great idea, thanks.'

He leaves her alone in the staffroom where she slowly finishes her coffee.

Chapter Four

As Dean leaves the prison he bumps into Pete, who's standing smoking just outside the front entrance.

'You've only just finished your break and you're having another one already?'

Pete drops his cigarette butt to the floor and stamps it out. 'What are you, my boss now? Hey, who's that woman? She's hot!'

Dean laughs. 'She's too good for you, buddy.'

'Oh, but not too good for you, I bet?' he says, not unkindly. 'Do you know if she's single?'

Dean thinks of the mild flirtation they had in the diner and assumes she is. 'She's just moved to town on her own and she's staying in the crappy apartment above the diner, so I'm guessing she's pretty single. For now, anyway.'

'Wow, you really could be a detective with those kind of deduction skills!' says Pete, laughing.

Dean feels irritated but he isn't sure why. 'So, about my Jane Doe. Do you think she could be related to anyone in here or not?'

'I haven't heard anyone mention a suicide yet but it's still early. Once you put it out to the press the media attention will get the inmates yapping. I guarantee we'll know who she is within twenty-four hours of the press release.'

Dean doesn't think that'll be the case this time. 'I hope so. Good to see you.' He walks back to his car as Pete tries to talk him into going out for a few drinks later.

'I can't. I'm on the night shift, remember? And you know I don't drink.'

Pete shakes his head as he walks back into the prison. 'Guess it'll just be me and Miss Smith then!' he jokes.

As Dean sits behind the wheel, and before he pulls out of

the prison grounds, he feels a stab of jealously that Pete is single and able to ask Beth out. It's that kind of thinking that got him into the mess he's in now with Linda. He decides to ring his wife, to check in with her.

She answers on the third ring. 'Hi.'

'Hey, how are you? Did you make it to Chrissie's okay?'

Her sister lives almost a hundred miles away, near the coast.

'Yeah, fine. I'm exhausted though. I can't stop going through everything in my head. Did you remember to feed Bella? She needs feeding twice a day and she needs lots of attention. Don't just ignore her.'

Dean smiles. 'Yeah, she wouldn't let me forget about her. She woke me up with her purring earlier. That cat has the loudest purr on the planet.' It's an ongoing joke with them. 'I bet Chrissie loved telling you she was right about me?'

He can tell Linda's hesitating. 'I haven't actually told her why I'm visiting. I said I just need a break from work, which is true in a way. It's been a nightmare lately.'

Dean feels for her. Working as a court clerk means she has to deal with the public on a daily basis and nearly all of them are pissed off by the time they see her. It's a horrible job and one she always said she would quit when they have kids. Dean can't imagine them having kids anytime soon though.

'Sorry to hear that, and sorry again for everything. I honestly don't know what I was thinking and I mean it when I say it's over with her.'

He can tell Linda's holding back more tears on the other end of the line. 'The thing is, Dean, you know I've always believed everything happens for a reason and I think maybe this happened to show us we aren't meant to be together any more.'

His stomach flips and he doesn't know what to say to her. After a few seconds of silence, he tries to change the subject. 'Listen, have a few days away, enjoy yourself by the sea, don't think about work. Then see how you feel after that.

26

You should know by then whether you're looking forward to coming home or not. I still love you, Linda, but if you think we've reached the end of the line then that's something we'll need to talk about when you get back.'

Although he doesn't want them to split up, he's a different man now to when they first met seven years ago, and it isn't just his brother's death that has changed things between them. He knows Linda hasn't been happy for the last two years because she's been drinking a lot more than she used to. She used to be teetotal. He suddenly remembers what Beth said earlier about accepting self-referrals for anyone who wants counselling. Not that he'd want Linda to see Beth, but a different counsellor might work. He doesn't want Beth knowing all the gory details of his affair. Not that it should matter what she thinks, he barely knows her.

'We could even get you a counsellor if you think that might help?'

Linda's non-committal. 'Maybe. I just need some time away from home.'

'Okay, honey. Is Chrissie there? I'd like to speak to her quickly.'

'Why? You never talk to her voluntarily.'

'I just want to ask her something.'

He hears Linda walking through the house looking for her sister. They talk for a minute and then Chrissie comes on the line. 'Hi, Dean. What did you do this time?'

And she wonders why I don't like her, he thinks. 'Listen, I just wanted to ask you to make sure she doesn't drink too much these next few days. I know you'll be watching out for her but she can be good at hiding it so, please, keep your wine out of sight for a while?'

Dean knows how much Chrissie likes to knock it back so she won't appreciate his request, but she can't say anything about this with Linda standing next to her so she's curt. 'Understood. Bye.'

He puts his cell phone down and slumps back in the driver's seat. He can no longer tell which part of this sorry situation is his fault and which isn't. He wonders whether marriage should be this difficult. When his stomach rumbles he decides to drive to the diner for a late lunch before he starts his shift.

The diner's packed when he arrives but Rachel grabs him a freshly vacated booth by the large windows and pours him a caffeine-free Diet Coke. They only buy it in for Dean as no one else in this town has ever asked for the caffeine-free version. Hardly anyone asks for the diet version either.

'I know you're busy but are you able to spare me a few minutes?' he asks her.

She looks around at the line building at the cash register and then sits down opposite him. 'Sure, the part-timers can look after that lot without me. What's up?'

'We found a woman swinging from a tree in the woods early this morning. I don't suppose you've heard anyone talking about it?'

Rachel looks sad. 'No, nothing. Has it been on the news yet?'

'No, Miller will be doing that later to make the six o'clock bulletin.'

'Well if none of you recognise her and there's no talk amongst customers here yet then that's sure to mean she's either a tourist or it was a homicide made to look like a suicide.'

Dean can't help but smile. 'You do realise you're too good for this place, don't you? You put Miller to shame.'

'Yeah, but if I became a detective who would serve you your breakfast every day? I'm just thinking of you.' She smiles. It's a sad smile that says she wishes she had chosen a different career. He's told her before there's still plenty of time to be a high school English Literature teacher, but she won't hear of it. She lost her fiancé in a car crash on the day they graduated with their teaching degrees. That made her lose motivation for everything. She lives with her father not far from the diner and has only dated one person since losing her fiancé: Dean's brother.

'So, how's your "win back Linda" campaign going?'

He grimaces at her. 'It's not started in earnest yet. I've told her to take as much time as she needs but, to be honest, Rachel, it sounds to me like it could be over.'

'If you really do want to win her back get busy making babies. You know she's desperate to be a mother. You'd be a great dad.'

When they first got married they had every intention of having kids, but over the last few years it's been mentioned less and less. Dean could take it or leave it but Linda used to buy baby clothes in preparation. He supposes the fact she stopped mentioning kids is another warning sign he's missed, which suggests she's been thinking of leaving him for some time, even before his affair. Initially they wanted to wait until he wasn't a prison officer any more because it didn't pay well. Then, being a police officer didn't feel like a safe enough job for a father. But now they don't even talk about it. Dean realises he's been missing a lot of warning signs over the last few years and hopes that maybe his affair with Sheila isn't the only reason for their problems. That's just made them face facts sooner than they might have without the affair.

'So, what do you want? Spinach omelette with hash browns?'

'Am I that predictable?'

She laughs as she heads to the kitchen to give Frankie his order. After five minutes Frankie delivers his lunch personally and sits in Rachel's vacated seat. The strangely comforting smells of fried food and bad cologne hit Dean.

'So, Mr Cop. I'd like to report a theft.'

Dean tucks into his omelette and raises his eyebrows as a question mark.

'This morning,' Frankie continues, 'after the breakfast rush, I went out back to take out all the trash – please try not to get too jealous of my glamorous lifestyle – and I noticed my stepladder's missing. I can't find that son of a bitch anywhere. It may not mean anything, but I'm not comfortable letting small crimes go unreported because they tend to build up to larger crimes, as you should be aware.'

Dean stops chewing and wonders if Frankie's stepladder is the same one Jane Doe used to reach the branch she was hanging from. 'Was it definitely there yesterday?' he asks.

'Yeah, it must've been because Marshall's son, Jason, came in to clean the walk-in freezer. He's meant to clean the top shelf, which is higher than all of us. He uses the ladder for that.'

Dean gets his notebook out. He may be off duty but he carries it everywhere. 'Was it the standard silver metal type?'

'The steps were silver but the plastic sides were white. It's always greasy as hell because it sits right behind the kitchen air conditioner and soaks up all the fat from my greasy delicacies.'

Dean doesn't laugh because his mind is in overdrive. The stepladder Jane used was silver and white. It was also greasy. Does that mean the victim came here on her way to hang herself? Or, if Rachel's theory is plausible, maybe the murderer came here on his way to killing Jane.

'Have you got CCTV out back?' he asks.

Frankie laughs in mock exasperation. 'I don't have CCTV anywhere! In case you haven't noticed, we don't live in New York City, Deano! This is small town New Hampshire, why would I need CCTV?'

Dean smiles. 'In case someone steals your stepladder, of course.'

Frankie rolls his eyes, gets up and walks back to the kitchen, mumbling something.

Dean's disappointed there's no CCTV at the diner and

considers the route from here to the woods, trying to think of anywhere the victim or murderer may have passed on the way. But, as the diner is on the edge of town, there's not much in the way of gas stations or shops in between here and the woods so there's no hope of footage being found. He slowly finishes his lunch, settles the bill with Rachel and then drives home to feed the cat and get ready for work.

'There you are,' says Miller, as if Dean has walked in two hours late. 'I'm waiting to do this press conference so I need everything you've got on our swinging sister, Jane Doe.'

Dean has only just clocked in and silently walks right by Miller, resisting the urge to say, 'I thought you were the detective.'

'Well? What have you got?' Miller sits on the edge of Dean's desk and they can all hear the wood straining to hold what must be the two hundred and fifty pounds of fat that is Detective Miller.

'I finished my shift straight after we found her. You're the one who's on the day shift so how would I have more information than you?'

Miller's face reddens. Dean notices that Steve, who arrived straight after him, overhears them from his desk and immediately looks up and stops what he's doing. Steve knows there's been tension between him and Miller for a long time, ever since Detective Jones retired and Dean strongly opposed Miller being his replacement. Everyone knows Jones was a good mentor to Dean, whereas Miller's just a pain in the ass.

Miller throws his notepad down in front of Dean's face. 'Write down everything you know before you do anything else, like change your tampon. You moody piece of shit.'

He struggles off the desk and walks away looking like a bull heading towards a matador. The desk breathes a sigh of relief and Dean resists the urge to throw the notepad at Miller's back.

'You okay?' asks Steve.

'Why am I expected to do his work for him? I've got enough work to do already, plus whatever else comes in tonight.'

'Go and dump some of your paperwork on his desk and see how he likes it.'

Dean smiles. 'Yeah, right. He'd have a heart attack if he ever had to do some real work.'

He writes down the very basics of what they know so far and thinks about leaving out the part about the stepladder potentially coming from Frankie's. He doesn't want to give Miller leads that he would never have found otherwise, but he knows he has to put his dislike of him aside for the sake of the victim. He walks to Miller's desk, notepad in hand, and watches him stuff a whole Twinkie in his mouth as he grabs the notepad with sugary fingers.

'I'd like to attend the press conference. I've not done one before and—'

Miller cuts him off. 'You haven't done one before, *Officer*, because you're not a detective.' He spits Twinkie as he talks.

Dean tries not to react and turns away.

'But what do I care, come and watch the professionals at work by all means. You might learn something.'

Steve shoots Dean a 'what a prick' look as he walks back to his desk.

The windowless room they hold press conferences in is tiny on purpose. The police dislike the press and the feeling is mutual, so the less journalists they can fit into the room, the better. In Dean's experience the press fills in the missing gaps with fabrications, which is guaranteed to make his job harder. The department only usually hold press conferences for things like murder, kidnap or armed robberies, which really don't happen much around here, but if he's ever to make detective one day, Dean knows he'll have to be a confident speaker in front of cameras and crowds.

He stands at the back of the room and looks to see who's there. There's the usual journalist and intern from the local newspaper, Craig and Jackie, both well known to the department and actually not the worst journalists they've ever come across at the station. Tina, the police department's administrator and media relations assistant, is sitting in the front row, ready with her recorder so she can deny anything that's made up about the press conference later. There are also a couple of people he doesn't recognise, possibly from larger out of town newspapers or online news sites. He's not sure why they think they're here, or how much they know already, but press conferences always garner a lot of media attention so you get a lot of vultures circling at these things.

Miller and Captain Brown are standing at the front of the room, facing the journalists and a cameraman, with camera, from a news station. Even from here Dean can spot the Twinkie sugar around Miller's mouth. Jenny slips in and stands next to him at the back. When things are quiet on the phones, she takes the opportunity to keep tabs on what's going on beyond her desk. *The sign of a dedicated employee*, he thinks.

She nods at him and then spots Miller's sugary mouth. 'What a douche!' she whispers.

He can't help but smile to himself and think how the whole town will see how greedy Miller is.

The cameraman finishes taking a call and stands up. 'Okay, Terry says we're going to film this live for a news flash, instead of this being a recording for later. There's to be absolutely no swearing and make it good because there are no second takes!'

He approaches the camera and waits for the thirty second 'going live' warning. Captain Brown doesn't flinch; he's a seasoned professional, but Dean thinks Miller looks like he might just soil himself.

The cameraman looks at his watch. 'Okay, I'll give you a ten second countdown when we're good to go.'

Miller quickly starts sweating heavily. Dean and Jenny exchange a look of bemusement. He really doesn't look like his normal overconfident self.

'Ten, nine, eight, seven, six …'

Miller's face is no longer pale, it's now bright red and his eyes are bulging.

'Five, four, three …'

Numbers 'two' and 'one' are mouthed silently and all eyes turn to Miller. He's supposed to start talking. He manages a few words, 'I'm Detective Miller,' before he collapses live on air. He doesn't just fall down in a slow faint; he drops like a dead weight and everyone feels the floor shake. Jenny leaps forward to where he's sprawled, ready to administer first aid.

'Shit,' says Dean and calls an ambulance on his cell phone as fast as his confused fingers will let him.

The cameraman is still filming until his phone rings and he takes orders to stop. Jenny undoes Miller's tie and top shirt button and then listens for breathing. She looks at Captain Brown, who's trying to hold Miller's head in his lap but it keeps rolling off onto the floor. Even his head is heavy. Dean see's panic in Jenny's eyes and, as she starts resuscitation attempts, an audience of cops forms at the door. They probably heard, and felt, the fall.

An hour later they are all standing around Jenny's desk waiting for news from the hospital and checking YouTube to see if anyone has uploaded a video of Miller's collapse yet. They've received plenty of tweets about it but no video, as yet. If Jenny had resuscitated anyone else at the station she would be a hero but with Miller, there's been some teasing about her kind efforts with some, not Dean, suggesting they were 'misplaced'.

A call comes in and Jenny takes the details without giving anything away to the silent crowd. After ending the call, she checks the rota, writes down some notes and hands her piece of paper to Dean. 'You're up!'

So much for spending the evening catching up on things, he thinks. He reads the note and groans. 'Seriously? Tammy Gordon again?'

Everyone tuts, shaking their heads as they disperse to where they should be, leaving Dean to deal with Tammy Gordon. Tammy's well known to the department having served time on multiple occasions already, and she's still only twenty-nine years old.

'Child services took a distressed call from Emily. Sounds like Tammy's at it again. Derek's already there.'

At the thought of fourteen-year-old Emily, Dean makes a move and rushes to Tammy's house, a fifteen-minute drive away.

Chapter Five

'Open up, Tammy! I won't ask again.' He's shouting through her back door, as the front door is crudely nailed shut. She previously insisted it's nailed because she's afraid of being burgled, but that makes no sense to anyone. Dean has a creeping suspicion it won't be long before the back door and windows are also nailed shut and poor Emily will have no way out. He speaks to Derek, the family's social worker, as they wait.

'It's like déjà vu whenever I arrive at this house,' says Dean. 'Why is Emily still here, can't you do anything about this?'

It's a rhetorical question as they know that both departments' hands are tied and neither of them have the power to do anything without Emily or Tammy's cooperation. Not until Tammy takes things up a notch.

Derek, a family social worker for over twenty years, looks exasperated and resigned at the same time. 'Listen.' He gets ready to have the same conversation they have every time they're called out to this house. 'We've both tried everything but Emily won't stand by anything she tells us, not when it matters, so the family court can't help me move her to foster care. You know I want to get her taken off her mother for good, but Tammy's grip is too tight over her. Tammy's told her she'll find her wherever she goes so I guess from Emily's point of view, she might as well live like this.'

The back door opens but only because Emily has plucked up the courage to open it. To Dean, she looks skinnier every time he visits. This time her face is bruised and her lank brown hair has been cut roughly, making her look like a rag doll. The bruise on her jaw hasn't turned purple yet but it's swollen and will obviously get a hell of a lot worse overnight. Tammy normally goes for the arms or legs, which can be easily covered up. *She must be off her medication to do this*, thinks Dean.

'Hey, honey. Come out here and say hello to us.' Emily loves Derek. They've spent a lot of time together over the years, so after just a few seconds' hesitation she tiptoes out of the house, looking back the whole time. She's only wearing a thin nightgown and open sandals, on what is an icy cold day with the sun about to set. It makes Dean shiver just to look at her.

'Where's your mum, Emily?' asks Dean.

'In her bedroom,' she says, in her tiny voice. 'I think she's passed out.'

As well as prescribed medication for her personality disorder, Tammy also self-medicates with drugs and alcohol. Dean pushes open the back door and heads into the kitchen, while Derek grabs some warmer clothes and shoes for Emily from the back porch.

The kitchen smells of something bad, something artificial, but overall it looks pretty organised and clean. The smell isn't dirt related. Dean assumes Emily's in charge of housekeeping. The house is freezing cold. He'd bet the heating hasn't been on for days, maybe longer. Just the thought of it makes him shiver again. He walks through the hallway to the stairs where their large Rottweiler, Rocky, is cowering under a shelf.

'Hey, boy! Come here,' he coaxes. The dog starts wagging his tail loudly, hitting the table with a rhythmic thud. Dean's surprised Tammy never docked his tail, but he's really glad she didn't. Knowing Tammy, she would've butchered the poor dog trying to do it herself whilst drunk or high. Rocky's coat is matted and dull. He needs a bath and a brush. Eventually, he slowly inches towards Dean. On a good day, he'd leap at Dean and unintentionally smother him with his chunky body but today he starts slow, licking his hand, moving up to his face, confidence growing with every second.

'Oh my God, you're killing me.'

Dean loves dogs and would have preferred one over a cat. Bella's kind of special in her own way but he'd rehome Rocky in a heartbeat. Probably Emily too, if truth be told. He's not sure how Linda would feel about that though.

'Hey, Derek?'

Derek comes in through the kitchen doorway, ducking his head as he's so tall.

'Could you and Emily feed Rocky and let him out back to get some air? And throw a ball for him. He needs some affection right now.'

He knows this will help Emily relax too. She tries her best to take care of Rocky but she hasn't exactly got a good role model. Dean looks up the stairs and wonders how to handle the situation. Emily has clearly been beaten. The fact she phoned Derek at Child Services to tell him means it must've been pretty scary this time. She doesn't normally rat on her mum unless it's bad. He feels the weight of responsibility on him as he struggles to think of a way to break the cycle. Even arresting Tammy will be temporary as Emily will refuse to repeat what she told them over the phone, so they'll have to release her. Tammy will be angry at the short jail stay and take it out on Emily as soon as she gets home. *Rocky will get in the way as he tries to defend Emily and we'll be right back where we are now*, he thinks.

He hears them playing out back. Rocky's happily barking with anticipation of the ball being thrown for him. *If only kids recovered that quickly*. As he enters Tammy's bedroom, thoughts of Beth spring to mind. Maybe she could work some magic on Tammy by dealing with the root cause of her aggression. For now, however, all he can do is arrest her. She's lying on her back on the messy bed, with a needle still in her hand. The room smells of cannabis and the curtains are pulled closed. There are dirty clothes all over the floor. He moves next to the bed and starts shaking her hard, trying to wake her out of her drug induced sleep. He's surprised when she comes around relatively quickly and then notices the needle is still full. She probably passed out from booze before she had the chance to inject herself. Shaking his head in disgust, he very carefully moves it away from them. Having attended Tammy before when she's been drunk, he knows to handcuff her while she rouses.

'What the fuck are you doing?' she mumbles.

He sits her up and passes her a glass of water that looks like it's been next to her bed for weeks.

'Wake up, Tammy. We're going for a ride to the station.'

Once she's fully awake, she turns feisty but she doesn't put up a fight for long. 'At least let me get dressed first,' she says, with tears forming. He's never seen her emotional before, just fired up and angry, the way Emily must see her all the time. He un-cuffs her, takes the needle from her bedside table and waits outside her room, having given her two minutes to get dressed and sort out her dishevelled black hair.

When she opens the door there's no fight in her. She's still bedraggled and smells like she hasn't showered in weeks, but she's clothed at least. She won't look at Dean as he re-cuffs her and leads her downstairs. Rocky has run into the house all excited, tail high, but when he sees Tammy he turns around and runs straight back outside. Derek has put Emily in his car, away from her mother.

'Tammy, you can't keep doing this,' says Derek. 'You're ruining her life.'

She breaks down and Dean has to hold her up. 'I just want to die,' she sobs. Then she shouts over to Emily, 'I'm so sorry, sweetheart. Mama will make it up to you when she gets back! Don't tell them anything!'

'That's enough of that,' snaps Dean as he leads her over to his car and roughly sits her in the back. Derek drives Emily to the police station as Dean coaxes Rocky back into the house. After checking he has enough food and some clean water he gives him a hug and then locks the back door, leaving Rocky inside. He'll let the local shelter know they need to swing by and home Rocky for the night.

After Dean has finished booking Tammy in at the station he phones the animal shelter to let them know they can pick up Tammy's house keys from the front desk. Then he seeks an update on Miller. Jenny has gone home and the other dispatchers are all busy on the phones, so he looks for Marty.

'Heart attack. How clichéd, right? I could've told him he'd have one.'

'Is he going to be okay?' asks Dean.

'Of course he is; guys like that always are. They eat what they want, do no exercise, get us to run around after them and you can bet your ass it will be us who has a fatal while he just has a little "warning". Son of a bitch has someone up there looking over him.' Then he whispers. 'Still, I'm glad it happened on TV. Is that bad?'

Dean stifles a laugh and then notices Captain Brown is watching from his office. 'Thanks for the update, Marty. See you later.'

'I'll send you a link to the video as soon as it appears!' shouts Marty behind him.

He heads next door to the morgue, to see Sheila. He needs to ask her to come over and take photos of Emily's bruises. Sheila may be the medical examiner but she's also the nearest thing they have to a police photographer since the latest round of budget cuts. She's good at spotting patterns and medical clues that the cops sometimes miss. Plus, she's the only one on the team who can stomach looking closely at dead and battered people and their injuries all day, whether in photos or in person. Before they leave the morgue to head back to the station, Dean feels it's time to address the elephant in the room. While Sheila washes her hands, he tries to plan what he's going to say.

'Sheila? I just want you to know that I wasn't using you

these last few months, well not intentionally, and I feel lousy about where we are right now.'

Her shoulders relax and she smiles at him. She looks relieved he's mentioned it. 'Look, we had a good time. Was it wrong? Well, for you, yes, because you're married, but for me it was a bit of fun that's run its course. There aren't that many hot cops around here, in case you hadn't noticed. Now I've ticked that fantasy off my bucket list, I can move on.'

He laughs. 'Well, I'm glad I helped you fulfil a fantasy. But seriously, I didn't mean to become the man who cheats on his wife, I was just …'

'I know,' she says. 'You were going through a hard time and you needed something that would take your mind off it.'

She puts her hand on his face and he feels it would be really easy to kiss her right now. She surprises him by leaning in and teasingly kissing the corner of his mouth. Before he can react, she moves away.

'But the fact that you're willing to give up this,' she says, indicating her body and doing a little wiggle, 'tells me you're getting over your grief and putting things into perspective again. Trust me, that's a good thing. I know you're a good man and Linda will remember that once she stops throwing things at you.'

He laughs again, which releases a lot of tension he's been holding over the last few months. If only Linda understood all this too. Or is he just expecting too much? Maybe what she said on the phone was right; their relationship has run its course and it might be time to move on.

'Come on then, lover boy. Let's go and see little Emily again. I'm just glad I'm taking photos of her alive and not dead.'

After a long night of helping Derek sort out a temporary foster home for Emily, checking in on Tammy, being called out to a burglary and catching up on paperwork, Dean leaves the station at six on Monday morning. It's still cold and dark, with a heavy damp mist in the air threatening rain. Not wanting to head home to a near-empty house straight away, he heads to the diner for his dinner, or what others are calling breakfast.

The diner is welcoming with its bright lights, red and white decor and sweet smell of warm waffles. As he walks in he spots Beth at a table by herself in the far corner, reading a book. Her reading glasses make her look academic. He heads to the counter to speak to Rachel but Frankie spots him first.

'Hey, Deano! You found my stepladder yet?'

Dean laughs and rolls his eyes. 'No, Frankie, I've got more pressing things to deal with.' He doesn't want to have to be the one to tell Frankie his ladder was used in a suicide. He'll leave that to Miller, if he ever returns to work.

'And you call yourself a detective!'

'No, I don't! I'm just a cop.' He notices Beth looking up. The breakfast rush hasn't started yet so there aren't many customers.

'Well, we all saw Detective Miller collapse on TV last night so maybe you can take his place? Although, if you can't even track down a stolen stepladder, you might not be the man for the job.' He winks at Dean as he laughs.

'Shut up, Frankie!' says Rachel. 'Do you want the usual?'

'No, I'm starving, give me a full grilled breakfast.'

She raises her eyebrows. 'Really? I think you've only had that twice in the last two years. You could do with a little fattening up. Sit down and I'll bring it over before the rush starts.'

'Linda's not here to give me a hard time about what I eat so while the cat's away …' He turns to sit down but then turns back. 'You know what, give me a coffee too. Cream and sugar.'

That stops Rachel in her tracks.

'I had a call out to Tammy Gordon,' he says, by way of explanation. 'That's enough to make anyone want a caffeine fix.'

Rachel looks concerned. 'Is Emily all right?'

'Emily won't be all right until we get her taken off Tammy for good. But she's safe for now.'

He turns and looks at the seating options available to him. Before he gets a chance to sit alone, Beth draws him over to her with her friendly smile.

'Good morning. How are you?'

Her breakfast plate is discarded and she's nursing a cappuccino. The book she's reading is thick, something about the neural networks of the brain. Dean feels less intelligent all of a sudden. 'I'm okay, thanks. You?'

'Good, thanks. I'm just plucking up the courage to go to work.'

'Oh yeah? Why do you need courage?'

'No reason really, I'm just being silly. I still haven't had any takers for my counselling sessions so I'm starting to get paranoid. I'm worried Sue's on the verge of firing me.'

'Come on, it's only been a week. Give it some time. Did you try the lunchtime talk I suggested?'

'No, but I will today.' She smiles. 'I overheard you mention you had a rough night. Are you allowed to talk about it?'

Dean wonders if she's counselling him or if he's the one being paranoid. Someone once told him they felt guilty just talking to a cop, even though they knew they hadn't done anything wrong. Now he knows what they meant. He feels like he's being analysed just talking to a psychiatrist. He wonders if she can switch off her professional curiosity any better than he can. Rachel puts his coffee down in front of him and heads back to the kitchen.

'I suppose you kind of work in the same business as me so I guess I can tell you about Tammy Gordon. Everyone else around here already knows about her and her poor kid. I was actually thinking of referring her to you.'

Beth's eyes light up and she leans forward.

'Tammy has demons. Anger being the worst. She beats her

little girl, Emily, and I'm starting to think she beats her dog too, and to be honest with you, the lines are so blurred I don't know which of those is more fucked up.'

'Trust me, they're both fucked up.'

He smiles at hearing her say the F word. It doesn't sound as offensive in a British accent. She's easy to talk to, despite her attractiveness and his feelings of intellectual inadequacy.

'Why's she so angry? Any history that you're aware of?' she asks.

'Only the usual; she married a loser and when he skipped town she was left with a house she can't afford and a kid she never really wanted. It makes me angry because Emily doesn't have a hope in hell of ever being normal. But every time we arrest her mum, Emily covers for her so we can't prosecute Tammy or rehome Emily. It's a long, complicated story.'

Beth tenses and gets a look in her eye that Dean can't read.

'It's a sad cycle I've seen many times, I expect you have too,' she says. 'Someone needs to figure out the cause of her anger to try and change her behaviour. How many times has this cycle happened?'

He tries to think how many times he or one of the others have attended the Gordon house over the last couple of years. He can't even remember. But he can remember being told about the first time Tammy was arrested for hurting Emily.

'I've lost count. But it started when Emily was a baby.'

He notices Beth pulling repeatedly at her blouse button. 'That's terrible.'

He doesn't tell her that Tammy was arrested for shaking baby Emily into unconsciousness. Nobody should have to know mothers like that exist. 'Apparently, she has a personality disorder and has seen all sorts of health professionals, but it hasn't changed what she does to Emily, and so far she's been resistant to external help. Would you work with her if I ask Captain Brown to make it part of the conditions of her release that she has to see a counsellor? I know she's not technically

44

an inmate but she has been before and no doubt will be again.'

Beth drops her shoulders and relaxes back in her seat, all smiles again. 'Of course I will. I have a completely clear diary so I can meet with her whenever she wants. Will you be holding her for much longer?'

'I don't think so. The social worker says Emily has already backtracked by saying she fell, so we can't charge her. We have no evidence it was Tammy's work.'

'So, will she be released today?'

'I should think she'll be home by lunchtime. Emily will spend one more night in foster care though, while Tammy cools down. It also means she'll get a good meal and a warm bed two nights in a row. It's not much but it's a bit of a break for her.'

'How tragic that this is her life. Let me know if you manage to make it compulsory and then Tammy can pay me a visit at the prison sometime this week. I wouldn't want to visit her at home on my own, it doesn't sound like she's a safe person to be around when she's angry.'

Rachel places Dean's grilled breakfast in front of him and his stomach growls at the smells. He's even hungrier than he thought. Beth puts her book and glasses into her bag and gets up to leave.

'Ring me on my mobile number when it's all arranged. Enjoy your breakfast.'

She flashes him that wonderful smile and, as he takes a sip of his coffee, he watches her walk away.

Chapter Six

Beth gets to work late because of her talk with Dean. Her mind is working overtime. She's thinking about how to resolve Tammy's cycle of abuse. When she unlocks her office door she sees some post that has been pushed through the crack underneath. One of the letters is from the employee council telling her again about the benefits of the on-site gym. The other letter is handwritten.

Can I meet with you today? I got a lot of issues I need your help with. Shania C. Riley. B Block, cell 114. Don't make it obvious.

Beth assumes Shania means she doesn't want the other inmates knowing she's asked for help. She feels excited at the thought of her first client. She starts up her computer and switches the small electric heater on. It's so cold in here there are icicles hanging off the window. Still, at least she has a room with no black mould. That would be bad for her asthma. She logs in to the prison record database and looks up the inmate. There's no photo, but there is a long list of despicable crimes. She wonders whether or not Shania is going to declare her innocence or whether she wants help coming to terms with what she's done. As part of her induction, and until she's proven herself, the warden asked that any counselling sessions she holds within the first two weeks are overseen by a corrections officer. Presumably for safety reasons. She heads to the guard's office to seek a chaperone.

As she lets herself in with her security pass, she spots Dean's attractive friend Pete on the phone and patiently waits near enough for him to notice her. It doesn't take long, as he quickly ends his call.

'Hi, how are you settling in?'

She observes him trying to look her up and down, in a nerdy 'don't let me get caught' way. She notices there's no wedding ring on his hand. He's not as attractive as Dean and perhaps a little younger.

'Not bad, thanks. Things have been a little slow but today I got this from an inmate.' She hands him Shania's note.

'Well, I've got to agree with her, she's got issues!' He laughs. As Beth doesn't laugh, he seems to think twice about joking. 'I assume you need someone to sit in with you?'

'Unfortunately, yes. I'm sure I'll be fine but Sue and Scotty insist, just for the first couple of sessions.'

'Good. They're right to insist. Do you want to see her right away?'

'Yes, please. Do you mind fetching her to me so the others don't know where she's going?'

'No problem. We'll meet you at your office.'

On her way back, Beth makes coffees for all three of them. She expected to feel nervous with her first inmate but she's calm and keen to get started. Once she's placed her notepad and pen on the table, she retrieves her asthma inhaler from her handbag. She manages two quick puffs before Pete knocks at the door and opens it. Shania is an older looking white woman with wild long grey hair. Beth would age her at about fifty-five, but her record shows she's only forty-six. Shania hesitates at the door.

'Come on in. I've made coffee.'

Pete leads her in and Beth quickly feels claustrophobic.

'I'm sorry my office is so small. Normally it would just be me and you, Shania, but as I'm new I have to have Officer Neale here to make sure I'm not doing anything wrong. Officer Neale? You can sit at my desk, Shania and I will sit on the comfy seats.'

They all sit down and Shania takes a sip of her coffee. Beth knows it's nicer than the brand the inmates get to drink.

The inmate looks her up and down, eyes hovering on her expensive watch and rings and then moving down her legs to her designer high heels. Beth notices everything.

'So, Shania, how can I help you?'

Shania laughs. 'Well, in case you ain't noticed, I'm locked up!'

Pete stifles a laugh behind his hand, but Beth doesn't react. She just stares, waiting for more. She's experienced enough to know the good stuff comes out during the silences.

'I'm in for neglect.' She waits for a reaction from Beth. Some look of disgust maybe, or an awkward cough, but Beth doesn't react. 'They said I neglected my children. But it's the state that neglected them because they don't pay me enough welfare to feed and clothe them properly. I don't know how they get away with calling it welfare.'

That isn't all she's been charged with according to the prison records Beth looked at. She wonders whether or not Shania will admit the rest to her.

'I've tried all sorts of jobs but I always get fired eventually. Budget cuts have ruined this country. No one can afford to have kids any more. Where's your accent from? You ain't from around here, I can tell that.'

Not wanting to give much away about herself, Beth replies with a curt. 'England.'

'Yeah? Is your country as fucked up as ours?'

Pete chimes in. 'You're supposed to be answering questions, not asking them.'

Beth stays focussed. 'So how long have you got left to serve?'

'Three months, which may not sound long to you but to me it is. I've already served two years and two months. Just for having skinny kids who grow out of their clothes too fast. They'll be nearly all grown up by the time I see them again.' She starts crying silently, without tears.

Beth hands her a tissue. 'Are you able to see it from your children's point of view?'

Shania's crying stops immediately and she turns hostile. 'They ain't got no point of view, they're kids. They made up a load of crap about how I let my boyfriend – someone who was good enough to take them on when they ain't even his – abuse them. Sexually. Little shits are just trying to get back at me because they don't want to see me happy.'

'But you wouldn't have been found guilty with no evidence.'

Shania's eyes are going wild, looking between Beth and Pete and bulging out of her eye sockets.

'What are you, a judge? Juries get things wrong all the time. I just couldn't afford a decent lawyer, that's what got me in here.'

'And where's your partner now?'

That shuts Shania up. She drinks some of her coffee.

'He's dead,' says Pete. 'Got stabbed in the men's state prison. Inmates don't like child molesters; they're considered the lowest of the low in their messed up criminal hierarchy.'

Shania's shaking her head and tapping her feet in unison. 'He was *not* a child molester.'

Beth senses she's not going to get Shania to come to any realisations if she doesn't get her to calm down a bit.

'Are you grieving for him? Is that why you've come to see me?'

The crying starts again but this time with tears. 'I'm worried about what's going to happen when I get out. I don't have anyone waiting for me apart from the kids and how can I trust them now? They turned on me.'

Beth's eyes widen. 'You mean they'll be coming back to live with you upon your release?' She looks at Pete. 'How is that possible, given the charges?'

Pete sighs. 'She's served her time. Plus, the abuser is no longer a threat. Child services are as stretched as everyone else.'

Beth is speechless for a few minutes as Shania makes a big deal out of blowing her nose and wiping her eyes. She really wants to reach for her inhaler again. Women like this make her so mad.

'You're judging me, ain't you?'

'No, I'm just concerned that you couldn't afford to keep your children well fed and clothed before so I'm wondering if there are any organisations that could donate clothes. There must be a local food bank who could help top up your weekly food shop? It's practicalities like this that, once in place, can help your children as well as you.'

'Well, if you find any, you send them my way. I need all the help I can get. Cigarettes are so expensive now, it's ridiculous.'

Beth struggles to hide contempt from her face. Pete's mobile phone rings and he gets up to take it, squeezing past the women to get out of the room. He holds the door open behind him a crack, so he can keep an eye on Shania. Beth leans in to Shania and quietly asks, 'How does it feel to neglect your children? To let a man molest them? Can you see why you deserve to be in here?'

Shania suddenly erupts in anger and demands to finish the session. She storms out and stands next to Pete as he ends his call.

'Take me back to my cell, I've had enough.' Glaring at Beth she says. 'You better watch it, talking that way to me.'

Pete looks at Beth, obviously confused. She signals it's fine for Shania to leave, so he escorts her away, leaving the office door to slam shut behind them. Beth sits back in her chair and sighs. She's never surprised by how well people delude themselves when it comes to accepting responsibility for their crimes.

She gets up and heads to the recreation room where there are a good number of inmates hanging around reading papers, watching TV and whispering in small groups. There are four guards scattered around so she knows she's safe. She switches off the TV and ignores the hostile protests of the few who were watching it. She would never have thought criminals would be happy to sit watching *The Real Housewives of New Jersey*.

'I'm so sorry, ladies,' she says, with over-friendliness. 'I'll put it back on in just a minute. If I could have everyone's attention, please!'

She certainly gets everyone's attention. The whispering women move closer, wondering what she's going to say. The guards also move closer. Beth doesn't spot Shania anywhere.

'My name's Beth Smith and I'm the new prison counsellor.' She ignores the heckles and continues as if she has everyone's full attention. 'I'm offering all inmates completely free counselling sessions. What that means in reality is that for one whole hour a week you can leave the humdrum routine of your daily prison life to come and sit in my warm office and have a chat with me over a cup of expensive coffee. It can't be during your work time though, I'm afraid.'

'Why would we want to talk to you?' shouts out a redhead.

'Because believe it or not, talking is good for you! You can talk about whatever you like. For example, maybe you're depressed, stressed, anxious or bereaved. Maybe you want to turn your life around once you get released, or perhaps you just want to know why your partner keeps cheating on you.' This gets some laughs. 'Well, come and see me and I'll try my best to help you figure things out. It's completely confidential so whatever you say to me will not make it back to the warden.'

This is met with stronger variations of 'Yeah, right.'

'Unless of course you tell me you want to harm the warden, in which case you'd be a bit stupid and I'd be obliged to tell her.'

The guards laugh at this. She turns around and switches the TV back on. As she walks away she says, 'If you want to see me, just tell one of the guards.'

She confidently strides back to her office and spends the next couple of hours researching what local services are available to vulnerable people around here. She comes up with a short, depressing list. When she's finished, she phones the warden.

'Hi, Sue, how are you?'

They shoot the shit for a while until Beth asks if she can go out on an errand. She tells Sue she wants to meet some of the co-ordinators of these organisations so she knows how to refer her clients to them when necessary.

'That's a great idea,' says Sue. 'Start with Healing Hands and ask for Gregory. He's lovely and always willing to point people in the right direction, service wise. How are bookings for your sessions going?'

'Not great,' admits Beth. 'Just one woman so far, and she wasn't very receptive.'

'Don't worry, anything new is always a slow burner. I bet within a couple of weeks you'll have them queuing down the hallway. Especially when they realise they get nicer coffee at yours.'

Beth laughs. 'Thanks. I'll head out now.'

She puts her coat, scarf, gloves and hat on and walks outside to her car, which is already covered in ice. She scrapes off what she can and goes for a drive.

Chapter Seven

Dean is woken by Bella just after lunchtime, as she rubs her face all over his and purrs loudly in his ear. She's reminding him it's time for her to go out and roam. Dean silently curses Linda for not letting him fit a cat flap to the back door. She thought it might put off potential buyers if they ever wanted to sell the house. In his waking slumber, he wonders whether she was thinking about selling up and leaving him that early on. They've had Bella for two years now so he thinks it coincides with when things started changing between them. Not wanting to think about the situation with his wife, he gets up.

Once showered and dressed he feeds the cat and lets her out. He won't see her again until he gets home after tonight's shift. Their house is on the edge of some open land and water, which keeps Bella occupied for hours. He could do without the gifts she brings home for them though; rats and baby birds, mostly. He watches her disappear from view, into the long wild grass beyond their back garden, as he eats a lunch of microwave pasta.

Watching Bella reminds him of Rocky. He wonders how he dealt with a night in the kennels and decides to collect the dog himself on the way to visiting Tammy this afternoon. After his talk with Beth in the diner this morning, he called Captain Brown to ask if attending counselling could be made a prerequisite of Tammy's release. His voicemail messages tell him that request has been approved, plus Tammy was released and driven home by Marty at ten this morning, while Dean slept. He doesn't officially start work until three o'clock but figures it will be almost that time once he's collected Rocky and arrived at Tammy's. Spending time home alone isn't his idea of fun, so he heads out.

* * *

Rocky licks his neck from the back of the police cruiser as Dean giggles like a schoolgirl and tells him to knock it off.

'You're going to make me crash, Rocky!'

He wishes he could just drive Rocky home to live with them, but settles for a long walk around the nature reserve and a quick game of ball before they get back in the car to finish their journey to Tammy's. There's no answer from Tammy's back door, even after knocking loudly.

'Looks like your mum's taking a nap,' he says to Rocky, who is sitting patiently next to him and starts wagging his tail at being addressed.

Dean starts to worry. He looks in through the kitchen windows but doesn't see anything different from yesterday and definitely no Tammy. She was dropped home just five hours ago and he wonders what trouble she could have gotten herself into since then. It's possible she's had a visit from her drug dealer already. He bangs as loud as he can but still there's no answer. He no longer has her key from yesterday but tries the door handle just in case it's unlocked. It turns easily. Knowing how paranoid she is about being burgled, he's surprised she would leave it unlocked, whether or not she's in the house.

'What do you think, Rocky? Shall we check inside?'

Rocky excitedly uses his nose to push open the door. He runs inside where he starts manically sniffing all around the downstairs, obviously detecting a new smell. Then, changing tack completely, he runs to his empty food bowl. He sits down in front of it and looks up at Dean. Although he's on edge, this makes Dean laugh as he quickly hunts down Rocky's kibble and fills the bowl for him.

'Tammy?' he shouts.

There's no answer so he slowly walks to the bottom of the stairs, straining to hear any movement in the house. Rocky's chomping is the only noise so Dean starts up the stairs, calling for Tammy as he goes, warning her of his approach so she doesn't get scared and shoot him. It's dark and musty in the stairway and landing. She hasn't opened any curtains yet. When there's no answer from knocking on her bedroom door, he cautiously enters.

Tammy's lying on the bed almost exactly as she was when he found her yesterday. He can't see her face so he moves around to her side of the bed and wishes he hadn't. Her eyes are wide open in a startled, intense stare. He can immediately tell she's dead. He shakes her first and then feels for a pulse but it's too late. With shaking hands, he contacts the station and notifies them of her death.

Sheila's kneeling on the bed leaning over Tammy. Dean wonders how she can have such a morbid fascination with dead bodies.

'And you say she was exactly this way when you found her?' she asks Dean.

'Practically, yes. I tried shaking her first to rouse her but she didn't change position.'

Captain Brown is at the foot of the bed, listening. With Miller in hospital they're a detective down and, considering Miller was their only homicide detective, Brown has to pick up some of the work.

'What do you think, Sheila? Drug overdose?' he asks.

'Well, there's enough drug paraphernalia around this room to make it the obvious option, but I still need to perform an autopsy and run toxicology tests before I rule out any other causes. Although, she has so many bruises on her from needles that even if there was a struggle with someone it would be hard to know.'

'Hard, but not impossible. Right, Doctor?' he asks.

'Not for a seasoned professional like myself, Captain.' She smiles, climbing off the bed and getting her kit together. 'It's sad but inevitable. Don't repeat this to anyone, but I can't help but feel glad for Emily.'

Dean nods. He knows they're all thinking the same thing, callous as it would sound to an outsider.

'Just imagine the new life she can have now,' she continues.

Brown speaks up. 'Not necessarily. Foster care can be just as tough and she's too old for adoption. She's had fourteen years of this mess, you think that's going to change overnight for her? It'll haunt her forever.'

The small ball of hope Dean had building in his chest evaporates. Captain Brown's right, he's seen it happen before. They all have. Kids from bad homes who can't get on in foster care so everyone gives up on them, leaving them homeless and loveless. It's a cliché for a reason. He wishes there was something good waiting for Emily but she's going to need a lot of help. He thinks of Beth again. Maybe she's arrived in town at exactly the right time for Emily. He makes a mental note to swap his counselling referral from Tammy to her daughter.

'Matheson, can I have a minute?' Brown leads them downstairs and out to the back garden where Rocky is digging a large hole. His nose and legs are covered in mud and he doesn't even notice them. Once again, he brings light relief to Dean.

'Miller's going to be out of action for at least a month, possibly more, because he's going to milk his heart attack for all it's worth,' says Brown and then adds under his breath, 'the son of a bitch.'

'Okay.'

'We need to get our Jane Doe case wrapped up, because Miller's little dance on TV has made headlines, which has itself raised the coverage of why he was on TV in the first place: to identify her.'

After Miller's collapse on live TV ruined the press conference, the station issued a press release about the woman in the woods. This went out in yesterday's papers and online.

'We've had fifteen phone calls from people who might

know her, although all we could put in the press release was that she was young and blonde so I doubt many of these callers are credible, but we've got to start somewhere.'

'Okay,' repeats Dean. He's not sure why Brown is telling him all this considering he's not meant to be on the case.

'You look confused, so let me tell you what I'm getting at.' Brown sighs heavily. 'I don't have time to be doing Miller's work for him and the department doesn't have the money to hire another detective to cover Miller's extended leave of absence. You already know recruitment is on hold for a second homicide detective, until the powers that be tell me we can go ahead. Not that it'll be easy to find someone who wants to work with Miller. However, we do have a small pot of money that would cover extra hours, if you'd like to step in to Miller's oversized shoes just to close the suicide case.'

Dean raises his eyebrows and can't hide a smile. 'Wow, really? What about Steve?'

'You know he's not interested in being a detective, he's after my job instead, but he did say he's willing to help you out if you need it.'

Dean knows he can't turn this opportunity down. 'I'd love to.'

Brown laughs. 'I knew that would make your day, although why you want to be a detective I'll never know. It's the most depressing job known to man, if you ask me. You'd still be an officer and the overtime would be on officer pay I'm afraid, but you can work days instead of nights until the case is solved, starting now. And whenever you have a lead, you can go off and pursue that. We'll find cover for your other duties as and when needed. Do you think you can juggle the two?'

Trying to play it cool but not managing very well, Dean says yes and thinks about where this could lead if he manages to solve the case quickly and efficiently. Rocky comes running over to them and jumps all over Dean, smearing him with dirt.

'The dog likes you. Make sure you drop him at the shelter before you leave here,' says Brown as he walks away to his car. 'Then go home and get some rest ready for changing your shift pattern to days.'

'Yes, sir.'

Once he's gone, Dean leads Rocky into the back porch to clean him off. He doesn't want the mud in his car. Sheila comes downstairs and spots them on her way out.

'Oh my God, you two are too cute for words!' She takes her cell phone out and snaps a photo. Both Dean and Rocky are covered in mud. When she shows Dean the photo he decides to take Rocky home with him rather than drop him off at the shelter. He wouldn't be able to sleep knowing Rocky was sitting in one of those awful kennels on his own. Bella won't be happy, but, with the confidence of someone who's never owned a dog before, he's pretty sure he can keep her and Rocky in separate parts of the house if he has to.

After Rocky's exciting day, and after sniffing the entire house as soon as he gets through the door, it takes just minutes to find Dean's couch where he jumps up, spreads out and quickly falls asleep. Dean changes out of his muddy uniform and into jeans and a T-shirt and settles on the couch next to the dog. There's no sign of Bella yet. He hasn't had an evening off for a long time, let alone an evening on his own. He picks up his cell phone and thinks about calling Pete to see if he wants to come over and hang out. That's when he sees a text from Linda that she sent a couple of hours ago.

On my way home. Should be there by six. See you in the morning, after your shift.

He looks at his watch; it's five-thirty. He looks at Rocky who is drooling, spreadeagled and barking in his sleep, front legs twitching.

'Shit. How am I going to explain you?'

Chapter Eight

When they hear Linda's car pull up in the driveway just after six o'clock, Rocky and Dean both jump up and head to the front door. Rocky barks a few times, excited about having a visitor coming to see him. This makes Dean cringe. Linda's not a dog person, hence Bella, so he knows she'll be furious. He grabs Rocky by his old leather collar and sits crouched down next to him as Linda hesitantly opens the front door. She must've heard the barking over the wind outside. Her eyes widen when she sees Rocky and then he lunges for her, all mouth and paws. Dean only just manages to keep hold of him.

'What's going on?' she asks, with a bemused smile.

'Sorry, he needed a home for a few nights. It's Rocky.' He looks at her expectantly. 'You remember? The dog I tell you about every time I'm called out to Tammy Gordon's place?'

'This is *her* dog? Surely he's not safe to be around if he's been brought up in that house?'

'Trust me, he's fine. Tammy overdosed today, she's dead.'

'Oh my God, that's terrible.' She closes the front door against the harsh wind and heavy rain. After thinking about what it means she adds, 'But good for Emily?'

Dean grimaces to suggest he agrees but feels bad for agreeing. Rocky can't stand being held back any longer. He makes one giant lunge at Linda, which pushes her backwards into the front door. Dean expects her to go crazy but Rocky's covering her in big wet slobbering kisses and it's making her laugh.

'Oh my God, you're adorable. But so heavy! Get down, Rocky. What does Bella think of him?'

Rocky starts to calm down and lays at their feet on his back, accepting stomach rubs as they talk.

'She's not met him yet, although it sounds like it's just started raining, so she'll probably be home soon. I doubt she'll be happy but we can keep Rocky in the kitchen if we need to.'

'Don't bank on it,' says Linda. 'Chrissie used to have a Doberman and it ate through her kitchen door in a bid to join them on the couch.'

Dean hasn't seen her this relaxed for a long time and wonders why she came home earlier than expected. Her hair and make-up look different, like she's made a real effort. He feels flattered that she'd go to some effort for her return. He leads Rocky back to the lounge and tells him to settle down in front of the couch. Rocky does exactly what he's told and quickly falls asleep again, every now and then opening his eyes to check he's not alone. Dean makes them both a green tea and they sit on the couch together.

'So, how are you?' he asks, not sure whether he should kiss her or not. 'You look great. I'm surprised you've come back so soon though, I thought you'd be gone for at least a week.'

She's twisting her watch around her wrist and not looking at him.

'I'm okay. I had some reiki yesterday. Chrissie has a friend who's practicing it for his course, so he offered it to me for free. It was really good actually. They say it helps you make important decisions. I think it did help.'

'Good.' An awkwardness settles over them as they both stare at the dog and think of what to say next. 'Well, I have news,' says Dean. She looks up at him, eyebrows raised. 'Thanks to our favourite detective having a heart attack live on TV—'

'Oh yes, I heard about that. Is he going to be okay?'

'Yes, unfortunately.'

'Dean! Don't say that!' She laughs.

'Come on, the guy's a douche who's had it in for me since he got promoted. Anyway, thanks to his penchant for fatty foods and his aversion to exercise, Captain Brown today asked me to take over one of Miller's cases, the Jane Doe we found hanging in the woods.'

She smiles at him and to Dean she looks genuinely pleased that he'll get to play at being a detective. This makes him feel hopeful that they can work things out.

'That's great! Does that mean extra money?'

'Not really, maybe a few extra hours if I need it. But he did say I can change to days from now on, until the case is settled, which is why I'm home at this time by the way.' *She didn't seem surprised to see me at home when she arrived*, he thinks. He wonders whether that means anything but doesn't want to think the worst. 'Which means we have all evening together,' he adds.

She smiles but he can't tell whether she's happy about that or not.

'I've got to ask, when we last spoke on the phone you practically said you think it might be time to call it quits. Do you still feel that way?'

She takes a deep breath and then sighs. Taking his hands in hers she says, 'I really don't want to hurt you and I've tried to put this off for as long as possible, hoping things would get better. I'm so sorry, Dean, but I don't think I'm in love with you any more.'

She starts crying and Rocky looks up at her, confused. He keeps his head up for a few minutes before laying it down again but he doesn't close his eyes. Dean feels sick. He suddenly wants a drink. A proper drink.

'I'm sorry. It's not just because of what you did with that woman, although that hasn't helped. I haven't been happy for a while now, you must've noticed? You're never here in the evenings, which means I've been lonely. I didn't feel like a married woman any more and ...' She hesitates for a second and looks down at their hands, clearly trying to hold back more tears. 'There's something I've got to tell you.'

He pulls his hands away from hers. He doesn't want to

listen to her but he knows he has to. Rocky gets up and sits next to him, putting his massive head in his lap. Dean wonders whether Rocky's telling him that he needs to go outside.

Linda strokes Rocky's head absently. 'Two years ago, I started a relationship with someone else.' She looks at Dean for a reaction.

He stares at her with his mouth wide open. He really wasn't expecting to hear that. 'Who?' he whispers.

'It doesn't matter who. It was wrong of me and I regret going behind your back. I didn't handle it well, but it was hard because—'

'It matters to me,' he says, with images of all the town's men zooming through his mind. From the men she works with to his friends, and the lawyers who pass through the courthouse.

'Dean, that's not the worst of it.' She covers her face with her hands as if trying to stop him from seeing her.

Rocky pulls back his head and gives Dean his paw instead, which he strokes. It's soothing.

'I got pregnant, but I miscarried the baby early on.' She breaks down again. Tears and snot this time.

Dean's had enough revelations. 'I've got to take Rocky out.'

He jumps up and strides out of the lounge, through the kitchen and out the back door. The cold rain hits him hard but he doesn't go back in for a jacket. He couldn't bear going back in there right now. Rocky follows him out of the side gate and they walk quickly together, through the dark streets. He stays close to Dean's side and only stops once to quickly relieve himself. A few cars honk their horns at Dean in recognition when their headlights light him up in the dark as they pass, but he doesn't wave to anyone. Eventually, they reach the children's playground and Dean sits on a swing in the wet darkness. The swing next to him rattles as if an invisible child is playing with it. Rocky sits next to him and doesn't move.

So that's why she hasn't been trying to get pregnant with

me, he thinks. *How did I not see it? When did she have time to have an affair?* He immediately feels stupid, remembering he's worked the night shift for over two years now. She's had almost every single evening spare. The drinking must have started after the miscarriage. *Is this why she couldn't comfort me when John died, because she was grieving for her unborn baby?* The wind picks up and slams rain into his numb face. He doesn't know what to think or what to do so he strokes Rocky. After a while, with a damp chill setting into his bones, he gets up.

'Come on, boy. Let's go home.'

When they get back Linda warns Dean that Bella's home, but Rocky spots the cat before they can be separated. He runs over with his tail wagging but Bella immediately doubles her size by puffing up like a blow-dried poodle and hisses a warning to the dog. Rocky stops and looks back at Dean. Then, deciding to try saying hello again, this time he walks slowly towards Bella instead of running. She swipes out at him with her claws whilst emitting a deep, guttural growl. This sends Rocky running into the kitchen whilst Bella escapes upstairs.

Dean glares at Linda. 'So what are you two girls going to do now then? Move in with your other man? Or is he married too?'

Linda's eyes are swollen and her nicely applied eye make-up is smudged. He doesn't care. She gave him such a hard time when he told her about Sheila that he can't bring himself to worry about her feelings now he knows she's been a complete hypocrite.

'Chrissie says I can move in with her while we sell the house.'

At the thought of having to sell his home he gets angry. 'I thought she was allergic to cats?'

Linda looks at him, puzzled. 'She is. I thought Bella could stay here with you until the house sells and I can afford my own place.'

Dean laughs but it's not pleasant. 'No way! It could take a year to sell this place. Rocky needs a home and I'm going to keep him. Bella's your cat, you take her. A bit of itchy eye won't kill your sister. Her eyes can bleed for all I care.'

'Dean! It's not her fault any of this happened!'

'No, but it's her fault she didn't tell me about your affair. She's always been a complete bitch to me so go and live with your alcoholic sister and your stupid cat and leave me and the dog alone. I want you gone by the time I get back from the diner. We'll settle the divorce and house sale through a lawyer. Hopefully, not one you're sleeping with.'

Linda takes a step backwards, shocked at his attitude. 'But it's awful out there. I don't want to be driving all the way back to the coast tonight, I've only just got here.'

'Tough. You could've told me your dirty little secret over the phone. That would've been better for everyone. If you don't want to drive back to your sister's, then stay in a hotel. I might be bringing Sheila back here tonight so you really don't want to be here when I get back.'

He immediately regrets saying that because he has no intention of calling Sheila, but he wants to hurt her. He calls Rocky out from the kitchen and slams the front door on his way out to the car. Rocky jumps in the back seat unprompted and Dean drives them through the rain to the diner.

Chapter Nine

Linda watches Dean storm out of the house with the dog. She isn't sure what to do next. She's cried so much over the last year that she feels physically exhausted. Her hair has been thinning and she's put on over a stone in weight, although not with food. She heads to the kitchen to look for something to drink. Slamming cupboard doors behind her in frustration, she quickly realises there's no liquor in the house, or if there is Dean has hidden it from her. She crumples into a breakfast bar chair and puts her head in her hands.

Dean hadn't reacted the way she expected him to. She thought he'd be relieved. He'd had his own affair so she thought that meant he wanted out of their marriage too. He'd been working nights for so long they almost never saw each other any more. It was rare to get a day off together, let alone to go out on a date. She was lonely and bored so much of the time that it made her feel isolated. She had expected to have children by now but, for whatever reason, it had never happened with Dean. After a year or two of half-heartedly trying to get pregnant, she could feel she was slowly losing him to his work.

Linda feels something brush past her and looks up. It's Bella, having come down from her hiding place. She's wiggling her bum and purring loudly against Linda, which makes her smile.

'Does Daddy ever feed you or does that crazy dog take priority now?'

Bella answers with a long high-pitched meow; her 'feed me' meow. Linda gets up and looks for the food bowl and cat pouches. As she pours the food, Bella seems on edge, looking over her shoulder in the direction of her meeting with Rocky.

'It's okay, princess. They've both gone for now.'

The cat eats heartily while Linda watches and sighs. 'What are we going to do, Bella? Do you want to come and live near the sea? There's plenty of fish and gulls to play with. And no dogs.'

Bella ignores her as she eats, so Linda heads upstairs to start packing a few things. In their bedroom, on top of the wardrobe, she finds their suitcases. She puts the largest one on their bed, opens it and then starts looking through drawers for things to take with her. Underwear, T-shirts and jeans all go in, followed by what little jewellery she has. On their dresser is a photo of them on their wedding day and she hesitates, not knowing whether she should take it.

They had been the happiest newlyweds, with so many plans for the future. They never wanted to travel the world or live a lavish lifestyle, but they did want to start a family and have a house big enough to invite everyone over for special holidays. But Dean's job always got in the way of holidays and special occasions. She was always terrified he wouldn't come home after his shifts, worried that he'd be harmed by a drink driver or stabbed whilst breaking up a bar fight. She felt it wouldn't be fair for their children to lose their dad, so she eventually stopped making any effort to get pregnant.

She sits down on their bed, looking at the photo as if they are a couple of strangers. 'What happened to us?'

With so much time alone at home without him, it was easy to be seduced by another man. Neither of them had wanted to go behind Dean's back. Every single minute of it felt wrong but they were drawn to each other. Both unhappy with their lives and seeking a physical connection. He worked as a lawyer so his hours were more predictable than Dean's. He was always available in the evenings to provide companionship. When she fell pregnant they were both ecstatic for the first few minutes until they realised they'd have to tell Dean everything. But for Linda even that couldn't overshadow the joy of being an expectant mum. She knew immediately a child was what was missing from her life with Dean. They were still so young that she resented living a lonely, passionless marriage.

Fighting back tears, Linda stands up and throws the final few items into the suitcase: hair bush, toiletries and some shoes. She puts the photo back on the dresser, face down. Those people are gone.

After carrying the suitcase to the front door, she grabs her handbag, puts her thick winter boots on and wraps up in her coat, hat and scarf. She grabs Bella before she can make a run for it and quickly crams her into her plastic carry case. Bella meows non-stop the minute she's closed in. She associates the carry case with veterinary visits.

Taking everything outside to the car, Linda straps Bella and her carry case into the front passenger seat and closes the door. She walks up the porch steps and locks their front door for the last time. Noticing snowflakes starting to gently fall, Linda takes a step back and looks up at the house she shared with Dean for so long. Although she's sad, there are no tears now. This had to be done at some point and she should have done it much sooner. Thoughts of the medical examiner who Dean slept with pop into her head. Linda had met her numerous times at Dean's work events and got on with her fine, although she felt a little intimidated by her obvious attractiveness and her intelligence. She couldn't really blame Dean for being tempted by her, especially during a time when he was grieving for his brother and not receiving any emotional support from her. But Linda couldn't support him through John's death; she was grieving for him herself. Grieving for John and their unborn baby.

Linda climbs into her car, checks that Bella is secure and backs out of the driveway. She has one last look at the house before pulling away.

Chapter Ten

Beth's Tuesday doesn't get off to a promising start. She's received a threatening note from an anonymous inmate warning her that if her one and only client, Shania, gives up any of her prison secrets during their counselling sessions, and those secrets get repeated to the guards, Beth will be held accountable. She laughs out loud as she reads the poorly written note.

'Bring it on,' she says to herself.

Shania has an appointment with her this morning, in fifteen minutes, but Beth doubts she'll turn up. She had sent Shania a note telling her when she would like to see her again, but Shania probably received a similar poorly written threat to her own. Wondering how the note got past the guards, but glad it did, she sits at her desk and reads a textbook about what causes mothers to treat their children badly and how this differs from fathers who abuse their children. After just twenty minutes she gets bored and checks her emails and texts. She has no personal messages from anyone, just junk mail. When she's deleted everything, she looks up at the clock and realises Shania should have been here by now. Annoyed that she'd be so easily intimidated, she goes to track her down, bumping into Toad on the way. She's not keen on Toad. He's boring and local, and she can tell he's never left this town, never mind the States.

'Could you accompany me to Shania C. Riley please? She's missing her counselling session.'

Toad is happy to oblige and lets Beth through the maze of locked doors.

'We're going out to the Tavern tonight and you're welcome to join us, seeing as you're now part of our big happy family,' says Toad.

Beth's taken by surprise and can't think of an excuse quick enough. 'Who's "we"?'

'Some of the guards, a few of the admin staff, maybe some of the police department. It's just dinner and a few drinks, where we let off steam.'

She doesn't particularly want to go. She remembers driving past the Tavern when she first arrived in town and it didn't appeal to her at all. It looked run-down and dingy, so she's non-committal. 'Thanks for inviting me, I'll swing by if I get a chance.'

They find Shania in her cell. When she sees them, she starts shaking her head. 'No way, I ain't interested in any more discussions with you!'

Beth's irritation grows. 'Shania, you can't let the other inmates intimidate you. You're trying to better yourself which is only a *good* thing.'

'I ain't intimidated by them! It's you. You're evil. I don't want any more time in that office of yours, making me think about things that should be buried.'

Toad looks at Beth and raises his eyebrows. She rolls her eyes as if to say, 'She's overreacting.'

'Shania, look, I promise I'll go easy on you today. We'll just talk about what you want to talk about. I won't even mention your children.'

She doesn't look convinced. 'Will the guards be there again, listening to everything I say? I thought this shit was meant to be confidential?'

Toad confirms someone has to be there with them but Beth overrides him. She needs clients and is happy to take the risk of Shania going berserk on her. Beth knows she can look after herself.

'Not if you don't want them there, no. I know it's uncomfortable enough talking about your feelings, even without having a guard listening.'

'Er, I can't let you agree to that,' says Toad.

'How about you stand outside the door, just in case we need you?' asks Beth. 'I'm sure Shania's not going to be any trouble.'

'I suppose that would be okay,' he says, unsure of himself.

'Shania? Ready?'

Shania reluctantly gets up and walks behind them to Beth's office whilst muttering obscenities as if she's being forced, when in reality she must know these sessions are an opportunity to get away from her cellmate for an hour. Beth's sure any interruption to the monotony of daily prison life isn't to be scoffed at. On the way, she stops to make drinks. When she reaches her office, she passes Toad his coffee and he stands outside the door.

'If I hear any raised voices, I'm coming in and you'll be locked in your cell,' he tells Shania.

Beth thinks how easy it was to get a guard to break the first rule of safety and security as listed in Scottie Taylor's procedure manual. She doesn't think Pete would have let this happen.

'Here you go.' She hands Shania her coffee.

'I must admit, you do make good coffee. I thought you Brits were all tea drinkers?'

Beth laughs. 'We used to be! But we've been taken over by your American coffee shops so we're all as addicted as you now.' As Beth settles into the comfy chair and picks up her notepad and pen, Shania looks nervous.

'I don't appreciate the way you made me out to be a bad person last time. I've got enough people judging me already, thanks.'

'I'm sorry you feel that way. My chosen form of counselling involves the client accepting what they've done wrong in order to move forward and become better people. But I can tell that's not going to work for you as it makes you uncomfortable, so how would you like to try some hypnotherapy?'

Shania sits forward in her chair intrigued. 'You can do that shit? You can put me to sleep and get me to talk about past lives and stuff? I love all that paranormal shit! There was this show on TV about it. Me and my boyfriend were hooked!'

Beth resists the urge to laugh at her stupidity. 'Well, I don't know if I believe in past lives and the paranormal, but I can try to reach your subconscious to see why you behave in certain ways. That can help us to change your behaviour in the future. It's an experimental method that I use, not exactly by the book, so to speak.'

Shania doesn't have to be convinced. She's clearly a believer and is lapping up the attention.

'You wait 'til I tell Tricky – that's my cellmate – when I get back. She's going to be so jealous!'

This time Beth does laugh. She can hear Toad watching videos on his phone just outside the door and hopes he doesn't walk in as she hypnotises Shania.

As Beth drives home from work later, it's already dark, even though it's only just turned five o'clock. There is slush everywhere from the snowfall and she had to scrape it off her windscreen before she could drive. She parks at the back of the diner and spots a police car as she walks up the external stairs to her flat, trying hard not to slip up. She wonders whether it's Dean. Deciding to have a look, she dumps her briefcase in the living room and then heads back downstairs and into the diner. It isn't Dean, it's a female officer, one she's never met. As she waits in line to order some dinner she thinks about Toad's invite to go to the Tavern with her colleagues. She's getting bored of spending her evenings alone or in here, so she decides to get to know her colleagues better and leaves the queue.

Pulling up outside the Tavern, she sees another police car. When she walks in she spots Dean sitting at the bar next to some people she doesn't recognise. He's nursing an empty beer bottle with a well-thumbed notepad next to him, closed.

'Hello,' she says as she sits next to him.

'Hi, how are you?' He looks tired and cranky and on the verge of leaving.

'I'm not bad thanks. Had an interesting day to say the least.'

71

'Oh yeah? What happened?'

She senses he's asking out of duty rather than because he really wants to know. 'Oh, just inmate drama. The usual.'

'Yeah.' He laughs. 'I know it so well!'

He seems to relax a bit so when the barmaid asks Beth what she wants, she orders herself a bottle of Budweiser and a top up of whatever Dean was drinking, which happens to be zero alcohol beer. He doesn't object.

'I was expecting a call about that lady you mentioned the other morning; Tammy, was it?'

'Oh shit, yeah, I forgot to tell you.' He looks around as if he wants to check who else is listening. It's getting busy at the bar so he motions to Beth for them to move to a table in the corner. They leave Dean's colleagues to their conversation. Once they're seated, the aging barmaid brings their drinks over, along with the notepad Dean left on the counter.

'There's been a change of plan. Unfortunately, or fortunately depending on your point of view, Tammy died yesterday. Within a few hours of release.'

Beth sits back in her chair and looks out of the window.

'We think she overdosed. Her dealer must've paid her a visit the minute she got home.'

'That poor woman. It sounds like she had plenty of demons.'

'You can say that again. Anyway, that leaves us with her daughter, Emily, who I'd like to refer to you, if that's okay?'

Beth's taken aback and stutters over her words. 'But I don't really … I mean I've never … well, I haven't counselled children before. I don't know if I'm the best person.'

Dean smiles at her. 'Listen, you're the best person in the whole town to help Emily because you never met her mother. It'll be like a fresh start for her. She knows everyone around here gossips about her mother, so she's not going to want to open up to anyone else.'

She can't help but think how warm and kind Dean is. He's clearly having a busy week, with two deaths to deal with in a short space of time, yet he's still working off the clock to make sure a child is looked after. She wonders how many other cops would do the same.

'Well, if you think that's what's best for her, okay. Write down the name and contact number of her social worker and I'll introduce myself.'

'Great.' He takes the pen she hands him and tears a piece of paper out of his notepad. When she takes the pen back from him she deliberately touches his hand. He doesn't react so she's not sure he even noticed. She's noticed he's not wearing his wedding ring tonight.

'How come you're in here at this time? I thought you worked nights?'

He takes a deep breath and fills her in on Miller's heart attack and his own temporary promotion. 'It's just to help close this one case, the suicide, then I have to go back to nights.'

'This sounds wrong when someone's had a heart attack but … congratulations?' They laugh. 'I bet your wife will enjoy having you home in the evenings. I always find evenings to be the loneliest time.'

He looks surprised when she says this. 'My wife won't be around for the foreseeable future so I'll get time to work on the case. Oh, and I've inherited Emily's dog, Rocky, so I'll have to walk him every night.'

'I love dogs. They're much more trustworthy than humans. So, do you have any leads on who the Jane Doe is?'

'No, nothing. Apparently, the article in the press has garnered some interest so I have some call backs to make, but I'm none the wiser on identity or reason for this young woman to kill herself.'

'I have books in my apartment on the subject of suicide. If you like, we could go and have a look through them to see if anything sparks a new lead?'

She notices Dean appears uncomfortable at the suggestion. He takes a few sips of his fake beer and sits back. 'I've got to get back to Rocky soon. I've been warned dogs destroy furniture when they're left alone for too long. I was at work all day so I really shouldn't be out now.'

Beth wonders again where his wife is. 'Do you mind if I ask you a personal question? You can tell me to mind my own business if you like.'

He beats her to it. 'Where's my wife?'

She smiles. 'Yes! Sorry, I know it's nothing to do with me but I have no friends in town yet and you're the closest I've got to making one so far, so I just wanted to know a little bit more about you without putting my foot in it.'

He laughs which relaxes his body language. 'It's complicated, but basically we're very newly separated. Like, as of last night. It's just me and Rocky now.'

She can tell there's a lot more to the story but feels she's probably pushed her luck too much already. 'I'm sorry to hear that,' she says, not really sorry at all. 'Hey, look at it this way; at least that gives you plenty of spare time to try and solve your case.'

'I was thinking of going back to the woods where she hanged herself. It's a good walking spot for Rocky and it might prompt a flash of inspiration while I'm there. It's a bit gruesome but you're welcome to join us if you like?'

'Well, I would like to meet Rocky.' She smiles.

'Sure, that's the reason you'd like to come,' he teases.

She thinks he's implying she's attracted to him, but he quickly clarifies.

'You psychiatrists have a morbid fascination with crime scenes.'

'You mean assuming it was a crime and not just a suicide,' she says.

'That's what we need to figure out.'

They finish their drinks and say goodbye to Dean's colleagues, who look like they're going to start talking about them the minute they leave.

Chapter Eleven

Separately, Dean and Beth head to the diner to return her car and so she can change into warm walking clothes. Dean waits outside in his police cruiser. It's completely dark now and snowing on and off so he needs to keep clearing his windshield. He watches as she locks her door and walks down the steps towards his car.

'Do you not have your own car so that you can travel inconspicuously?' she asks, as they pull out of the diner's parking lot. 'I bet you can't go anywhere in secret.'

'What, on my pay?' He laughs. 'We share Linda's car sometimes but she's obviously used it to get to wherever she's gone.'

'You don't even know where she's staying? It must have been a messy argument.'

Dean figures he's told her so much already he might as well tell her the rest on the way to his house. 'I kicked her out after she announced she's been cheating on me. For two years.' He looks over at Beth. Her eyes are full of concern. 'I've cheated on her too.'

'Oh, right.'

She looks ahead as he drives. He thinks he sees a smile on her face even though it's dark. Unsure why she's smiling, he doesn't say anything else.

When they pull up at his house and open his front door, Rocky comes bounding over to them. He only gives Dean a quick sniff and chooses to jump all over Beth instead.

'Rocky, get down!' shouts Dean.

Beth doesn't seem to mind him slobbering all over her jeans. She kneels on the floor to give him a hug and he immediately rolls onto his back, legs spread, not embarrassed to show himself off. Beth's laughing as Dean wraps up warmer for their walk. Eventually, they all pile back into the cruiser and Dean drives them to the woods.

He parks in the clearing on the edge of Maple Woods and retrieves two flashlights from the trunk of his car, so they can light their way. It's pitch black without them, even the moon is obscured by thick clouds. As they walk, Beth seems comfortable in his presence but he's feeling a little uptight. It feels weird to be going on a walk with someone other than Linda. Even weirder now he has a dog. As he tries to locate the tree in the dark, it starts snowing again. Beth's face lights up like a small child's at Christmas.

'I love snow!' She spins around in it.

'Even though you get it all the time in England?'

'We actually don't get it as much as you probably think. Not every Christmas is a white one, unfortunately.'

'I heard that when you get snow, the whole country grinds to a halt and you all use it as an excuse not to make it into work?' he teases. He did actually hear this on the news one Christmas. Linda was tutting heavily beside him. Probably because winters here can be long and cruel, and if everyone stopped for a bit of snow they wouldn't be able to function.

'Well, yes, that can be true,' she replies with a laugh. 'But remember, we aren't equipped like you are. We don't have snow chains, ploughs and things like that. We're lucky if we see a gritter all winter! Anyway, why would you want to go to work when you can spend the day making snowmen and drinking hot chocolate?'

He laughs and feels more comfortable. *This is just an innocent walk in the woods with my new friend and my new dog*, he tells himself.

Rocky's running backwards and forwards around them, sometimes disappearing but not for long. Dean hasn't gotten around to buying him a leash yet. He recognises the tree where they found the woman. 'This is it.'

Beth starts looking around the base of the trunk to see if

76

anything was missed by the police. This amuses him as he knows he and the others looked carefully and didn't find anything. She disappears behind the tree and crouches down. Rocky joins her and Dean sees dirt flying through Rocky's back legs while his tail wags.

'Dean, look at this!'

Beth has a small muddy card in her hand, like a credit card.

'You're kidding me? How did we miss that?'

'It was Rocky – he must have picked up a scent because he just started digging around this.'

He takes it from her. The name on it states 'Vicky Carpenter'. There's no photo and it's not a driver's licence or ID card so he can't tell if it's their woman. He rubs some of the mud off to read more. Charlestown Library Card.

'I've never heard of Charlestown, have you?' Beth asks.

'It's a popular town name so it could be from any state. I don't know a Charlestown around here, but it could still be in New Hampshire.'

Dean looks at the card, puzzled. It could be the victim's or it could have been lost here by anyone, perhaps after the suicide. At least it's one more lead than he had earlier, something to look into at last. He sees if Rocky will dig anywhere else by letting him have a good sniff of the card.

'Fetch boy!'

Rocky starts barking with excitement, not quite understanding what Dean means but desperately wanting to be of service.

'I think he'll need a bit more training before he qualifies as a police dog,' says Beth.

They both scour the area again using the flashlights but they don't find anything else and the snow is starting to settle. Rocky chases a squirrel, disappears for five minutes and then reappears with a mouth full of bird feathers, which Dean quickly makes him drop so he doesn't choke on them. He checks his watch; it's now just passed nine o'clock.

'I'm starving,' says Beth. 'I was going to order dinner at the Tavern but I didn't get a chance to.'

Dean agrees, he hasn't had dinner yet either. He wonders whether to invite her back for dinner at his house but he's conscious it would sound like a cheap chat-up line.

'Have you got any soup at yours? I could murder a nice hot tomato soup.'

He laughs at her brazenness. 'You're in luck. We always have soup in.'

'Great!'

They head back to the cruiser as the snow flurries thicken.

By the time they get to Dean's house, the snow is heavier. They shake off their coats outside the front door and Dean leads them into the warm kitchen. He looks at the growing pile of dirty dishes with embarrassment but doesn't say anything for fear of drawing her attention to them.

'Take a seat, I'll get the soup on.'

He gets some bread rolls out of the freezer and uses the microwave to defrost them. While he waits for them and for the soup to heat up he fills Rocky's new food bowl, previously Linda's favourite pasta bowl, with plenty of freshly bought chicken and rice flavoured kibble. Beth takes her thick sweater off, revealing a tight white T-shirt underneath. He tries not to look. Rocky wolfs down his food.

When the soup's ready they sit opposite each other at the dining table. Dean suddenly wishes he'd put the radio on to avoid awkward silences.

'So, help me out here, what causes a young woman who has her whole life ahead of her to kill herself?'

Beth puts her spoon down while she gives it some thought. The steam from her soup makes her skin look dewy.

'There could be so many reasons. She could be a victim of domestic abuse, she might have lost her child or miscarried a baby, she could have split up with her partner, or she could have been suffering from clinical depression or any number of mental health issues.'

This makes Dean think of Linda and her miscarriage. Thank God she didn't do anything stupid. 'But to go to the trouble of stealing a stepladder, walking to the middle of some woods by yourself and then trying to tie a rope into the right loop *in the dark* with no flashlight.' He shakes his head. 'You saw how dark it was out there tonight, I would've gotten lost without a flashlight. The whole set up suggests to me she was thinking rationally as she did it, so she couldn't have been too upset at the time because it required planning.'

'I know what you're saying, but she couldn't have been thinking rationally or otherwise she wouldn't have been barefoot.'

Dean nods. 'True.'

As they finish their soup Dean's wondering what to do next; offer coffee? A glass of wine? A lift home? His cell phone rings. The caller display tells him it's Sheila. *Shit*, he thinks. *I'm sitting in my wife's kitchen, eating dinner with an attractive female, taking a call from my ex-lover. I need to simplify my life.*

'I better take this, it's work.'

She nods and gets up to rinse their bowls and plates while he moves to the doorway.

He watches her as he takes the call. 'Hey, what's up?'

'Hi,' says Sheila. 'Sorry to bother you at night now you're on days, but I've got Tammy's toxicology results.'

She sounds excited to Dean, out of breath like she wants to explode with information. 'And?'

'First of all, what drugs have you ever seized from Tammy's house before?' she asks.

'She's purely a meth and cannabis user. She always said anything else made her skin bad. I know, right? The irony.'

Beth turns around and raises her eyebrows at him, smiling slightly. This must sound weird from her point of view.

Sheila continues. 'Thought so. Well get this; she was loaded up on cocaine and heroin at the time of her death. And she has bruising on her arms to suggest she was held down. Plus, the needle marks on her arms are more bruised than you would expect from a regular drug addict, which says to me that someone forced those drugs into her.'

Dean reaches for a chair and sits back down. 'You're kidding me?'

'I wish I was. If you ask me, which you would because I'm the medical examiner, I would say Tammy was murdered.'

Dean exhales loudly. 'Holy shit.'

'You want to come in and take a look at her and the report?'

She doesn't really need to ask, he's already moving. 'I'll come straight over.'

'Okay, I'll stick around.'

He puts his phone in his pocket and looks at Beth, who looks like she knows what's coming.

'You've got to go to the station?'

The look of disappointment on her face makes him think she was hoping something would happen here tonight.

'I'm sorry, I've just had some big news and it can't wait until the morning. But I'll drop you off on my way.'

She smiles. 'I love how seriously you take your work.'

That's what Linda used to say, he thinks.

They wrap up warm again and Dean brings Rocky with them seeing as he doesn't know when he'll be home. In the car, Beth offers to take Rocky overnight.

'I couldn't ask you to do that, he's crazy!'

'I honestly don't mind. He's lovely and it would be like having a security guard with me all night. It sounds like there might be a murderer loose?'

He knows she probably overheard everything Sheila told him anyway, so he can't lie.

'It's probably one of her dealers who got pissed when she

didn't pay him on time, so don't worry too much. But, yeah, don't let anyone in unless you know them.'

They pull up at the diner.

'Well, thanks for dinner, it was lovely,' she says.

He wants to lean in and kiss her goodnight but doesn't think that would be a good idea. He only separated from Linda twenty-four hours ago.

'No problem. Thanks for taking Rocky. Take him to Frankie's for breakfast, he loves feeding waifs and strays. I'll give you a call when I can collect him.'

'Okay. Goodnight.'

She gets out the car and opens the back door for Rocky to jump down. Dean watches them run up the steps to her apartment. Rocky looks around at the car before he heads inside, probably wondering why Dean's not following them. *Yeah, I'm wondering that myself, buddy*. He reverses out of the parking lot and heads to the station.

Sheila's leaning closely over Tammy's naked torso.

'See? Tell me that's not abnormal bruising?'

Dean leans in for a look. 'I'm not the expert here, Sheila, but, yeah, it almost looks like fingermarks where they've applied pressure to her arms. Maybe he was sitting on top of her holding her down with his body weight and then he held her arms down as the drugs took hold. Tammy would've been hard to pin down though, she certainly was when she was drunk anyway.'

'Could be. Have you told Captain Brown yet?'

'No, I came straight down here. I'll go and see if he's still in.'

He heads next door to the station and notices a light on in Brown's office before he sees him through the glass, sitting back in his chair and on the phone. He signals it's okay for Dean to enter.

'Understood. I'll get right on that, sir.' Brown puts the

phone down. 'Right after I go home for dinner and get some sleep, asshole.'

Dean laughs. 'The District Attorney?'

'Isn't it always? What do you want, Matheson? Have you found the identity of our Jane Doe yet?'

'Maybe, Captain. I found this next to the tree tonight. I'll chase it up first thing tomorrow.'

He shows Brown the library card but he doesn't seem very interested. He hands it back to Dean, switches his computer off and starts putting his coat on.

'The reason I've popped by is that Sheila thinks Tammy Gordon was murdered.'

Brown has his back to Dean and his arms in the air, about to put them through his coat sleeves. When he hears the word 'murder' his body slouches forward and his arms drop. He turns around to face Dean.

'Are you shitting me? Homicide? Matheson it's ten o'clock! Why couldn't you have waited until tomorrow morning to tell me this?'

Dean knows he doesn't mean it.

'I was looking forward to a delicious home cooked meal with my adoring wife. Well, a microwavable frozen meal with a woman who hates me, but now I've got to stay longer.' He sits down.

'You go home as planned. I just wanted you to know as soon as we found out. We can handle it from here.'

'But you're not a homicide detective, Matheson. I only gave you that one case due to desperation.'

Dean decides to put his neck on the line. 'Captain? I knew Tammy better than any cop here because, for some reason, I almost always got the call out. I know Emily well and I want to see this through to the end for her. I would really like to solve this case and find the person who killed her mum.'

Unbelievably, Brown seems to consider it.

'What about that wife of yours, is she going to ring me at

all hours blaming me for you never being home? I've got one wife annoyed at me already, I don't need two.'

'Not a problem any more. We're separated, so I'm responsible to no one. Well, apart from Tammy's dog.'

Brown doesn't flinch at the news that Dean has separated from Linda. Sadly, it's all too common for the force to get in the way of marriage. But when he hears about the dog, he reacts. 'Rocky?'

'Yeah. He's become a house guest. But he can come with me if I need to go anywhere, he's no trouble at all.'

Brown has no problem with dogs at the station. He used to be a police dog handler and has used dogs in the field for a long time. Ever since Hadley, his loyal German Shepherd, died nine years ago he's wanted to replace him but couldn't bring himself to let go. He'd told Dean and Steve that getting a new dog would feel like betraying Hadley.

'Okay, listen up. You and Rocky can take the Tammy Gordon case but you have exactly one month to solve that and the Jane Doe case. If you don't manage it then I'll need to give them to someone else.'

Dean's grateful. 'Thanks. You won't regret it.'

Brown doesn't seem so sure. 'I'm going home. Don't stay here all night, wife or not, it's not good for you.'

They leave his office, which Brown locks behind him. Dean heads over to his desk. It's almost midnight and he knows he won't be able to function tomorrow if he doesn't get any sleep so, after writing down some notes and making a list of what he needs to do in the morning, he switches off his desk lamp and heads home.

Chapter Twelve

On Wednesday morning, Beth's day off, she and Rocky have breakfast in her apartment, courtesy of Frankie's take-out service. Beth has scrambled egg bagels and Frankie cooked up some leftover bacon fat and pancakes for Rocky, who is now lying on his side slowly farting out this strange new food.

'You need to go for a walk to burn off that breakfast,' she says to him. He starts wagging his tail lazily and then farts again.

'Eeugh! Come on, that's it! I'm taking you for a very long walk.'

Although she told Dean she likes dogs, she's actually allergic to all animal fur. Her nose hasn't stopped running since she's been around Rocky and her eyes are itching constantly. She can't wait to clean her apartment once he's gone. She swallows some allergy pills with water and looks out of the window. Last night's snow is frozen on the ground but the sun is rising and slowly turning it to slush. She wraps up in as many layers as she can fit under her jacket. As she gets her boots on, her mobile phone rings. It takes her by surprise and makes her jump. She's assuming its Dean.

'Hello?'

'Hi, my name's Derek Jackson, from Child Services. Officer Matheson gave me your number. I hope you don't mind me calling this early?'

It's nine-thirty so not that early but Beth's disappointed it's not Dean calling.

'Hi, what can I do for you?'

'Well, I was hoping you could squeeze in a counselling session with Emily Gordon today at some point? You see, she's not reacted at all to the news of her mother's death and I'm a little worried about her.'

Beth sighs heavily. She was hoping to enjoy her day off and Dean only asked her last night if she'd help Emily, so she wasn't expecting to have to do it so soon. She doesn't have any prior experience of working with children and feels a little uncomfortable at everyone pinning their hopes on her. They're all assuming she can work magic on a child who has been mistreated from birth. Beth knows from experience that there's no cure for a childhood of crazy.

'Erm, well I have Rocky to look after today so it wouldn't be a good time, perhaps tomorrow?'

'No, that's great timing! Emily's been asking after her dog and I think if she could take him for a walk it would bring her out of her shell a little. You could have an informal chat with her during the walk, get to know her a little and see if you think you'll be able to help?'

Beth feels like she can't say no and realises her plans for today will have to wait.

'Okay, I was about to take Rocky out right now actually. Do you want to meet us somewhere?'

'That's great, thanks. I really appreciate it. Do you know where the children's park is? It's on the route to Dean's house actually, I don't know if you've been to Dean's house before?'

She ignores the comment, knowing full well he's trying to gauge just how friendly she and Dean are. She's not used to the small-town rumour mill but can see through it all the same. She tells him she knows where the park is and they agree to meet up in an hour; he'll bring Emily and she'll bring Rocky.

'You're about to see your little friend, Rocky.'

He gets up and walks over to her for some attention.

'Let's grab some coffee while we wait.'

They head downstairs to the diner where Frankie tells Rocky he has to sit in the corner under a table so that none of the customers complain.

'Me? I'm a dog person, but the health inspector? He's a cat person. What can I tell you?'

Beth laughs and waits for her tall skinny cappuccino to be brought over. Rocky sits licking up crumbs off the floor by her feet. He's so chunky he could move this whole table if he decided to run off.

'Hey, how are you?'

Pete, from work, has walked up behind her. She thinks he looks different without his work uniform on. He looks more relaxed and younger. She hadn't realised how tall he was before.

'I'm good thanks. How are you?'

'Not bad. Is this your day off too?'

'Well, it's supposed to be but it looks like I'll be doing some work this morning, although not prison related at least.'

He sits down, uninvited, but she doesn't mind too much. He pets Rocky under the table and one of the waitresses brings Beth's coffee over.

'Is this Rocky?'

'Yes, do you know him too? He seems to be a bit of a celebrity around here.'

Pete laughs. 'Yeah well, when he was a puppy he was forever escaping and would end up miles away in other people's gardens, so we all got to know him over the first couple of years of his life. Until Tammy started locking him in. He must be about five years old by now. I've not seen you for ages have I, boy?' Rocky licks his hand affectionately. 'So how are you enjoying working at the prison? I hope the inmates are playing nicely?'

'It's fine, thanks,' she says. 'It's a friendly place to work actually, considering. That could be because I haven't met many inmates yet though.'

He smiles and then starts playing with the sugar dispenser in a self-conscious way.

'I don't know what your plans are for later but I wondered if you would like to go for a drink maybe? Some of us go to the Tavern most nights and I haven't been for a while so I thought I'd make an appearance. You're welcome to join me.'

He speaks too fast which makes Beth realise he's hitting on her. She feels embarrassed for him and wonders whether to accept his offer or not.

'I don't have any plans yet but I'm not sure how today's going to pan out now I have a new client. How about you give me your number and I'll call you if I'm able to make it?'

He looks surprised, as if he was expecting an outright rejection. She wonders whether he thought she was interested in Dean. She is, but Pete doesn't need to know that. He writes his number on a napkin and leaves it on the table as he gets up to leave with his take-out order.

'There you go. Hope to see you later. Have a good day,' he says as he walks away, smiling.

She turns around to watch him leave and then follows him with her gaze to see which car he gets into. It's an old beat up dodge, nothing impressive. She waits for him to drive off and then takes Rocky out to her car to go and meet Derek and Emily.

When she pulls up at the park, Rocky starts barking and whining. He can spot Emily standing next to Derek's car. Before Beth even manages to get out of her car Emily has run over and opened Rocky's door.

'Rocky! Here, boy!'

He excitably sniffs her all over and then lays upside down at her feet, tail wagging fast. Emily's hugging him and showering him with kisses. Beth has to admit, it's a touching moment. *At least she's not completely emotionally stunted*, she thinks.

'Hi, I'm Derek.'

She's never liked social workers. In her experience, they don't do much good. Derek looks more like a boxer. He's tall and broad, with big hands. As she shakes his hand she smiles at him. 'Beth. Pleased to meet you. And you must be Emily?' She leans over and gives Emily a hug. Emily stiffens immediately and doesn't reciprocate, but she doesn't pull away either. 'I bet you've missed Rocky, haven't you? You must tell me all about him!'

Beth and Derek lead the way, along the path that skirts the entire children's park. Emily doesn't say anything.

'For instance, tell me why Rocky's so smelly when he eats pancakes!'

Emily giggles into her hand and for the first time she looks up at Beth, who notices she's wearing clothes that are too big for her and her hair is tangled and messy. Beth thinks she looks anaemic judging by how pale she is, which wouldn't be surprising seeing as anaemia usually goes hand in hand with malnutrition. She's also extremely thin.

'He sure likes to fart doesn't he, Emily?' Derek is laughing too.

'He isn't supposed to eat human food, that's why!' says Emily, very timidly. Then she runs off in front, seemingly relaxed, as Rocky follows her.

'I hope you're not expecting miracles,' says Beth as she and Derek watch the pair running around them.

'Not at all. We know she's obviously been affected by recent events and will need long term help to overcome some difficult experiences. But for now, we just want to help her grieve suitably and I don't know where to start. It's her mum's funeral next week. Do you think it's safe to take her along or would that just overwhelm her?'

Beth thinks about it. She knows from experience that not being able to attend your mother's funeral is devastating enough as an adult. Although for a child, it could protect them from feelings they're not mature enough to cope with.

'It depends. What was her relationship like with her mother? Was there any affection at all between them or does Emily speak poorly of her?'

They come to a bench and Derek sits down so Beth joins him. She can feel the icy cold wood through her clothes and it makes her shudder. Emily's throwing sticks for Rocky nearby.

'She's devoted to her mother. She makes excuses for her and she always expresses guilt and anxiety when she's asked to tell us what Tammy was up to all day in that house, about how they survived. That's why we could never get her away from the situation, because Emily didn't want to get away.'

When you grow up with crazy, it's your normality, thinks Beth. She feels tears welling in her eyes but won't let them fall. She turns away from Derek and tries to compose herself.

'That's because she doesn't know any different. Her life is normal to her. It's very hard to speak badly of your parents when you're a child.'

Derek takes this in but doesn't respond.

'Is there a father around?'

'No. He's not been around for years. I don't know where he's living any more.'

'Did she have a regular boyfriend who Emily might feel comfortable with?'

'No. I've never heard of any. Tammy suffered with paranoia and didn't like anyone in her home. Most of the time it was just her and Emily. She bought Rocky to be a guard dog but that was clearly a mistake as he's the friendliest dog in town. The worst he could do to an intruder is lick him to death, or sit on him.'

They laugh. Emily's gone over to the play area now and Beth stands up. 'Give me a few minutes alone with her.'

'No problem.'

She walks over to the swings. 'Do you want me to push you?'

Emily jumps, clearly startled. She hadn't noticed her approaching, which makes Beth think she must be living in her head. She gets onto the swing Beth's standing behind but she doesn't look particularly keen.

'You don't have to have a go on the swings just because I asked. It's completely up to you.'

'That's okay, you can push me if you want.'

Beth gently pulls the swing back and let's go. Emily holds on tight.

'I can go higher than that, I'm fourteen you know.'

This makes Beth laugh. 'Wow, fourteen? I better push you harder then! Make sure you hold on tight!'

Emily laughs as she goes higher and higher. To Beth she looks and acts about nine or ten years old. Both her psychological and physical development is delayed.

'Are you not scared?'

'No! It's fun!'

Beth stops pushing and stands to the side so she can talk to Emily while she's relaxed and enjoying the swing.

'Emily? Derek has told me about your mum passing away. I'm so sorry to hear that. You must miss her a lot.'

Emily doesn't say anything; she just keeps the swing momentum up.

'My mum also passed away but I was a bit older than you. I still miss her now.'

Emily looks concerned. 'You mean it never goes away?'

'No, it never goes away unfortunately, but it gets a tiny bit easier every day that goes by. That doesn't mean you don't still love them, but you start to accept it better.'

Emily slows down. 'She was only in jail because of me. If she wasn't in jail that morning, she might not have fallen sick.'

Beth's alarmed at her thought process. 'No, Emily, that's not true. Your mum didn't catch a bug from being in jail. Your mum died of other causes, which you'll be able to understand better as you get a little older. But it definitely wasn't anything to do with you or with her being in jail that day, do you understand?'

The swing has stopped now and Emily's face is blank, Beth can't read what she's thinking.

'Why won't anyone tell me how she died?'

Shit, Derek could've warned me, thinks Beth. *What am I supposed to tell her?* She takes Emily's hands and kneels down in front of her.

'I honestly don't know all the details but here's what I do know; your mum had been sick for a while because she had an addiction to something that was bad for her body. I think on this particular day she took too much of that substance and her body couldn't handle it. But, Emily, this could have happened on any day of her life. It has nothing to do with her being in jail. Addiction is a horrible disease that no one who has it can control, they usually need help.'

Emily's listening closely to every word. Beth hopes she's not speaking out of line by telling her about the suspected drug overdose. She doesn't think Dean would have told Derek yet about his new suspicions of murder.

'So why didn't Derek tell me that? They think I can't handle anything but I'm not a baby.'

Beth smiles at her. 'He wants to protect you because he's worried about you. You're very lucky to have him looking out for you.'

Emily looks around to see Derek, who's currently being trampled by Rocky. This makes her laugh. 'When can I live at home again?'

Beth has no idea what to say to this so she signals Derek to come and join them, to let him answer those questions. 'Let's ask the boss, shall we?'

'He won't tell me, I've already asked.'

Derek approaches them.

'Derek, Emily's been telling me how she feels grown up enough to be told the truth and I think she's right.' Derek looks increasingly alarmed. 'I've told her how her mum was struggling with addiction and that's what unfortunately caused her death.'

'Okay,' says Derek, slowly, looking from her to Emily and back to her again.

'But now Emily wants to know when she can move back home again. I'm not sure what happens next so I thought you'd be the best person to answer that.'

He gives Beth a look that suggests he feels he can't discuss it in front of Emily. 'Honey, I've already told you, none of that is figured out yet.'

Emily looks disappointed and loses interest in their conversation so Beth speaks up for her.

'What do you think happens next though, Derek, given your experience? It's important you keep Emily in the loop. After all, this is her life we're trying to sort out.'

Derek sighs and looks at Emily who is looking surprised at what Beth said on her behalf.

'To be really honest with you, Emily, and I'm only telling you this because you think you can deal with the truth and I really hope you can, it's unlikely you'll be able to live in your old house again.'

Emily looks down at the ground and they both spot the tears she's trying to hold back. 'Why?'

'Because it will have to be sold by the bank to pay off the mortgage your mum owed on it. However, you and I will go there at some point in the near future to collect all your things and anything of your mum's that you want to keep. I promise it won't be sold before you get a chance to go there again, you don't need to worry about that. And then, you will continue living with Julie and Simon until everything is sorted. It could be that you stay there for a few months or a few years, we just don't know yet. But you like Julie and Simon, right?'

She smiles. 'They let me go on the internet. We don't have the internet at home. Plus, Julie makes me cupcakes.'

Beth laughs. 'You're a girl after my own heart; I love cupcakes too!'

'But Julie's allergic to dogs so Rocky can't live with me there.'

'You don't need to worry about Rocky,' says Beth. 'Officer Matheson is happy to home him for the time being. You know Officer Matheson, don't you?'

Derek interjects. 'You know him as Officer Dean, don't you, Emily?'

She nods. 'When I was little he used to give me piggyback rides around the back garden whenever he came to visit. He's funny.'

'Well, he'll bring Rocky to visit you, so you don't have to worry about that,' says Beth. 'I know it's all change for you at the moment, but things will get better soon.'

Emily smiles but it looks like there's not much happiness behind it. In the spirit of keeping her in the loop, Derek mentions her mum's funeral.

'It's your mum's funeral on Monday. I want you to have a think about whether or not you want to attend. It's completely up to you and not a decision anyone wants to make for you.'

Emily fidgets in the swing.

'Have you ever been to a funeral before, Emily?' asks Beth.

'No, we don't have any relatives.'

'Let me explain what happens at a funeral then. First of all, everyone gathers in the church for prayers and maybe a few hymns. Then your mum will be buried in the cemetery while the Reverend gives a reading and everyone stands beside your mum's coffin. That's when people get their chance to say their own goodbyes. Then, they usually go back to someone's house to have a bite to eat together. Derek, who will be at the funeral that Emily will know?'

He tries to shrug his shoulders without Emily seeing but realises he can't and fakes positivity instead. 'Well, I'll be there, of course, and we can see if Officer Dean wants to come. If Emily comes then Julie and Simon will be there. Erm, I'm not sure who else as you don't have many relatives, but if we put a notice in the newspaper it should attract some other people who knew your mum.'

Beth thinks that Emily probably knows no one else in the town would want to attend.

'Would you come too?' she asks Beth.

Now it's Beth's turn to feel uncomfortable. 'Er, well, you know what? If you want to go and you want me there then, yes, I'll go.' Then, to change the subject, she adds, 'But Rocky can't come! He won't be allowed in the church as he'll probably knock all the flowers over!'

Emily quietly giggles into her hand and Rocky, after hearing his name mentioned, comes bounding over and sits next to them.

'Have a think about it, honey. You don't have to decide today,' says Derek.

'I do want to go. I don't need to think about it. I need to say goodbye to my mum.'

Derek exchanges a look with Beth that suggests he hopes she's right about this. 'Great, I'll get all the arrangements sorted then.'

'And I'll invite Officer Dean when he comes to collect Rocky later,' says Beth, feigning happiness.

'Great! Come on then, it's time for some lunch. Julie will be wondering where we are,' says Derek.

They walk to Derek's car and say their goodbyes. After Derek and Emily drive away, Beth gets Rocky into her car and drives back to the diner, desperately wishing she wasn't invited to Tammy's funeral.

Chapter Thirteen

Something's nagging at Dean but he can't put his finger on it. It was something said during his last conversation with Beth, while they were at his house, but then Sheila phoned him, which seemed more important. Maybe it's a lead he's not thought of or a link to something he's missed. He knows it'll come to him eventually, but for now it's irritating him.

He's spent all morning returning calls from people who phoned the station claiming to know something about Jane Doe. As he ends a call from a psychic who claims to know who she is, and will tell him for a specially reduced 'police discounted fee' of just five hundred dollars, he's about ready to give up on the case for today and start working on Tammy's case instead. However, before he switches cases, it's lunchtime and he's ready for a break so he offers to do the station's lunch run.

'Okay, I'm off to Frankie's. Who wants what?'

Marty jumps up to retrieve his wallet from his back pocket. 'Why is it always Frankie's? Why not Taco Bell or Mickey D's?'

'Because Frankie's food is real. If you have a problem with my choice of eatery, then go fetch your own lunch.'

Marty, Jenny and a few others give him long convoluted lists of what they want. With half the station claiming to be allergic to either wheat, gluten or dairy, he has a full page of notes with him by the time he leaves the station. He thinks how ironic it is that none of them seem to have allergies when ordering off the set menu at McDonald's. On the way to the diner he suddenly remembers he should have contacted Beth about collecting Rocky. As he pulls into the parking lot, he spots her entering her apartment with Rocky following behind. He assumes they've been out for a walk and decides to knock on her door, unannounced.

'Hi,' is all he manages when Beth opens the door because Rocky jumps all over him.

'Come on in,' Beth says, smiling. 'He's covered in slush because we were at that park near yours earlier.'

Dean pushes Rocky down and wipes his feet a bit longer than he would have if entering his own house. He tries not to look as Beth strips out of layers of sweaters, but when her T-shirt almost gets pulled off with them, he can't help but notice her body.

'It's always so warm inside when you get back from a walk, isn't it?' she says as she takes off her boots. He follows her lead and takes his shoes off. He notices her apartment doesn't have much in it. Dean knows for a fact that even when empty of tenants, this apartment comes furnished with a bed, a bookcase, a television and a small two-seater couch. He knows this from spending time here after arguments with Linda. Frankie's always welcoming on these occasions and says he likes having a cop looking after the place. Looking around now, other than some books, a few clothes here and there and some food shopping scattered about, it's pretty sparse. He wonders if she's waiting to see whether she likes New Hampshire life before she gets her belongings shipped over from England.

'Would you like a cup of tea or coffee?' she asks from the tiny kitchenette.

'I don't have long. I'm meant to be picking up everyone's lunches, but I suppose I could squeeze in a cup of English tea.'

'Actually, it's American tea. Did you think I brought a load over with me?' she replies with a laugh. 'Take a seat.'

'I'm sorry I didn't call you earlier about collecting Rocky. I've been talking to whackos all morning so it slipped my mind.'

'That's okay, I was out anyway.' She strokes Rocky's head. He's settled down on the only rug in the apartment, tired from this morning's exercise. 'I met with Derek and Emily this morning.'

She brings their drinks over to the coffee table and sits next to Dean on the couch. It's so small their knees touch.

'That was quick, I thought it might take a while for you to fit her in.'

'Derek phoned me this morning and we decided a walk with Rocky was just what she needed.'

'I hope you don't mind me giving him your number? He was really keen on my idea of having a counsellor talk to Emily.' He sips his tea, which is a nice change from the coffee he's started drinking again lately. Beth has switched the electric heater on. It's warming the small space quickly and Dean thinks he could quite easily spend the afternoon here rather than go back to the station. 'How did she seem to you?'

'Actually, not as messed up as I would have expected considering her background. She's definitely in touch with her emotions, which is a good thing, but she doesn't know how to grieve for her mum. Oh, which reminds me, you and I have been invited to her mum's funeral on Monday.'

'That's okay, I was planning to go anyway. Not necessarily for Tammy but I should keep an eye on who else turns up, if anyone. Now I'm looking for a murderer I've got to keep my eyes and ears open and, you never know, the perp may show up at the funeral.'

'That would be pretty twisted if they did,' she says.

'I know, but I saw it happen in a movie once and that's where I get all my best ideas,' he teases.

'Shut up! No, you don't.'

They sip their tea and watch Rocky sleep.

'Do you know for definite whether Emily's mum was murdered?'

'The medical examiner has told me she's ninety-nine per cent sure she was, so that's what I'm working on this afternoon.'

'Where will you even start?' asks Beth.

'I know who her main drug dealer was, so me and Marty

will be paying her a visit.' He finishes his tea. 'Anyway, I need to pick up lunch for everyone and then head back to the station. Unless you want to keep him, I can take Rocky back with me if you like?'

'As much as I would love to spend more quality time with him, Pete's asked me to join him for drinks at the Tavern tonight so Rocky would be alone for a while if you leave him here.'

Dean doesn't know what to say. He didn't realise Pete was such a fast mover.

'Is that okay?'

'Sure, that's fine!' says Dean, trying to look fine with it. 'Pete's a good guy. Divorced. Two kids. It was a messy split but I'm pretty sure his ex-wife has moved on with her life now she's taken him for everything he had.' He's not sure why he told her that. Well, he is. He's jealous. Even though he knows he shouldn't get involved with anyone new this soon after separating from Linda, that doesn't stop him wondering whether he should have made a move on her sooner. Realising once again that he knows nothing about women, he gets up to leave.

'It's just drinks,' she says, casually. 'He said the others from work will be there so I could do with getting to know them better if I decide to stick around.'

He looks back at her as he puts his boots on. 'You haven't decided whether to stay yet?'

She looks like she wants to talk about it in depth but doesn't want to keep him.

'I'm not sure yet, no.'

'Well, at least give it a little longer. Despite the recent suicide and possible murder, Maple Valley's really not a bad place to live.' He laughs.

She opens the front door for him. 'I'll have to take your word for that.'

'Come on, Rocky. Sorry to drag you out into the cold again but you've outstayed your welcome.'

Beth gets down to give the dog a hug as he lazily makes his way up from the floor and over to the door.

'Don't listen to him, Rocky. You're welcome here anytime.' She looks up at Dean, 'You both are.'

He wants to go back in and kiss her. Instead, he leaves with Rocky following behind. They walk down the steps and over to his car, through the slush. He puts Rocky in the back and then suddenly remembers his lunch list and heads into the diner.

At three o'clock that afternoon, with Rocky asleep under Captain Brown's desk, Dean and Marty pull up outside a trailer park on the outskirts of town.

'This place always reminds me of a shanty town,' says Marty as he gets out of the cruiser.

'I know what you mean. They've been pretty quiet lately though. I haven't been called out here for a while. Have you?'

'No, you're right. Somehow that makes me uneasy. I prefer it when we know what they're up to.'

They approach the badly painted black trailer first as that's the last known address they have for Skylar, Tammy's drug dealer. Marty knocks on the door. He has to knock hard to be heard over the loud television that's blaring out infomercials. When there's no response, he tries knocking on the plastic windows.

An elderly white woman wearing a bad purple wig answers the door. 'What?'

Dean lets Marty do the talking.

'We're looking for Skylar.'

'Don't know anyone called that.' She slams the door on them.

They laugh and knock again. This time she's even less friendly. 'What the fuck? Are you deaf? She doesn't live here any more.'

'I thought you didn't know her?' quips Marty.

'Listen, wise-ass, she moved out ages ago. Her and that disease of a boyfriend earn so much money selling drugs that they moved to town, in that big white house near the lake. You know, the one that crooked councillor used to own? That's how I ended up in this palace.'

Dean thinks she's telling the truth so he turns away. 'Thanks for your help, ma'am.'

'Fuck off!' she says as she slams the door on them for a second time.

'Charming! Can you believe that?' Marty asks. 'They choose to deal drugs for a living and they can afford a nicer house than either of us. We're in the wrong job.'

'Tell me about it.'

As they get in the car and drive back into town, Marty plucks up the courage to ask Dean about Linda.

'I've heard she's moved out and is staying with her sister, thanks to my wife being the town gossip. Are you two getting divorced?'

He takes a deep breath. 'To be honest, I don't know yet. Maybe.'

'Is it because you were tapping Sheila? Please tell me you were tapping Sheila?'

Dean can't help but laugh.

'I have to live my life vicariously through you, man, so give me something to think about in the shower!'

'What?' exclaims Dean. 'You better not be thinking about me in the shower, you freak!'

'You wish! I mean Sheila. She's so hot and now I know she has a weakness for cops I might stand a chance of getting a little action this year. Assuming you two are over now?'

Dean knows Marty's joking. 'Sheila would slap a sexual harassment charge on you the second you even look in her direction. You know she hates the way you joke about women.'

'I'm just kidding. I also heard there's a new British chick in town and you've been spotted gazing into each other's eyes over lunch at Frankie's?'

Dean isn't surprised his every move is being watched. It's hard to be inconspicuous in this town, especially when you're a cop.

'What does your wife do, follow me around all day and live tweet my every move?'

'No, but be careful, man. She's friends with Linda remember, and it wouldn't surprise me if she's telling her the same things as she's telling me every time I try to watch TV.'

Dean's annoyed. 'You can tell your wife that I've only been talking to Beth, the British woman, because she's helping Emily Gordon. There's nothing going on with us. In fact, she's going out for drinks with Pete tonight.'

'Pete? Is he dating again already? Last time I saw him he said he'd never touch another woman after what his wife did to him.'

'Yeah, well, wait until you meet Beth. She's hard to resist.'

Marty laughs. 'I better tell Pete to keep his hands off her.'

Dean laughs and doesn't protest. He'd quite like to tell Pete that himself. They pull up outside the lake house. It's old but it's a nice detached property with a bit of land. Dean spots a couple of kids running around outside without shoes or trousers, just socks, underpants and T-shirts. Considering it's been snowing, they must be freezing.

'Looks like she was right. There's Skylar's kids.'

'Money can't buy you class,' says Marty as he spots the kids playing in slush.

They approach the house and Dean takes the hands of the little boy and girl and leads them to the porch, out of the wet slush. *They must be no more than three years old*, he thinks. Marty knocks on the open front door.

'Skylar? It's Officers Matheson and Swan.'

It doesn't take long for Skylar to appear through a cloud of fruit flies hovering around the doorway. Dean tries not to think about what might have attracted them. Skylar's an attractive girl and Dean knows from experience she's intelligent, not your average drug dealer. Unfortunately, she just happens to fall for the wrong men. All of her previous boyfriends have done time for drug dealing. Her latest boyfriend, Beau, gets her to do his dirty work for him. Luckily for him, she's better at not getting caught than he is, which is good for business. She's practically an entrepreneur, hence their new home. She comes to the door with shoes and clothes for the kids. Probably only because the police are here. She doesn't say hello, she just grabs the kids and starts dressing them on the doorstep.

'Have you heard about Tammy yet?' asks Marty.

'Yeah, stupid bitch can't handle her drugs. Seriously, who OD's in this day and age?'

'Nice. Real sympathetic,' says Marty. 'I bet you're going to lose quite a bit of business now?'

She looks at them for the first time. 'You think I need her business? Have you seen the house I'm living in now? I've got better customers than her.'

Dean's irritated with her for flaunting what she does. He wishes he was wired. 'So where were you on the day she died? Did you pay her a visit the minute she got out of jail?'

She stops fussing with the kids and thinks about what Dean's asking. 'Are you trying to pin this on me? She didn't buy anything from me that whole week.'

'So where were you that day?' he asks again. He can tell she's tempted to slam the door in their faces, so he adds, 'You can either tell us here or tell us at the station while child services look after the kids. It's up to you.'

'For fuck's sake! Wait here.'

She storms off and disappears into the house. The kids look up at Dean and Marty, not quite knowing what to do. Dean picks up the boy and Marty picks up the girl.

'Jesus Christ, they're freezing,' says Marty.

They hug them close, to warm them up, and both kids immediately play with the police radios. Dean knows they can't step in the house as Skylar will freak out and start talking about suing the Police Department. When she gets back she doesn't even care that they're holding her kids. She has a diary in her hands and shows them that week.

'What does it say there? On the day she OD'd? Hospital appointment. You know how long it takes to drive to the hospital and back, especially when you've got two screaming kids wanting to stop every five minutes. We were out there nearly all day.'

Dean puts the boy down and gets his notepad out. 'What time was your appointment for?'

'Noon.'

'And which doctor did you see?'

'Doctor Crawford. It was for the kids' asthma check-up and vaccinations. And before you ask, Beau came with us.'

'What time did you leave the hospital?'

She starts getting annoyed. 'I can't remember that!'

'Maybe if you stopped smoking marijuana you'd have a better memory and your kids wouldn't have asthma. Think, Skylar.'

She ignores his comment and thinks out loud. 'It must've been about two because we had lunch in their coffee shop and by the time we got home it was already starting to get a little dark.'

Dean found Tammy dead just after three o'clock. There's no way Skylar could've made it home from the hospital and killed Tammy if she was really there for a noon appointment and stayed for lunch after. He puts his notepad away and Marty puts the girl down.

'Okay, we'll check that out. In the meantime, burn a little of your drug money on some heating; your kids are freezing.'

'Fuck you!'

For the third time today, they have a door slammed on them as they walk back to the cruiser.

'If it wasn't them then who else would've killed Tammy?' asks Marty as they pull away.

Dean sighs. 'Something tells me this is going to be more complicated than I thought.'

When they get back to the station Marty gets called out straightaway to deal with a theft at the nearby DIY store. Dean heads to his desk where he finds Sheila's full autopsy report waiting for him. She's now one hundred per cent certain Tammy was murdered, as the bruising on her arms is consistent with someone's hands holding her down. Sheila notes that the perp had 'small to average' sized hands. That could mean it was a woman. Maybe Skylar was lying to him about her alibi, in order to buy some time to flee. Although with her new set-up he doubts she would want to leave. But maybe she needs time to hide some evidence. He immediately looks up the number for the hospital switchboard to try to speak to someone who will verify Skylar's appointment.

'I'll put you through to Doctor Crawford's office,' says the switchboard operator.

Doctor Crawford's personal assistant answers on the first ring. 'Doctor Crawford's office, how may I help you?'

'Hi, my name's Officer Matheson from Maple Valley Police Department. I need you to confirm whether or not Skylar Hutton had an appointment with Doctor Crawford on Monday at noon.'

There's a slight hesitation in her response. 'I need to make sure you are who you say you are, sir, for data protection purposes. I'm going to have to call you back at your station. Are you there now?'

Dean sighs and sits back in his chair. Sometimes it feels like every law in this country is designed to slow the police down. 'Yes, I am. Do you want our switchboard number?'

'I'll find that myself, sir, as I have to make sure it's legitimate. No offence.'

Dean shakes his head. 'Oh, none taken, of course.'

'Give me two minutes and I'll call you right back.'

He puts the phone down and rolls his eyes. He watches Jenny who's not currently taking a call. He knows the hospital call will come through her. Within a few minutes she takes a call and looks over at him. She smiles as his phone starts to ring.

'I have the hospital on the phone for you. Is this your STD results day?'

He can't help but laugh. 'It sure is, keep your fingers crossed for me!'

He sees her laugh as she puts the call through.

'Hello, Officer Matheson. I'm just checking that name for you now; Skylar Hutton, wasn't it?'

'It was,' he says, patiently.

Dean hears a lot of typing and clicking from the end of the line.

'Here we are. Dr Crawford did have an appointment booked in at twelve noon that day, for two child vaccinations. The notes say the adult who attended was male though, not female.'

Well, what do you know? Thinks Dean. *Skylar sent Beau instead of her. He isn't even their father so that was a strange decision.*

'Are you sure?'

'Yes, his name was Beau Lachay.'

'Okay, thanks for that.'

He ends the call and sits back in his chair. Just because Skylar's alibi doesn't hold up, doesn't mean she killed Tammy. Detective Jones always told him it's good to get as many concrete facts as possible before going for an arrest warrant, otherwise you can look stupid come arrest time. But the false alibi and the 'small to average sized hands' from Sheila's autopsy report are two good facts. He'd like to find a third before he goes to Steve or Captain Brown with his theory.

Jenny looks over at him questioningly. He gives her a thumbs up and mouths, 'All clear!' She laughs.

Marty arrives back at the station and shakes snow from his jacket and boots.

'It's snowing again?'

'Yeah, starting to get heavy.'

'Great.' Dean sighs. 'What was the problem at the store?'

'George thinks he has a shoplifter. He's missing a few things, nothing big. It's probably just kids. He doesn't even know when it went missing so there's not much I can do. I've told him to watch his CCTV.'

This makes Dean think of Frankie's steps, but with Skylar on his mind he decides to focus on Tammy's murder for the rest of his shift.

Chapter Fourteen

Beth decides at the last minute to meet Pete for drinks at the Tavern this evening. She doesn't think Dean's ever going to make a move on her so she figures she might as well have some fun while she's in town. She deliberately wears a tight black dress with the highest heels she owns. The Tavern isn't a nightclub so she'll be overdressed, but as she isn't expecting to be in town forever, she isn't too bothered about what people think of her.

When she walks through the entrance, she looks around for Pete. She didn't bother calling him first to let him know she was coming. This way she's not his date. He's clearly been looking out for her though, as he's the first person to turn around from the bar. She smiles at the surprise on his face as he looks her up and down. Some of her other colleagues are playing pool and Sally from the admin team is sitting with Pete at the bar.

'I didn't think you'd come,' says Pete. 'Let me get you a drink.'

'That's nice of you, I'll have a bourbon and Diet Coke. Hi, Sally.'

She likes Sally because she's plain, boring and has shown no interest in getting to know her better. Beth likes people who aren't nosy.

'Wow, you look amazing. Far too good for this place!' says Sally. 'Are you planning on going somewhere after this?'

'Who knows, the night is young!'

Sally laughs and walks over to the pool table to join in with the others.

'So how was your day off in the end?' asks Pete.

Beth sits on a bar stool and waits for her drink. 'Quite relaxing, actually. I didn't really do much. How about you?'

'I was just studying most of the day,' he says.

'Really? What are you studying?' She's genuinely interested; she likes an educated man.

'Well, I don't want to put you off but I want to be a lawyer.'

He says it like he's embarrassed which makes her think he has self-esteem issues. Not attractive in a man. 'That's great! I bet that's difficult to study while you work full-time?'

She listens to him talking about his hopes and dreams but without really caring much. It's obvious to her that he'll never make it as a lawyer because he doesn't appear to have the money or the confidence to see it through to the end. Still, he's attractive and he's buying the drinks so she's happy to feign interest. As he talks she keeps one eye on the door, hoping Dean will turn up. When conversation runs dry she enquires about the inmates they work with.

'I haven't had much luck getting volunteers for my counselling sessions, apart from Shania. Is there anyone in particular who you think I should approach? Anyone who's really messed up and needs to be helped?'

Pete sips his beer and thinks. 'I mean, they're all pretty messed up, to be honest with you, that's why they're in prison in the first place. But the ones that get to me are the ones who don't even try to look after their kids, you know? Like Shania, for example. She doesn't even miss them while she's inside. That's sick, right?'

Beth agrees. 'So who else is like Shania then? Because I'm happy to approach people in private to see if they'd like my help.'

'There's Judy D'Angelo. Her kids have health problems because they're inbred, although she won't say who the father is, just that it's someone in her immediate family. She's protecting that man over her kids! She's obviously messed up because she's tried killing herself twice.'

'What's she in prison for?'

'Neglecting her kids. She went on a week-long holiday and

left her kids alone with just the family dog and a pantry full of chips and chocolate. The kids were starving when the cops broke down the door after a tip off.'

Beth takes a sip of her bourbon. 'Is she remorseful?'

'I can't tell, to be honest. It's a touchy subject with her, so maybe. But we all know the minute she gets out, although she won't get her kids back, she'll get pregnant with another one and the whole cycle starts again.'

She can tell he feels strongly about this as he's tearing the beer mat into strips as he talks. She decides to add Judy to her list of potential clients but, for now, she wants to lighten the mood so she orders them their second round of drinks and starts flirting with him. She doesn't know yet if she's going to sleep with him but she's not against the idea. Unless Dean shows up.

Chapter Fifteen

After a couple of busy days at work, trying to be both a cop and a detective, Dean needs an evening to himself where he's not doing overtime and he's not thinking about work. At eight o'clock on Friday night he leaves the station with Rocky, their bellies rumbling for dinner. On the way to the diner he thinks about Linda and how he hasn't heard a word from her since their last argument on Monday night. He's not even had a text. He knows she didn't take many of her belongings with her, so he's expecting her to want to arrange collection of the rest of her stuff at some point.

Then he thinks of Beth and wonders whether she's gone for drinks with Pete. Although he hopes she didn't, he knows he doesn't have time for another relationship himself, plus he's still got the mess with Linda to figure out. If Beth does start dating Pete it would be one less complication in his life, allowing him to concentrate on solving these cases and proving himself to be detective material. He's hoping Miller gets comfortable lying in bed all day, and that he might even decide to retire early. He pulls over at the diner to pick up some take-out. Leaving Rocky in the car, he queues, waiting for Rachel's attention at the counter.

'Hey, Dean. How are you doing tonight?' she asks.

'Good thanks, you?'

'Not too bad. You just missed the rush. What can I get you?'

'I've got Rocky in the car so just something to take out. What's Frankie making this evening?'

'He's got some lasagne and French toast left if that interests you?'

'Sounds great. And some bacon fat for Rocky.'

'Wait right there, it won't take me long to bag it up.'

As he waits, he hears the door open behind him. He turns around, wondering if he'll bump into Beth while he's here. Instead, Linda walks in as if they've pre-arranged to meet there. He's taken by surprise.

'Hi. How are you?' she asks.

'What are you doing here?' He doesn't know what she wants so he's not in the mood for small talk.

'I was on my way to the house when I saw your car outside. I've been missing you and I wanted to talk.'

He rolls his eyes and moves away from the counter so they don't give everyone a show.

'What?' She follows him. 'We are still married, you know. We need to talk all this through. I think we might have been too hasty last time we spoke.'

He turns around and leans against the wall as he looks at her. She looks tired. 'I thought you said your gut feeling was that we shouldn't be together? You said you don't love me any more and, oh wait, wasn't it you who had a two-year affair behind my back?' He sees she's about to protest about his affair but stops her before she can speak. 'Yes, I know I can't talk, but I was grieving for my brother. You got yourself pregnant with another man's baby!'

The remaining diners seem to simultaneously stop talking and eating at the same time and look over at Dean and Linda. Linda lowers her eyes in embarrassment and folds her hands over her stomach. He knows he's upset her but she doesn't say anything. He feels bad every time they speak to each other.

'Why are you really here, Linda?'

She looks surprised at his directness but this quickly turns to annoyance. 'Who's Beth Smith?' she asks.

'Oh, come on! I see you've been talking to Marty's wife. You know, we're technically separated so I don't need to answer that question.'

'We're still married!' she shoots back.

'She's no one! Just a new counsellor at the prison. I've

111

asked her to help Emily Gordon, that's it. I haven't slept with her, Linda, despite what Marty's wife says.'

'You mean you haven't slept with her *yet*.'

'Oh! That's funny, coming from you. Just how many men did you sleep with during our marriage? You still haven't told me who got you pregnant!' His voice has risen so loud the whole diner stops talking again.

Linda cringes, making Dean feel like a jerk. He doesn't know why they're doing this to each other. He knows he can't stay married to her after she broke the news of her affair, but he doesn't want their relationship to be like this. He wants a smooth break, where they both move on amicably. Rachel slides his take-out food across the counter towards them and smiles awkwardly. He's aware everyone's listening to them so he throws down some money and heads outside.

Linda follows him to his car and stares at her feet. 'Dean, I'm pregnant.'

He opens his mouth but nothing comes out. He closes it again and turns away from her.

'It's yours,' she adds.

'How do you know?' He thinks it's a perfectly reasonable question, but Linda obviously disagrees.

'You asshole! How dare you?'

He swings around to face her. 'What do you mean? Just a few days ago you told me you miscarried someone else's baby, so why wouldn't I ask that?'

Rocky's been watching them through the car window and starts barking as their voices rise. Dean feels bad for him; he's already lived through enough dysfunction and now they're making him anxious. He opens the back door and lets him out.

'Keep your voice down, he's agitated.'

'I've only slept with you in the last few months,' she hisses.

He resists the urge to say, 'Well, that's kind of you.' He can't remember when they last slept together. Thoughts of sex with Sheila blur the lines.

'God, we are two messed up people,' he says with a deep sigh.

She looks over at him and smiles. 'I know. What the hell are we going to do?'

He crouches down next to Rocky and tries to think. 'Do you want to keep the baby?'

'Yes, but I don't want to raise him or her alone. I always thought you'd be an amazing dad. Maybe if we have it, it will all work out.'

Dean feels sorry for her but he can't think about this right now. 'How about we sleep on it and meet up tomorrow? We need to decide separately what we want.'

Linda reluctantly agrees and slowly walks to her car. 'I'm staying at the Hinsdale Hotel tonight.'

As she drives away Dean notices the faces of the other diners watching them through the window. He puts Rocky back in the car and places their food in the front with him and then drives away, a little too fast.

When he gets in his front door, his cell phone rings.

'Hello?'

'Hi, it's Beth!'

She sounds drunk and he can hear music and voices in the background.

'Come and join us at the Tavern. I'll buy you a drink!'

After what just happened, he's no longer tempted to join them. 'Sorry, Beth, but I can't tonight.'

'Why not? Is everything okay?'

'Not really.' He sighs. 'My wife just came back to tell me she's pregnant with my child and she wants us to make a fresh start.' He's not sure why he's telling her this, it just comes out.

She becomes serious. 'Do you want me to come over? Honestly, it might help to talk about it.'

He smiles at her offer, but thinks inviting a hot drunk woman to his house tonight will only end in trouble.

'No, I'm fine. We're both going to take the evening to think about things and then meet up tomorrow to decide what happens next. I really need to do some serious thinking tonight.'

'Oh, okay. She's not staying with you tonight, is she?'

'No, she's staying at a hotel.'

'Okay. Well, if you need me, ring me.'

'Thanks. You carry on enjoying yourself.'

She laughs and then ends the call.

Dean gives Rocky his bacon fat and eats his own take-out food in front of the television, content to watch whatever's on without changing channels. When he's finished with dinner, he hunts down the liquor left over from last Christmas. They have unopened bourbon that Marty bought for him. He'd hidden it away from Linda. It's been a long time since Dean has touched alcohol.

'With the night we've had, we deserve it, don't we, boy?'

Rocky wags his tail and barks. Dean finds himself a glass and some ice and sits back down in front of the TV, pouring a full glass of bourbon, but only intending to sip that one glass all night. He puts his feet up and lets Rocky spread out next to him on the couch. Thinking about everything that's happened over the last week makes him drink faster than he intended.

It's been an awful year what with John dying, Linda's depression, his affair and then learning of Linda's affair and subsequent miscarriage. Now Linda says she's pregnant with his child. He refills his empty glass to the top without noticing. The thought of Linda coming back and trying to pretend everything is good with their relationship makes his chest ache. They can't trust each other any more and, if he's honest with himself, he resents her for not being someone he could lean on after John's death. It makes sense to him now though; she was sleeping with someone else at the time so she was splitting her time and affections. Plus, her miscarriage must've happened just before John's death. But the way John died was so traumatic for Dean, he feels she should've helped him through it, no matter what.

No one expected John to ever take his own life. He was a successful lawyer who loved his job and was always bragging to everyone about how much he billed his clients, and what new boy toys he'd spent his money on. When it was just him and Dean together, John was more real and down-to-earth. He always insisted he wanted a simple life with a wife and kids, living in suburbia, but his firm wanted him to be someone else, someone more aggressive and macho and this didn't come natural to John. He was more sensitive than that.

When John took a leave of absence from work for a few months and moved back to town, away from the distractions of the city, he changed quickly. Dean didn't see him as much even though he lived closer to them, and so he didn't know what was going on in his life. Whenever he suggested to Linda that they invite John around for dinner, she refused almost every time. She'd say she didn't want to spend all evening listening to them talk about work, as she spent enough time with lawyers as part of her job. On the few occasions John did come for dinner, Linda would practically ignore him. Dean thought she was jealous that he was spending his time off with someone other than just her.

When Dean got the call that John had died, Linda didn't even hug him. He couldn't forgive her for that. She just started avoiding him. Whereas Sheila was there for him when he needed it, and that's why the affair started. They'd both tried to resist, neither of them are stupid and they knew it would end in tears, but it helped Dean through the darkest days of his life. It gave him a distraction from dealing with the pain and from asking the same questions over and over in his head. Why did John do it? Why didn't he come to Dean first, and tell him what he was going through? Was Dean too selfish to notice John's life was falling apart? Could he have stopped it? These thoughts were relentless apart from when he was with Sheila, away from home and work.

He wonders who it was that Linda had an affair with but at the same time he doesn't want to know. He suspects it can't be anyone he knows well because he would have spotted it. Whenever he thinks about the possibilities a heavy feeling of dread in his stomach tells him it's best to let sleeping dogs lie. Especially if he decides to make a go of things with her.

He sighs out loud and tries to concentrate on the TV whilst knocking back his drinks. His vision is starting to get a little blurred. If he was really honest he would tell Linda tomorrow that he doesn't want them to try to save their marriage, baby or not. The one good thing to come out of the affair with Sheila was the realisation that lust can be thrilling and make you feel alive. What he has with Linda doesn't make him feel that way. Even spending time with Beth makes him feel young again. His identity has changed during their marriage, not through anyone's fault. He's just not himself any more, he's become a more boring version. All he does now is work. Maybe it's because of how much they've been through and maybe he owes it to her to try again. But he can't help thinking a baby is just going to emphasise their problems, not alleviate them. He takes another big sip of bourbon and rests his head on the cushion behind him. It's not long before the alcohol sends him to sleep.

He can't tell if that's his head banging or if it's something else. He tries to open his eyes but his eyelids are too heavy. Rocky's barking now. He jumps up and instinctively reaches for his gun, without knowing why. It takes what seems like ages for the fuzz to clear from his head and when it does he realises he's at home and someone is banging on his front door. Really loudly.

'Dean? Dean, open up!'

It sounds like Steve. Confused, and dizzy from getting up

too fast after a night of drinking, he dodges Rocky and opens the front door.

'What's the matter?' he asks Steve.

'Where have you been? It's eight-thirty! We've been ringing you for an hour!'

Dean looks at his watch. It feels like he's only just stopped drinking but it's Saturday morning and he should be at work.

'Shit! Sorry. Let me brush my teeth and I'll be there.' His mouth tastes of garlic and bourbon, and his throat is bone dry.

Steve follows him into the house.

'No, Dean, you don't understand. There's been an accident, out on the highway between here and the Hinsdale Hotel.'

Dean spins around. 'Is anybody hurt? What happened?'

'Where's your phone, man? Why haven't you answered our calls? Where have you been?'

Steve's looking at him strangely; he's also sniffing the air in front of them and looking in the lounge where the empty bottle of bourbon is sitting in front of the couch.

'I've been here, asleep! I must've fallen asleep in front of the TV last night. I don't really remember, ask Rocky!' He laughs, trying to downplay the drinking.

'I thought you didn't drink any more?' asks Steve.

'I don't, that's why it knocked me out. I don't know where my phone is though.' Steve's eyeing him with suspicion and it pisses him off. 'Will you just tell me what's going on? You can lecture me about drinking later.'

Steve gently pushes him down onto the couch by the shoulders.

'There was an RTA. Just one car that we know of right now. Dean, it was Linda.'

Dean looks puzzled and laughs. 'What do you mean? She was in the car or it was just her car?' His brain won't join the dots quick enough.

'She was in the car. She's sustained some injuries and she's been taken to the hospital. The paramedics worked on her at the scene because the fire department had to cut her out of the car. They don't know if she's going to be okay.'

Dean jumps up. 'But she's pregnant! She has to be okay!'

Steve looks alarmed. 'What was she doing up there then? Have you kicked her out or something? Was she staying at the hotel?'

'We're meant to meet up today to discuss things. Did she not tell you?'

Steve looks away. 'She's been unconscious the entire time. We're hoping she'll come around at the hospital and tell us what happened.'

'I need to go and see her,' says Dean as he leaves the house without his keys or a coat. Rocky barks. 'You have to take Rocky for me.'

Steve grabs Dean's coat and house keys and locks Rocky in the house for now.

'Here, take these.' He passes them to Dean who just throws them into Steve's car and then gets in the passenger seat.

'You want me to take you?' asks Steve.

'Yeah, sorry. I can't drive, I'm way over the limit.'

Steve looks at him in a way that suggests he's not sure what's going on with him. He gets in and drives Dean to the hospital.

Chapter Sixteen

When Steve arrives at the police station the following Friday afternoon, a week since Linda's accident, a crowd quickly forms around his desk. Dean's friends are keen to ask how Linda's funeral went, as Steve was the only one who got an invite. Not that anyone begrudges Dean's decisions at the moment. He has just lost his wife.

Steve throws his keys onto the desk, takes his black suit jacket off and collapses into his chair. 'Man, that was awful.'

Jenny puts her hand on his shoulder. 'How was he?'

'I can't tell. He didn't talk to anyone. He shook hands but wouldn't look up. It's like he was completely separate to Linda's family. None of them sat with him.'

'Why the hell not? The crash wasn't his fault,' says Marty.

Sheila passes through the office on her way out after a meeting. When she overhears Steve, she comes to join them. 'Tensions always run high between families at funerals. You've got to remember, apart from weddings and christenings, it's usually the only time the two families come together.'

'That's true,' agrees Captain Brown. 'Do we know any more about what caused the crash?'

Sheila sighs. 'CSI are still quiet at the moment, sifting through their photos and evidence. I'll keep chasing them. I know one thing's for sure; this town's keeping me and the coroner busy lately. Her office keeps ringing, pressuring me for more information about all these deaths so that they can arrange the inquests.'

'We're run off our feet over here too, especially now Dean's taking some bereavement leave and Miller's still off sick. This couldn't have happened at a worse time,' says Brown. 'I've got the D.A. on my back about Tammy's murder.'

Jenny agrees. 'I'm fielding so many calls from the press right now. They're trying to imply our town has itself a suicide problem. It's a good job they don't know about the murder yet, or they'd all be parked up outside.'

Brown shakes his head as he walks back to his office. Jenny goes back to the phones and Sheila sits down in-between Marty and Steve. Steve knows she's feeling guilty about her affair with Dean. When she heard about Linda's death she told him she blamed herself. She believes if she hadn't got involved with Dean, they'd still be together and Linda wouldn't have been out driving at that time of night.

'I'm worried about him,' she says. 'He didn't react well to John dying and for this to happen just a few months later means he's going to need our support.'

Steve agrees. 'He's definitely not himself. Even before this happened.'

'What do you mean?'

'When I went to find him that morning he was drinking, or drunk from the night before. I'm not sure which.'

Marty's surprised. 'But he never drinks. He always turns us down when we go for a night out. Did he say why he'd been drinking?'

Steve shakes his head. 'No. He stank of it though. Looks like he slept on the couch too. It would bother me normally, but because it was the night of Linda's crash, it bothers me even more.'

Sheila stands up, ready to get back to work. 'He needs his friends around him. Maybe one of you could ask him what's been going on lately.'

'I'm heading out so I'll walk with you,' says Marty as he grabs his coat.

They leave Steve sitting alone at his desk. He switches his computer on and forces himself to look again at the crash scene photos. They were taken while Linda was still alive, thankfully. It's not like he's not used to seeing deceased people, but when they're the wife of one of your closest friends, it's horrendous and something he's glad to be spared.

When he had arrived at the scene in the early hours of that morning, it was dark, cold and hard to understand what had happened. He hadn't recognised Linda because of the terrible bruising to her face and neck. Her neck was so swollen he had assumed she'd broken it. But when he checked for a pulse as he phoned the ambulance, he was amazed to find it strong. It's only when he lifted her hair off her face and stood back a bit that he recognised her and the car. His heart sank as he realised he'd have to tell Dean. She hadn't been wearing a seat belt, which is unusual for the wife of a cop. He hadn't noticed the skid marks on the road until it had gotten lighter. By then both the ambulance crew and the fire department had arrived and were working hard to get Linda out of the car alive.

He'd tried calling Dean repeatedly, but there was no answer. It looked to him like Linda had swerved into the tree to avoid someone or something, maybe a deer or, knowing Linda's love of animals, maybe she was swerving to avoid just a bird or a beaver; things other people would just run over. But the skid marks suggest someone might have run her off the road on purpose. He just hopes he's wrong, for Dean's sake.

Chapter Seventeen

Beth hasn't seen Dean in over a week. Understandably, she wasn't invited to his wife's funeral this morning and she had to attend Tammy's funeral without him. At least that was quick and painless. Only a handful of people turned up and Emily managed to hold it together. Beth has been eating breakfast and dinner at Frankie's every day in the hope of seeing Dean, but he hasn't come in.

'Have you not heard from him either?' she asks Rachel, as she eats her dinner at the counter that evening.

'No, I was at the funeral earlier but I didn't manage to speak to him. I just can't get over it, first John and now Linda. I wish we knew what happened. He wanted to sit by himself at the church. Linda's family avoided him because they think he should've gone after her. Someone told them about the argument that started in here that night and then continued outside. They think he shouldn't have let her stay at a hotel.'

'Someone should go and visit him to check he's okay being in that house alone,' says Beth.

'His colleague, Steve Dalkin, said he'd been to check on him a few times and Dean had let him in for a coffee, so he's not completely alone. Plus, he has Rocky. Steve offered to take Rocky with him but Dean wouldn't hear of it.'

'I did too. I've sent him a few texts but he hasn't responded to any of them. I guess we've only just met but I'm worried about him. He's such a good guy, the way he looks out for Emily and Rocky.'

'Yeah, he's one of a kind all right,' says Rachel. 'His neighbour, Mrs Busby, said she's been leaving casseroles on his front porch every single day so we know he's eating okay. Maybe when they stop he'll come and visit us.'

Frankie's been listening and comes over to join in. 'Aren't you a counsellor? Can't you go and counsel him?'

The thought has already crossed Beth's mind. 'When he's ready, he knows where I am. You can't help someone until they're ready to be helped. He's grieving at the moment and that can be a long, complicated process.'

'Maybe he doesn't know he needs help,' says Frankie. 'We know what he was like after his brother died; he fell to pieces and didn't ask for anyone's help. He had an affair, you know? Sometimes men need help but they can't ask for it so they do something crazy instead.'

Rachel nods her head. 'It's true.'

'Just do us a favour,' says Frankie. 'Pay him a visit. Pretend you're there to take the dog for a walk, or to bring him some food. I'll plate up some risotto for you.'

Beth feels like she can't say no but she doesn't mind too much as she does want to check up on him. 'Okay, if you think he won't mind.'

Frankie heads to the kitchen.

'In a twisted way, I hope Linda was speeding and lost control because of the ice and it wasn't some asshole who caused her to crash into that tree,' says Rachel.

Beth agrees. 'I know. I can't imagine someone around here doing that and not reporting it or staying to help her. I've never lived in such a friendly town before.'

'Don't worry, Dean's colleagues are making it their personal mission to find out. I think they're convinced there was someone else involved. I overheard them talking about how they're testing the second set of skid marks against different types of car tyres and all sorts. I guess they're just trying to help Dean.'

Beth doesn't say anything. Frankie emerges from the kitchen and gives her a bagged plate of food. 'Tell him we love him and we want to see him back,' he says.

'I will. Thanks for dinner.'

She leaves the diner and gets in her car. She thinks she should at least text Dean first in case he's adamant he doesn't want visitors.

Frankie's ordered me to bring you some food. I can be there in 10 mins, is that ok?

It takes just seconds for him to reply: *Fine.*

When he lets her in the house the first thing she notices is how tidy it is. She was expecting a smelly mess of dirty clothes and used dishes, but even Rocky is shiny.

'He uses my bath water after me. I know, right? Who'd have thought a Rottweiler liked taking baths? He loves the bubbles too.'

She can't help but laugh at that. 'You use bubble bath?'

'Of course. It's not a bath without bubbles, is it, Rocky?'

She notices they both smell the same; clean and floral. Dean's in pyjama bottoms and a T-shirt and the heating is up full blast, making her take her coat and jumper off. She knows that just because he's cracking jokes, it isn't necessarily a good sign. The pale skin and dark shadows under his eyes tell a different story. He gestures to the couch and offers her a glass of orange juice, which she takes. He sits down one seat away from her on the couch.

'I know everyone must ask this but how are you doing? I can't imagine how hard this morning was for you. I wish I could've been there.'

He's quick to reply. 'Don't worry, I'm fine. I can't believe she's dead. I don't want to believe it. This morning was surreal. I had to jump in the bath as soon as I got home to try to wash the guilt off me.'

'Why do you feel guilty? What could you have done to stop it?'

He looks away and sips his drink, which she's pretty sure has more than orange juice in it.

'You're not counselling me, are you? No offence, but I could really do without that.'

She's taken aback for a minute. It's hard not to probe him about his feelings when he's just lost his wife.

'I'm asking as a friend to you, not as a professional. But we don't have to talk about it. I've put Frankie's food on your side table. Maybe I should leave.'

She moves as if to get up but he grabs her hand.

'No, don't go. It's driving me crazy, being alone in this house. Rocky's great but he doesn't answer back. Well, not all the time.'

She stays where she is and he lets go of her hand.

'I'll stay on one condition.'

He looks at her questioningly.

'I want what you're drinking.'

His smile lights up his face and he instantly looks younger. He goes to the kitchen and gets a glass, some ice and the large bottle of vodka he's been drinking from.

'Tell me when to stop,' he says as he pours the vodka.

'All the way, please.'

They sit drinking together, just watching TV. Beth looks around the living room and sees signs of Linda everywhere: framed photos, a pink scarf with butterflies on and even her slippers are still here, like they're waiting for their owner to be right back. She knows everyone grieves differently, and maybe it's not properly hit him yet, but to her, Dean appears to be coping well.

'Do you have a cat?' she asks out of the blue, noticing the scratching post in the corner.

'Yeah, kind of. Linda's sister is looking after her. She told me at the funeral that she's going to come by after the weekend and collect some of Linda's stuff. She insinuated I was going to throw it all out and move another woman in straight away.'

He sounds bitter.

'She doesn't blame you, does she?'

'She blames me for everything. She knows I had a brief

affair so she's using that to blame me for Linda's drinking. Ironically, it turns out Linda started drinking heavily two years ago so they can't pin that one on me. Plus, Linda told me the jerk she was having an affair with got her pregnant.' He looks over at Beth for a reaction.

'Oh,' is all she manages.

'Yep. She miscarried though.'

Beth's confused. 'So, when you told me that other night that she was pregnant, was she pregnant with your child or his?'

He laughs bitterly. 'That's what I asked and to be honest it didn't go down too well, especially in a diner full of our neighbours. She insisted it was mine.'

Beth tuts and reaches for his arm. 'Oh, Dean. You've certainly had an awful year, haven't you?'

He takes a long sip of his drink. 'Tell me about it.'

'I have to be a counsellor for just one minute. Please tell me why you feel guilty because that's not healthy.'

He turns his body on the couch, to face her.

'I've been through this before, recently. My brother died a few months ago. But I didn't feel the way I'm feeling now.'

'I'm so sorry about your brother. In what way are you feeling different?' She can tell he's struggling to find the right words.

'I loved Linda for a long time, but over the last few years we both changed a lot. It got to the point where we were living together but not as a couple. She was distant and now I know why; she was fucking someone else. But, to be honest, after the initial shock of her telling me that, it really didn't bother me as much as it should've. And when she told me she was pregnant with my child, I had no feelings about it at all. It didn't seem real somehow. I'm still not convinced it was mine because I don't even remember having sex with her recently.

'It was only when she said she wanted us to be together again that alarm bells started ringing in my head and I wanted to say no. I didn't want to hurt her feelings though, so I suggested we put it off for another night so I could think of a nice way to say "thanks, but no thanks". Although I would've been there for the baby no matter what. The thing is, if I'd have told her there and then that it was over, she wouldn't have been staying at that hotel for the night. She would've either been going back to Chrissie's or she could've stayed here until she was ready to leave. I don't even know why she was out on that stretch of road so late after she would've arrived for check-in. Maybe she was going back out to meet someone for a drink, I just don't know. The others are looking into it all for me because I just can't bear thinking about it.'

He stops and takes another sip of his drink. 'So, I feel guilty because I wanted a way out of our marriage and then she died.' He looks at her. 'Did I make that happen?' He breaks down.

Beth reaches forward and holds him tight while his grief pours out of him. She can feel the emotion leaving him as he heaves big breaths in and out, along with the tears. He smells lovely and feels strong in her arms but all she can think about is the pain he's feeling. She wishes she could tell him that what has happened is for the best.

Chapter Eighteen

When his clock chimes midnight, Dean's almost sober. He doesn't want to be a drunk and can feel how easy it would be to go down that road, so his last few drinks have been just Coke. Beth has switched to water.

The local weather report comes on TV and warns them of heavy snow outside. Beth gets up to look out of the front window.

'It wasn't snowing earlier. Oh shit, come and look at this!' she exclaims.

Dean walks up behind her, so close he can feel her body heat. The snow is already a foot deep. He feels guilty that having his heating on full blast has numbed them to how cold the temperature dropped over the evening.

'You're snowed in,' he says, laughing.

'Why are you laughing? You'll be the one carrying me home when I can't get my car out!'

'Maybe Rocky can pull you along on skis?'

Rocky doesn't even lift his head at the mention of his name. He's fast asleep on the armchair. When Beth doesn't laugh, he realises she's genuinely worried about getting home. 'You couldn't have driven anyway, you put away more liquor than me!'

'But I thought one of the perks of having a police officer as a friend was getting away with bad things.'

She pouts as she says this, which immediately turns him on. He's been fighting the attraction all night, which is partly why he stopped drinking. He didn't want to make any stupid moves. 'So that's the real reason you got to know me, is it?' He's trying desperately not to flirt back but can't help himself. He wants to feel different to how he's felt over the last couple of weeks. 'To get out of parking tickets and other "bad things".'

She laughs and becomes self-conscious, sitting back down and pretending she's hooked on the TV.

He has to ask her to stay the night seeing as she's snowed in, but he wonders how to do it without it sounding like a come-on. She beats him to it.

'Would it be okay if I crashed on the sofa tonight? I can be up and out early tomorrow without waking you.'

'But Rocky sleeps on the couch,' he says, deadpan, which makes her laugh.

'How about I sleep on the floor then? Because I wouldn't want to put Rocky out in any way.'

Her laughter's infectious and he wants to stay up all night with her. Then guilt kicks in again and he thinks about Linda. He can't invite Beth to sleep in the spare bedroom because it's full of Linda's things. He started moving stuff in there a few days ago but eventually lost steam.

'How about you sleep upstairs and I'll sleep with Rocky?' he suggests.

'Oh no, don't worry, I can sleep anywhere. I'm sure me and Rocky will both fit on here.'

He won't let her sleep on the couch.

'Look, this is going to sound really, really sleazy, but bear with me. I have a large king size bed—'

She laughs. 'Yeah, you're right. That's a sleazy way to start a sentence!'

'Let me finish!' he protests. 'There's room for all three of us and I promise there will be no "funny business", as you Brits like to say. Rocky will make sure of that. He's been wanting to get on that bed ever since he moved in so I'm pretty sure he'll be delighted to sleep in between us.'

Surprisingly, Beth agrees. 'Okay then. I promise to be good too.'

The way she looks at him suggests otherwise.

By the time Dean has let Rocky out for his evening toilet trip and tidied away the dishes, Beth's sitting up in his bed and from what he can see with just her shoulders above the duvet, she appears to be half-naked.

'What are you wearing?' he asks, genuinely wondering what she has on under the duvet.

'This is my camisole that I was wearing under my blouse, and I found a pair of your pyjama bottoms. Is that okay?'

He thinks it's very okay when the duvet slips down and he can see she has taken her bra off. He can see her breasts quite clearly through her camisole vest. He quickly turns and calls Rocky upstairs. Rocky jumps onto the bed with more ease than Dean would've expected from such a heavy dog. He's so excited he jumps all over Beth. After wearing himself out doing loops of the bed, eventually he calms down and, as Dean predicted, stretches long ways down the middle of the bed. Dean climbs in next to Rocky and looks at Beth.

'This is weird,' he says.

'I know! It's just for one night though. It'll be fine.'

'Wait until my neighbours realise your car has been here overnight. I won't be invited to church ever again.'

She laughs and lies down, stroking Rocky's face. Dean lies down too and stares at Beth. He wants to kiss her. He wants to touch her. Instead, he turns his bedside light out.

At some point in the night Rocky jumps down, probably too warm on the bed between them. Dean is wide awake and has been staring into the darkness for a while now.

'Something we said?' he jokes.

Beth laughs and reaches out to him. He moves closer and hugs her to him; her body heat feels comforting. It's so dark they can't see each other. After a few minutes of hesitation, as he listens to his conscience warning him not to do it, he uses his hand to gently feel his way down her face to her lips, where she kisses his fingers. He removes his hand and replaces it with his lips. She kisses differently to Linda, more passionately. It turns him on immediately. He tries not to think of all the reasons as to why this is wrong. It doesn't feel wrong, not like Sheila did. The way they touch each other feels perfect so he lets himself enjoy every second of getting to know her body.

Once Dean's asleep he has some disturbing dreams. He's cautiously approaching the woman they found hanging from the tree, but when he shines his flashlight on her face he sees Linda staring back at him.

'She took my shoes,' she says as he jumps back in fright.

He looks at her swinging feet, which are bare, just the way Jane Doe's were. Then Miller turns up, wearing just a hospital gown.

'I've just had a nice hospital visit from Sheila. She was helping me recuperate, if you know what I mean.' He laughs that horrid creepy laugh of his as Sheila appears naked next to him.

'Are you feeling better now, Detective?' she asks Miller.

Then the scene changes and Dean's driving a car faster than he's ever driven before, even faster than on emergency call-outs. He doesn't recognise the road or the scenery as he speeds through it, but it's pitch black except for his headlights. As he turns a sharp corner another car appears, heading straight towards him and it seems to be driving as fast as his. When his headlights reach it, he recognises it as Linda's car. But it's not her behind the wheel, it's him. He's staring at himself. This causes him to lose control of the car and drive head first into Linda's. The collision makes him jump awake.

Rocky's back on the bed leaning heavily on him but when Dean jumps, Rocky sits up and looks at him, fully alert. Dean puts out his hand to let him know he's all right. *Goddamn booze giving me nightmares*, he thinks. It's still dark in the room but the clock tells him it's almost six o'clock. He looks over at Beth. She's still sleeping. He just has time to wonder how awkward it will be when she wakes up but after just a few minutes, tiredness overtakes him again and he falls back to sleep.

Chapter Nineteen

When Dean walks into the station at ten o'clock the next morning, Steve's the first person to greet him.

'What are you doing here?' he asks. 'It's only been a week.'

'Don't worry, I'm ready. I need to occupy my mind before I go crazy.'

Captain Brown sees Dean arrive. He comes out of his office to join them.

'How are you doing, Matheson?' he asks.

'I'm okay. I want to be here as I still need to solve those two cases.'

'Given what's happened, I don't think that's a priority for you at the moment. And Miller's talking about coming back to pick up the Jane Doe case so don't worry about it.'

Dean's shocked. 'What? When? And why? I thought he'd be off for months?'

'I think his wife's sick of him being at home, to be honest with you. Sounds like no one likes that asshole. He said he was going to stop by after the weekend to flick through some paperwork. I doubt he'll do much but I can't exactly say no. I need all the staff I can get.'

This motivates Dean to want to get straight back to work to solve the case before Miller returns. 'Captain, I really want to be back. I know I'm still grieving and probably a bit screwed up but if I have something to concentrate on it will help me, honestly.'

Steve looks at Brown. 'I'll keep an eye on him.'

Dean laughs. 'I don't need looking after! Honestly, I'm fine.'

Brown gives in. 'Well, it would do me a favour so fine, if that's what you want. We need to get those two cases closed ASAP so get cracking.'

As Brown walks away Dean sits at his desk and mocks Steve for his 'I'll look after him' comment.

'Screw you!' Steve laughs. 'Some of us have been worried about you!'

Dean remembers the morning Steve came to find him, to give him the news about Linda's accident. Steve didn't see him at his best and probably assumes he's been drinking heavily ever since. 'Listen, I'm fine. I haven't been drinking if that's what you're worried about. Well, no more than a widower should be anyway. I've had Rocky to take care of. That dog needs three walks a day, he's killing me!'

Steve laughs again. 'Where is he today?'

'I wasn't sure I'd be in all day, what with it being my first day back, so I've left him at home for now. I'll pop back to let him out at lunchtime.'

Steve lowers his voice. 'Speaking of your house, I've been driving past randomly, just to keep tabs on you, and I noticed you had an overnight visitor last night.'

He looks as embarrassed saying this as Dean feels hearing it. 'You can stop with the surveillance, thanks. Like I've already said, I'm fine. My visitor got snowed in last night so they had to stay over.'

He wonders if Steve knows it was Beth's car or whether he's assuming it was a family member come to visit.

'Okay. Just wondering because you know how it is in this town. People talk.'

Dean dismisses this with his hand and switches his PC on. He spends the next couple of hours reviewing the reports about Jane Doe and Tammy's cases, but he's regularly interrupted by colleagues expressing their condolences. Jenny drops him a cupcake on his desk and gives him a long hug. It brings a lump to his throat so he shoos her away, pretending to be unaffected.

As he reads through Sheila's autopsy report again for Jane Doe, he's struck by a reminder of something from last night's weird dreams. 'She took my shoes.' That was what Linda said to him as she hung from the tree. Bare feet, he thinks. Why does that feel relevant somehow? It's like an itch he can't locate properly. He writes it down and stares at it for almost five minutes. His concentration isn't good at the moment. Frustrated, he throws his pen down and looks at his watch. It's past one o'clock so he heads home to take Rocky for a walk.

Dean has brought Rocky back to the tree, to see if that triggers the missing link. He wonders if her shoes are close by and were missed by the team. Rocky barks, making Dean realise he's been holding a stick for too long, absorbed by his thoughts.

'Get it!' He throws it as far as he can.

Then he stops cold. Bare feet. How did Beth know their victim had bare feet? He tries to remember when it was that they were discussing it. He remembers them eating soup in his kitchen the night they found the library card under the tree. He asked her opinion of why someone would kill themselves, and she was convinced the woman wasn't thinking rationally because she was out in the woods on a cold night with bare feet. He doesn't remember telling her the victim had bare feet but maybe it was part of the press release. He needs to read the press release again when he gets back to work. She could've heard it through town gossip as well. Maybe Eric Petty had been talking about his discovery while he was eating at the diner. He can ask her himself seeing as she's invited him over to dinner on Monday night.

He carries on with the walk and tries to get back to thinking about who this dead woman could be. Steve said he looked into the library card while Dean was off work, but it hasn't amounted to anything at all. Dean's convinced it was dropped there by a tourist at some point. Either that or it was a fake ID meant to send him off on a wild goose chase. But that would mean the victim was murdered and it wasn't suicide. He hasn't seriously considered this option yet but as he's desperate for a break in the case, he decides to head back to work and look at it from a different angle. He leads Rocky back to the cruiser.

When he gets back to the station Captain Brown insists on having Rocky in his office. 'So you can focus on work.' Dean knows that's not the real reason, but is grateful anyway. He spends a half hour writing down the facts from the perspective of it being a homicide instead of a suicide and then passes his notepad to Steve to compare the two pages.

'Have a look and tell me whether you think, just from those facts alone, this looks more like a suicide or a homicide.'

Steve takes the notepad and reads everything twice. He sits back in his chair. 'What does your instinct tell you?'

'To be honest, I genuinely thought it was a regular suicide. But now I've considered the other angle I'm thinking she was murdered and it was set up to look like a suicide.'

'I know what you mean. It's the bare feet that get me. Would anyone really walk anywhere outdoors barefoot? Especially with how cold it's been here lately. The fact we haven't found her car or purse or anything about her makes it completely plausible that she was killed.'

Dean feels excited and nervous, like he's on the verge of a breakthrough. 'You know Tammy's death looked like it was an accidental drug overdose. I know that's not the same as suicide but Sheila's convinced she was murdered.'

Steve sits up straight in his chair. 'Do you think—'

'You know what? I'm not a detective but I think we might have ourselves a serial killer.'

It sounds stupid when he says it out loud, but Steve's taking it seriously so he tries not to talk himself out of the possibility. On the other hand, he doesn't want to jump to any rookie conclusions which could cost him the chance to make detective.

'You need to tell Brown your theory. He's got more experience than anyone else here.'

Dean thinks about it for a minute and looks over at Brown's office where he can see him feeding Rocky cookies. 'He may be the most experienced member of our current team but I think I want to run this by Jones first.'

'Do you think that's a good idea? He's meant to be retired and all.'

'Come on, cops never really retire. I bet he'd love to hear it.' He gets up and grabs his car keys. 'If Brown asks where I've gone, tell him I'm following a lead and I won't be long. I'll come back for Rocky.'

'I think he'd prefer if you didn't,' says Steve as he watches Brown trying to teach Rocky some tricks.

Dean leaves the station and calls Jones on his way to his car.

'Hey, Matheson! Twice in one month? I'm honoured.'

Jones and his wife, Barbara, attended Linda's funeral.

'Yeah, I can't stay away. Thanks for the condolence bourbon, by the way.'

'No problem. I still can't believe she's gone. Neither can Barb. Have you found the asshole who did it yet?'

'No, not yet. The others are looking into it. I can't even think about that right now, to be honest. It was probably a drunk tourist who's long gone. Anyway, I want to run something by you. Can I come over?'

Jones perks right up. 'Sure you can. I'd make you a coffee but I know you think it's dirty!'

'Not any more. In fact, the stronger the better. Get the coffee on, I'm on my way.'

Jones greets him with a bear hug, which is quickly followed by Barbara giving him a gentle, motherly hug. To Dean it feels like visiting home at Thanksgiving. *This is the most normal couple I know*, he thinks. His parents had him and his brother later in their lives and, as a consequence, didn't live long enough to see them turn thirty. They were great role models but Dean wishes he'd had longer with them. When he was younger he resented them being older parents and accused them of being selfish, but now he's glad they missed John's death. It would've killed them knowing he took his own life for no apparent reason.

He sits down and accepts some of Barbara's apple pie. Jones has obviously asked Barbara to make herself scarce, because she quickly excuses herself after telling Dean again how lovely she thought Linda's funeral was. He doesn't remember much of it himself. He kept his eyes closed most of the way through and focussed hard on keeping it together in front of Linda's family, whose collective eyes were burning a hole in the back of his head, or so he imagined. Once Barbara leaves the living room, Dean relaxes and sips at his coffee as Jones takes a seat opposite him.

'Do you know, I watch that clip of Miller having a heart attack every single day?' he says. 'It has me in stitches! It's the best medicine a man can have.'

Dean almost spits out his coffee as this makes him laugh. He knows Jones has no respect for Miller but he didn't expect that comment. He hopes he's joking but suspects he's not.

'It worked out pretty good for me as I've been given two cases to look into,' he explains.

'Really? They didn't draft anyone in from a different station?'

'No, I asked to cover them. I need some experience. One is the Jane Doe we found hanging in the woods and the other is Tammy Gordon.'

Jones looks shocked. 'You mean Tammy didn't OD?'

'Nope. Sheila says she was held down and the drugs were forced into her.'

'Shit. That's karma for you. How's Emily doing now?'

'Not too bad, actually. She's getting counselling and she's in a nice foster home, for now. Apparently, she handled her mum's funeral well and is getting stuck into her new school at the moment. She's already made some friends. You know what? I think she might make it out of all this okay.'

Dean didn't make it to Tammy's funeral. He had Linda's to drag himself to.

'Let's hope so. Do you need some help with the cases?'

Dean looks down and wonders how to put his theory to Jones. He doesn't want to make a fool of himself. 'Okay, humour me for a minute. I think the hanging in the woods could've been a murder. And with Tammy being murdered in the same week, I'm wondering if we could have a serial killer on our hands. Someone who doesn't like women very much.'

Jones whistles and sits back in his seat. 'So, your first case as a trainee detective and you leap to the conclusion that there's a serial killer on the loose? You do know that's what every single rookie detective wants their first case to be, right?'

If this was coming from anyone else Dean would be irritated, but he respects Jones and would rather be put in his place now than waste time heading down the wrong path.

'I know how it sounds.'

'Why do you think the two cases are related?'

'I don't think there's any link between the victims at all. Jane Doe isn't local; no one has reported a woman missing and we didn't get any good leads from the press coverage. She could've been in the wrong place at the wrong time. With Tammy, you would think it was Skylar Hutton who killed her, but she says she has an alibi. It's not rock solid at this point but she's got herself a good set-up so I don't think she would murder someone just for a small bit of drug money. Besides, why would she force drugs into Tammy? She'd just be losing more money.'

He can tell Jones is getting excited about helping him solve this. His eyes are all lit up and he's moved to the edge of his seat.

'But why would a serial killer, someone completely random, kill Tammy with drugs? A serial killer would want us to know they were out there. They would probably kill by more gruesome methods: strangulation, stabbing and maybe even rape the victim first. Was Tammy molested?'

'Sheila said there was no evidence that Tammy had sex within the twenty-four hours before she died.'

'Hmm,' says Jones. 'Interesting. If it wasn't her dealer I'd be surprised. Tammy was a recluse, wasn't she? She didn't let anyone in her house. So, whoever it was, they either got invited in, which her dealer would've been, or they broke in.'

'There were no signs of a forced entry. He back door was unlocked though.'

'So, the killer knocked on her door and then forced their way in the minute Tammy opened it. Maybe they pretended to be the mail man or someone from child services.'

'Once the cause of death changed from overdose to homicide, the CSI team went back and scoured the house for prints, hair and stranger DNA, but found nothing out of the ordinary.'

'That's not unusual,' explains Jones. 'It just suggests the killer wore gloves and a hat.'

'Which suggests to me that he or she is a pro, and therefore a possible serial killer.'

Jones smiles. 'You would be a lucky son of a bitch if you got a serial killer on your first case.'

Dean laughs. 'Your idea of "lucky" varies somewhat to mine.'

'Tell me about Jane Doe. What do you know?'

'Did you read the press releases?'

'Of course.'

'Well, that's about it,' says Dean. 'We haven't found anything else of relevance. I don't know if it mentioned it in the papers but she was barefoot. And we found a library card buried under the tree but Steve says it's not relevant.'

'Was she molested?'

'Nope.'

Jones sits back and thinks for a while, trying to piece together the two puzzles in his head.

'I honestly don't think the two cases are related. It would probably be a mistake to continue down that path as it might close your eyes to other potential leads. I would get a drawing of Jane Doe out wider than the state, to see if anyone comes forward. Put her on all the missing person websites. She could've been a tourist staying in a town close by who got abducted and then discarded here. You'll start getting calls straight away but they'll mostly be people who desperately want her to be their missing daughter or sister. Get someone else to field the calls, they're time consuming and soul destroying. Only call back those who recognise the description of the clothes she was wearing.'

Dean's furiously writing all this down like a student taking notes. It does feel like he's being schooled but he doesn't mind one bit.

'As for Tammy, well maybe she did really OD. But try to find out from Emily whether her mum made any new friends over the last few months. You never know, there could be a new boyfriend we don't know about.'

Dean looks up and smiles. 'We?'

Jones laughs. 'Yeah, I feel like I'm right back at work with you. Only it's more fun playing detective from my armchair. I don't have to listen to assholes like Miller and I can drink while I think.'

Dean grimaces. 'Apparently Miller's coming back next week. He wants to pick up this Jane Doe case.'

'Well, you can't let him. Don't tell him anything you know, just keep working on it yourself. You'll beat him to the answers, I'm sure of it. Then you can bug Brown to give you a promotion. I'll back you.'

'Thanks.' He gets up. 'I better be heading back. This has been really useful, I appreciate it.'

'Anytime. I'll post you my consultancy invoice!'

Dean laughs as he leaves the house. 'And I'll post it right back.'

Chapter Twenty

Beth has been busy with new clients ever since her talk to the inmates in the recreation room. Half of those she has been seeing have just wanted an excuse to get away from their cells, so she hasn't invited the time wasters back for a second session. Some of the others who have asked to see her, including Pete's recommended inmate Judy, have some complex issues, which is great for her to gain experience.

For this afternoon's session, however, she has to put up with Shania again. Beth decides she can't listen any longer to her moaning about how she's been wronged all her life by everyone around her, and how nothing is her fault. She decides it's time to take action. Now she's been at the prison for three weeks without any safety incidents, she doesn't have to be chaperoned by any of the guards during her counselling sessions, so she finally has free rein to run her sessions however she likes, with no interferences.

'Today, Shania, I thought we would try hypnotherapy again. Does that sound okay with you?'

'I don't care what we do as long as it works,' she says. She's jittery, unable to keep still.

'Well, if you want it to work you need to calm yourself down. Start with the deep breathing exercise from last time.'

For the second time, Beth explains to her the deep relaxation techniques she was taught by someone she used to live with. They're not exactly legitimate techniques but they help to hypnotise people within seconds. It doesn't take Shania long to respond. Her breathing slows down almost to the point of snoring. Beth has to grab the coffee cup from Shania's hand as her grip relaxes. She's never had such a suggestible patient.

'How do you feel now?' asks Beth.

'I just want to stop dreaming those dreams about the kids.

It's wrong. I don't want to sleep any more,' she says, dreamily. 'My life's easier when I'm awake.'

'That's your conscience telling you you've done something wrong. You'll keep dreaming about them and thinking about them until you admit you're an unfit mother.'

'An unfit mother?' She sounds like she's seriously considering this.

'Shania, not only have you starved your children and not clothed them suitably, you knowingly let your boyfriend abuse them. Then, when they found the courage to speak up and tell you about it, you chose to disbelieve them. You believed the words of a near-stranger over your own flesh and blood.'

Shania begins crying but Beth is just getting started.

'Do you understand that makes you a terrible person? Just because you gave birth to them doesn't make you a mother. Do you understand you let your children down and they'll never get over what you and your boyfriend did to them?'

Shania is gently shaking her head side to side and crying harder. 'Am I a bad mother?'

Beth's voice deepens as she says what she really thinks of her. 'You're not a mother. You never mothered those children a day in their lives and they will be so much better off without you.'

Shania stops shaking her head.

'If you want to be a good mother you should kill yourself.'

Shania considers this. 'I should kill myself?'

'Your children will thank you for it. They'll remember you fondly if you put them out of their misery by killing yourself while they're young,' goads Beth. She's panting as she speaks now, worked up and angry. Ever since she was taught these hypnotherapy techniques, she's been amazed at how effectively they work.

'They'll love me?'

'Yes, they'll love you if you die now. If you stay alive any longer they'll just remember you as a criminal who didn't love them, because they'll be exposed to you every day.'

Shania starts nodding her head slowly, as if she's having an epiphany.

'You could use a bed sheet to hang yourself in your cell.'

'I could cut my wrists.'

'You could. You'd have to be careful that Tricky didn't walk in on you though. Time it right.'

'I could kill myself.'

'You should kill yourself, yes. You should kill yourself, Shania.'

Beth leans back in her chair and doesn't speak, to give time for this to sink in to Shania's subconscious and to give herself time to calm down. She thinks of her own mother, Susan: a pitiful, wretched woman who would do anything for attention after the death of her first daughter. Jessica's cot death at six months of age devastated her mother, but the kind and generous attention she received from medical staff and her friends caused her grief to twist her thoughts. Desperate for that attention again, she immediately fell pregnant, this time with Beth. From the very beginning of Beth's life, her mother pretended she had all kinds of ailments so that they had to make regular trips to the hospital. During these trips, she would soak up all the attention she received as the worried mother. Beth wasn't really ill so her mother had to fake a lot of the symptoms. She eventually had to leave Beth's father so that there was no one to witness and expose her twisted deceit.

Her mother should have put her first, protected her, but by this point she was on her downward spiral, not that Beth knew this then. As a child, she just couldn't understand why she was in hospital all the time. There were so many blood tests, so many pills to take and so many tears from her mother. They built a special bond during those years spent in various hospitals and surgeries. It took until her teenage years to realise what her mother had become. Before that she had been fiercely protective of her when teachers and doctors finally tried to intervene after suspecting the worst.

Once she was old enough to understand how sick her mother had been, Beth realised her whole life so far had been a lie. A cruel lie her mother had concocted for attention. Trying not to let thoughts of her mother take her back to that dark time, she wakes Shania and phones for a guard.

As Shania, weepy and dazed, leaves her office with a female guard to be led back to her cell, Beth decides it's time to leave for the day. It's six o'clock on Saturday night and although she isn't seeing Dean tonight, she fancies a night out at the Tavern to distance herself from thoughts of her deceased mother. It's time to build strong bonds with her colleagues that will withstand potential inmate accusations.

When she walks into the Tavern two hours later she notices how busy it is. Saturday night brings out all the clubbers, even in a small town like this. She spots Pete and Toad at the pool table and grabs all three of them a drink on her way over. They both look her up and down as she hands them their Buds, taking in her long bare legs and her very tight dress. She wonders whether Pete thinks he might strike it lucky tonight. She let him down gently last time.

After some small talk, she sits and watches them play pool. Pete keeps coming over to check on her.

'How was your day?'

'A bit stressful, actually. My last client was Shania and she got very upset. I think we had a breakthrough but I'm still worried about her. The poor thing seems to have demons that are hard to expel.'

'Does talking about things actually do any good?'

'Oh, you'd be surprised,' she explains. 'Once someone admits what they've done wrong it can set them free and change not only their lives but their children's lives too.'

Just then, Pete's phone rings at the same time as Toad's. She watches them react to their callers

'Who?'

'You're joking?'

'Shit. Be right there.'

'What is it?' she asks Pete.

'Suicide at the prison. You'll never guess who?'

She raises her eyebrows in question.

'Your friend, Shania.'

She puts her drink down and acts as if she's going dizzy. Toad lets her lean against him as she catches her breath. 'Oh my God, that's awful.'

Pete takes her hand. 'I'm going to head over there.'

'Me too,' says Toad.

'I should come too,' says Beth.

'No, I don't think that's a good idea,' worries Pete.

'But I was probably the last person to have a proper conversation with her so the police will want to see me. So will the warden.'

Pete and Toad exchange a concerned look but she's insistent so Pete drives her to the prison while Toad follows in his car.

When they arrive two police officers are already with Shania's body in her cell. They acknowledge Pete and Beth's arrival and Pete introduces them to her.

'This is Marty and Steve.'

'Captain Brown's on his way,' says Steve.

Pete tries to hold Beth back so she doesn't see the mess Shania has made of slitting her wrists, but she pushes forward to see.

'Oh my God. I don't believe it,' she gasps.

Pete hugs her to him and moves her away, trying to protect her. She has to bite her tongue to avoid telling him how sexist he's being right now. He doesn't know she's seen much worse without being fazed.

Steve's keeping everyone out of the cell when the medical examiner arrives. Beth hasn't met her before but knows she had an affair with Dean. As Pete introduces them, she notices Sheila checking her out.

'Who found her?' Sheila asks, as she enters the cell and carefully crouches down next to Shania, expertly avoiding stepping in the blood.

'Her cellmate,' answers Steve. 'She's adamant Shania would never even consider killing herself but the CCTV cameras show Shania cutting her own wrists.' He turns to the guards. 'You need to see why no one was watching her. Maybe she set up a distraction in the rec room; got someone fighting to give her some privacy.'

'You also need to find out where she got some glass from,' says Sheila. 'It looks like she used a glass soda bottle. She knew to cut downwards instead of across.'

'I'm on it,' says Toad as he heads to the security office.

'Scottie's going to be well pissed off,' says Pete. 'I bet he'll make us all retrain.'

'Poor Shania,' says Beth.

Pete strokes her back. 'You were saying talking works earlier. Doesn't look like it worked this time.'

Beth doesn't say anything. She wonders whether the warden is still going to want to invest in a counsellor after this.

Chapter Twenty-One

Dean didn't hear about the inmate's suicide until Sunday morning, when he arrived at work. As he isn't working nights any more he didn't have to attend. Captain Brown told him it's being treated as a simple suicide, which is a relief for Dean because he doesn't think he can manage any more murder cases. He knows that if he doesn't solve the two cases he's already got, he'll have to relinquish them to Miller or the new detective when they finally get one. Steve's handling the paperwork for Shania's death so he doesn't need to get involved at all. After he heard about it on Sunday, he tried phoning Beth to see if she was okay but she didn't pick up all day. Eventually, he thought it best to let her have a day to herself.

By Monday morning he still hasn't heard from her and wonders if their dinner date is still on for tonight. He arrives at the station, fixes himself a strong coffee and then sets to work following the advice Jones gave him. He spends a couple of hours meticulously entering the description of Jane Doe onto every relevant missing person's website he can find. He includes the digital drawing of Jane that their sketch artist created for him yesterday, plus a photo of the mannequin they dressed in her clothes, to help with identification. He writes an updated briefing for the media, to see if that will provide any new leads and is even thinking of bringing Eric Petty in to re-interview him. At this point, even he could be a suspect.

Whilst he's browsing the missing person's websites he can't help but look at some of the people who are listed as missing, as opposed to deceased and unidentified. It's heartbreaking seeing their smiling photos and reading the descriptions underneath. When he was training to be a cop they did some work on missing people and they were told that a depressingly large number of them aren't really missing, they choose to leave their lives behind with no word to their family to reassure them that they're fine. This seems cruel to Dean. But the rest, a higher proportion of which are women and children, seem to have vanished into thin air, many never to be seen again by anyone. He knows most of these will be murdered, their bodies dumped in woods, under concrete or in rivers. If he ever thought about it too much he wouldn't be able to do this job.

By lunchtime, the station is getting phone calls from people who have been on the websites and think they know who Jane is. Remembering Jones' advice about letting someone else field these calls, he tries not to get his hopes raised. Marty drew the short straw when they were deciding who would take the calls. Dean can overhear some of the conversations he's having.

'You think she's foreign? Uh huh. Yeah. Which nationality? You don't know. What do you think her name is? Why the hell not? Why would she be in New Hampshire? Uh huh. And what's your name?' The conversation stops suddenly which means the caller wants his anonymity.

Dean walks over to Marty, 'Did they say they think she's foreign?'

'Yeah, but come on. How likely is that?'

Dean thinks of Beth. 'Did they have a name?'

'He wouldn't say. He also wouldn't give me any of his personal information.'

He walks back to his desk and adds 'Foreign?' to his notes, although if this is like any of the other crack callers they've had, it's unlikely this will lead anywhere. As it's almost one o'clock he has to go and meet Emily and Derek at the park to walk Rocky. He wants to ask Emily about any new friends her mum might've made before her death.

Rocky lunges at Emily as soon as he sees her and almost

knocks her over. She doesn't seem to mind. She's looking much healthier than the last time Dean saw her. She has new clothes on that actually fit properly and the dark circles under her eyes have gone. Even her bad haircut is hidden under hair clips. She still doesn't look fourteen to him though.

'You look great, kid. How are you doing?'

'I'm okay. I miss Rocky though.'

'I know, but at least you don't have to pick up his poop any more!'

This makes her laugh. Derek suggests they sit down at a picnic table. He gets out a flask of hot chocolate with three plastic cups. Although it's a bright day, the weather is bitterly cold with a hard frost twinkling on the ground. It's so cold that Emily's nose is bright red.

'First of all, Emily,' says Dean, 'I just want to say I'm really sorry I couldn't be at your mum's funeral. I had every intention of going but something happened which meant that I just couldn't.' His voice breaks slightly at the end. Derek lowers his eyes.

'What happened?' asks Emily, eyes widening.

He doesn't want to upset her by talking about another death, but he wants her to know he had a genuine reason for not being there.

'My wife died.' He had planned on saying more but he gets a lump in his throat and turns his face away from them.

Emily takes his hand in both of hers while Derek puts a hand on Dean's back.

'It's okay, you don't have to talk about it. It's hard, isn't it?' asks Emily.

Dean nods and regains his composure. 'It sure is. Now I kind of know how you've been feeling and it's awful. I get called out to a lot of messy situations and I think I've become hardened to it, you know?' He's talking to both of them and they both nod in agreement. 'But when something happens to you, it's only then that you truly know how all those people you've dealt with were feeling. So, I hope I said the right things after your mum passed away.'

Emily pats his hand. 'There isn't a right thing to say but it's nice to have people who care.'

Derek actually wipes a tear away after this comment, which makes Dean and Emily laugh. It breaks the melancholy atmosphere.

'Anyway,' says Dean, fully composed. 'I need to ask you a few questions but if you find them too upsetting then we can just change the subject. Is that okay?'

She hesitates but after he's just shared his feelings with her, he thinks that helps her trust him. She nods.

'I'm just trying to piece together the last month of your life at home and I need to know whether you or your mum had any visitors during that time?'

Emily makes a thinking face and comes up with Skylar's name immediately. But Dean doesn't think she knows the real reason Skylar used to visit.

'Anyone else? Did you or your mum make any new friends recently? Did she have any phone calls from anyone?'

Emily doesn't even have to think about it because there were no other visitors. He knew Tammy was an untrusting recluse but he thought maybe she'd been in touch with a relative at least. Emily thinks not.

'Okay. When was the last time Skylar visited your house?'

'Erm, a couple of days before ...' She stops herself and Dean can tell she wants to say a couple of days before her mum was jailed.

'Okay, that's great, you've been really helpful. And for that, you get this.'

He pulls a Hershey bar out of his pocket but Rocky lunges at it before he can give it to Emily.

'Rocky! Drop!' shouts Emily, and he does. The wrapper is a bit slimy but that doesn't put her off. She opens it and finishes it within seconds.

'Have you been to see Beth again recently? The lady with the funny accent?'

Emily's demeanour changes. 'I don't want to see her again.'

Dean looks at Derek who says, 'Oh yes. I need to talk to you about that. Why don't you and Rocky go and play over by the swings for me?' he asks Emily.

'Okay!' She's so used to being dismissed while adults talk about her that she gets straight up.

When she's gone Derek continues, 'While you were off work, we met with Beth in the diner. I left them alone for about five minutes while I chatted with Frankie. When I went back, Emily was crying and said she wanted to leave.'

Dean's surprised. 'I wonder if Beth hit a raw nerve, maybe?'

'Emily told me on the drive home that Beth had told her to be mindful that she's completely alone in this world and she should never trust anyone, not even Simon and Julie. She said everyone lets you down eventually and it's better she knows now than to go through life being disappointed.'

Dean raises his eyebrows. 'Beth said that?'

'According to Emily.'

'Do you believe her?'

Derek sighs and leans back. 'There's no doubt Emily's capable of making stuff up, but I don't see why she would.'

'Maybe she just doesn't like Beth for some reason, perhaps because she's being asked to talk about her mum. I don't know. I'm seeing Beth tonight so I'll ask her about it.'

Now it's Derek's turn to raise his eyebrows. 'Seeing her tonight? As in a date?'

Dean laughs. 'Do you realise you sound like a woman right now?'

'Hey, don't get defensive! I'm not judging you. She's got a great accent.'

'Hey, you're married. Hands off,' jokes Dean.

Dean arrives at Beth's apartment just before their agreed time of seven o'clock. He hasn't heard anything back from her so he's not sure if she still wants him to drop by for dinner or not. He thinks it best to check in on her either way, considering what happened at the prison. He almost bought flowers at the last minute but doubted himself and decided against it. Having been married for so long, he doesn't remember what the rules are after you've slept with someone just once. Technically, they're not even dating. As he's about to knock, Beth opens the door.

'Hello!' She greets him with a kiss on the lips and then pulls him into the apartment. 'How are you?'

'I'm great,' he says as he closes the front door behind him. Dinner smells good. 'How are you doing? I heard about what happened at the prison.'

'Oh, I know. Awful, wasn't it? I'm sorry I missed your calls, I was out of town yesterday.'

'Really? Where did you go?' he asks, genuinely curious. He's never heard her mention knowing anyone out of town. Then again, he's never heard her mention her friends or family either. He starts to realise how little he knows about her.

'I just went for a bit of exploring, to get to know the area better. I get cabin fever here sometimes as it's such a small town and I'm used to big cities.'

He didn't know that about her either. 'You need to tell me more about yourself as I'm starting to realise I've done that male thing of not asking you much at all.'

She smiles at him and waves her hand. 'Oh no, I'm a really boring topic. You're far more interesting.'

She leans in and kisses him again, this time for longer. He's starting to think it will lead somewhere when she stops and heads to her tiny kitchen area.

'I've made us a huge dinner, I really hope you'll like it. Although, I got halfway through cooking it when I had a terrible thought that you could be vegetarian, vegan or allergic to something. Please tell me you're not!'

He laughs as he walks over to see what she's been cooking. 'No, I'm not any of those things. What are you making? It smells amazing.'

'Roast dinner. I thought seeing as it's Thanksgiving this week I would attempt to celebrate it while I had a visitor. I've made chicken, roast potatoes and root vegetables, plus Yorkshire puddings with thick gravy. How does that sound?'

He's surprised at the effort she's gone to and had forgotten all about Thanksgiving, what with everything that's happened recently.

'That sounds amazing. I've never had Yorkshire puddings before. Actually, I've never had an English roast either. I'm glad I skipped lunch now.'

She tells him to sit at the tiny kitchen table as she starts dishing it up onto plates.

'Why did you skip lunch? I don't know how you can do your job with nothing to keep your energy levels up. I get shaky and faint if I don't eat every few hours.'

'Don't worry, it's not a regular occurrence. I've just had a really busy day.'

'Are you any closer to solving your cases yet?'

Not wanting to talk about work, he tries to change the subject. He's dreading asking her what happened with Emily in the diner and wants to save that for later. 'Never mind that, look at this food! Rocky would be so jealous.'

'Where is he?' she asks, as she puts their plates on the table and joins him.

'He's having a sleepover at his new uncle's house. My Captain has fallen in love with him so I doubt I'll see Rocky any time soon.'

She laughs. 'You can always take him home a doggy bag if you like, there's plenty of chicken left. I bet he'd love the bones.'

They start eating and temporarily go quiet as Dean savours the flavours. He didn't expect her to be such a good cook, just because he sees her eating in the diner so much. She seems happy to eat instead of talk. When they're finished, she tells him she has dessert in the fridge.

'Oh my God, I couldn't eat anything else,' he says. He notices his protruding stomach with shame. 'Well, I certainly feel like I just ate thanksgiving dinner.' He heads over to the couch while Beth lights some candles and passes him a glass of red wine before joining him.

'Tell me something about yourself, because all I know is that you work at the prison, you live here and you're British. Seriously, that's it!'

'But don't you like the mystery of not knowing who you're sleeping with?' she teases. 'Tell me about you instead,' she says.

He can't help but wonder why she's so reluctant to talk about herself and wonders if she's estranged from her family. Or maybe she's just incredibly shy. But he doesn't think that's it. 'Me? I'm boring; I'm from here, I work here, I went to school here, I got married here. I'll probably be here forever. The end. Now tell me about your family. Any brothers or sisters?' He thinks he sees her stiffen slightly. She takes a big sip of her wine.

'No brothers or sisters. My parents are both long gone. I was a sickly child, always ill with something. That meant I didn't have many school friends because I was kept home a lot. It's just me really. I never knew aunties and uncles or grandparents. Which is probably why it's so easy for me to move to a new country and start afresh.'

'At least tell me why, out of all the places you could've started afresh, why did you choose New Hampshire?'

She laughs. 'Well, with a licence plate motto of "live free or die", why wouldn't I choose New Hampshire? Actually, a friend at my university was from Connecticut and she told me how beautiful New England was, so when I graduated I decided to take a few holidays out here until I found the kind of town I wanted to live in. I'm not saying I'll be here forever, but it's perfect for now. I like how friendly and trusting everyone is.'

'Nowhere is completely crime free so don't be too trusting, especially at the moment. Don't you miss your friends back home?'

She turns away when he asks this.

'No. Friends come and go. Besides, I'm making new friends now. Like you.'

'Well, I've got to hand it to you, you're very brave to move to a new country on your own. It puts me to shame as I really haven't travelled much at all.'

They sit in silence for a few minutes. He doesn't feel it appropriate to keep pushing her to open up. He takes a sip of wine, needing courage to approach the Emily situation, as he doesn't want to offend her. 'I met with Derek and Emily earlier today.'

'How is she? She's so adorable. I really hope she's going to be able to get over her awful upbringing.'

'She's looking a lot better than she used to and she loves her foster home, but she said something that worried me.'

Beth looks at him as if she has no idea what he's going to say. 'She said she didn't want to meet with you again because you made her cry.'

Beth looks shocked. 'Me? When?'

'In the diner, apparently. Emily thinks you said some pretty harsh things to her while Derek was over at the counter talking to Frankie.'

Beth puts her wine glass down and then takes her sweater off. 'Sorry, cooking always makes me overheat. I can't imagine what she's referring to, I didn't even ask her anything about her mum. I think we just talked about Rocky.'

Dean's distracted by her body. She only has a tight T-shirt on under her sweater and he can't help but look at the curves it outlines.

'She must have just been feeling a bit upset that day and maybe misunderstood something you said.'

'Probably. I did warn you that I'm not a specialist in child psychology of any kind. I think it's best that you find someone else to counsel her, to be honest, because it's so important that there's a good rapport between counsellor and patient.' She continues to try to cool down by taking her shoes and socks off. She has bright red nail varnish on her toes. This reminds Dean he was going to ask her about Jane Doe.

'By the way, how did you know our hanged lady had bare feet?'

She stops midway through removing one sock and doesn't turn to face him. He feels like he's said the wrong thing. Eventually she continues and then leans in close to him.

'I don't remember how I know. Was it in one of the newspaper articles?'

'Maybe. I know a lot of people have been talking about it. Have you ever met Eric Petty?'

She thinks about it. 'His name rings a bell. I think I might have overheard him talking about it in the diner. Was he the one who found her?'

'Yes. We told him not to talk about it so it just goes to show no one listens to us.'

She stands up and surprises him by taking her T-shirt off, quickly followed by her jeans. Any further discussion he wanted to have about Jane Doe is now off the cards. He gets up from the couch and follows her into the bedroom.

Chapter Twenty-Two

When Beth arrives for work the next morning, she's still cursing herself for mentioning Sarah's feet were bare when they found her hanging in the woods. *How could I have let that slip?* It had been her intention ever since moving to Maple Valley to get close to one or two of the local police in an attempt to be on the inside of their investigations. When she first spotted Dean, in his police uniform, she was relieved at how attractive he was. It made her job easier. She had been worried she might need to sleep with an overweight, donut-eating, misogynistic pig.

In fact, Dean has been a revelation to her; not at all what she expected a small-town cop to be like. She hadn't expected to enjoy being involved with him, which obviously led to her guard being dropped. Now it's firmly back in place, as she can't afford to let that happen again. *It's a good job men are easily distracted*, she thinks, remembering the sex they had after dinner. She had wanted him to stop asking questions about Sarah, Emily Gordon and her personal life. She hadn't planned to kill Sarah, and had already warned her off twice, but the woman was relentless in following her every move. Beth had to kill her before she ruined her new life in Maple Valley.

When Dean left her this morning he seemed perfectly happy and didn't mention the bare feet remark again. Sitting in her office, she swallows her self-prescribed multitude of daily vitamins and homeopathic tinctures, as she considers how to progress with these monstrous women she has access to without arousing suspicion. She thinks it would be a good idea to make some proper friends here pretty quickly, so that she seems like one of the locals and less of an outsider. She needs to gain their trust and have a break before moving on to the next patient. She heads to the staffroom to make herself a drink and to see who she can win over.

Pete's making a coffee when she walks in. Her heart sinks a little as he's still pursuing her, which is making him watch her every move. She keeps bumping into him everywhere at work and that's annoying as she could really do without his attention right now.

'Hey, how are you this morning?' he asks. 'Can I get you a coffee?'

She knows she has to say something to make him back off. 'No, that's okay, I'll make myself one.'

'Really? It's no trouble.'

She starts making her own whilst trying not to show her disgust of how dirty the kitchen is. Normally, when there's no one else in the kitchen, she rubs everything down with her antibacterial wipes before using the communal kettle, coffee machine and spoons. The guards regularly touch the same objects as the inmates, who in Beth's opinion are utterly filthy, so it drives her crazy to think the inmates' germs are on the kitchen appliances she has to use.

Trying to ignore the germs, she turns to Pete. 'While you're here I just wanted to let you know that I've started seeing Dean. I only mention it because I know you used to work together and have remained friends, so I hope that's not going to be a problem?' She looks at him as if she's embarrassed to tell him.

His face flushes as he turns away from her, probably believing she's been leading him on all this time, which she knows she has. She wanted to make sure she had Dean interested first, and just used Pete as a back up.

'I didn't think he'd get involved with someone so soon after what happened to Linda,' he says.

Beth realises she may be able to use Pete's annoyance to her advantage sometime in the near future. 'It actually started while Linda was still around,' she lies. 'I'm not going to lie about it, there was some overlap. But mostly just as we were getting to know each other. Dean told me his wife was a complete bitch and he had wanted to leave her for a long time, even before I moved here. I don't know if you know of his other affair? With that doctor. Sheila, is it?'

Pete doesn't say anything but from the way his shoulders are tensed, she can tell he's holding his tongue and is pissed off with Dean.

'It sounds to me like he had been trying to get rid of his wife for a while but she was slow to take the hint. It's sad really.'

Pete turns around to look at her. 'So why did you flirt with me?'

She pretends she doesn't know what he's talking about. 'I wasn't flirting. I'm new in this town and I was trying to make friends. I'm really sorry that you misread the situation.'

'He needs to learn to keep it in his pants, if you ask me. He's going to get through every woman in this town before long.'

'Well, hopefully, now that we're together, he'll settle down a bit.'

Pete shakes his head as he picks up his coffee and leaves. 'See you around.'

She sighs and finishes making her drink. She wonders how long it will take the rest of the town to find out about her and Dean.

Her ten o'clock meeting with the warden is worrying her and as she walks into Sue's office, she realises she's right to be worried. Sue looks incredibly stern and doesn't crack a smile at all. Beth recently found out she's ex-army, which explains why she's sharper than most of the staff here. After some curt greetings, Sue gets straight to business.

'Beth, please help me to understand why Shania killed herself? Because you had told me that counselling helps *prevent* suicide, yet she was with you just hours before slitting her own wrists.'

She isn't intimidated by Sue, but she does want to keep her job. 'I hear what you're implying, Sue, but no one can predict how someone's going to react to counselling. I ask probing questions that are designed to get to the heart of their issues. This helps them to understand how they can turn things around and become better people. However, some people obviously can't deal with reality because what they've done is too awful to acknowledge. Shania was adamant that her problems weren't her fault and that her children were to blame. Now, I can't perform miracles, especially in the short time I was seeing her.'

Sue's face softens somewhat. She sits back in her chair and takes a sip of her tea. 'She certainly had issues. This wasn't her first time in here either.'

'Maybe there was something else going on that we don't know about,' says Beth. 'I've seen how the inmates work now. There's a lot of victimisation going on in here. Maybe someone had threatened her? Or maybe she was worried about leaving? I'm sure I don't have to tell you how inmates get used to the structure that prison provides. In fact, half the women who've been to see me do so because they're scared about returning home. They're scared to be reintroduced to the very problems that got them in here in the first place: drugs, boyfriends and other temptations.'

Sue shakes her head. 'No, I don't think any of that is what would cause Shania to do this. She was one of the tough ones, a lot of people were scared of her. I can't imagine any amount of threats would cause her to kill herself so close to her release date.'

Beth tries to hide her annoyance that she can't manipulate Sue as easily as she'd like.

'What happened in her session that day? Have you written up the notes yet?'

'No, I haven't had time. I'll do it as soon as I can and email you my report. Nothing too far out of the ordinary happened. It went pretty much the same way as her previous sessions. She would cry whenever she mentioned her boyfriend and get angry whenever she mentioned her kids. She did seem worried though,' she lies. 'I felt like something was wrong but she didn't want to tell me. She wasn't too keen to get back to her cell, which is why I think it had more to do with her fellow inmates than with her emotional state. Maybe they left her with no choice.'

Sue seems to consider this for a moment. 'You do realise that if anyone else commits suicide we have to have an external party come in to hold an investigation? They may even conclude that counselling is bad for the women, which would mean your job would be redundant. So, let's hope this doesn't happen again.'

Beth realises she's being dismissed like a naughty schoolgirl, even though Sue can't prove Shania's suicide is linked to her counselling sessions. She didn't realise they would hold an investigation if another inmate kills themselves. After all, these are just criminals they're dealing with. *Really*, she thinks as she closes Sue's door behind her, *who cares if they die?*

Chapter Twenty-Three

Dean is sitting in an interview room at the station trying to get some quiet time so that he can have one final crack at these cases. Detective Miller is due back tomorrow and he really doesn't want to hand over his work to him. He'd rather burn everything than help Miller, but professional integrity wouldn't let him. Brown has been very clear that today is Dean's last opportunity to prove himself. He has Marty checking all the responses on the missing person's websites and on social media, saving Dean a lot of wasted time.

He starts with Jane Doe and spreads out all of his notes in front of him on the table, along with the photos Sheila took of the body. He picks up a photo of the dead woman's face and just stares at it. Her only striking feature is the freckles on her shoulders. This makes Dean think of Beth. She has freckles all down her chest. Thinking of Beth reminds him about their conversation; she said she'd heard about the woman having bare feet in the press release they'd put out in the media. Dean finds this from his pile of papers and sits back to have a read of it:

Maple Valley's Police Department were called to an apparent suicide by hanging early on the morning of Sunday 7th November in Maple Valley woods. The victim was a white female, thought to be about twenty-five years old, with blonde hair, brown eyes and freckles on her shoulders. She was wearing a white skirt and blue blouse. We are seeking help in identifying this female, so that we can notify her family. Anyone with any information should contact the police immediately.

No mention of the bare feet, but there's also no mention

of shoe colour, so maybe Beth just assumed she was barefoot. A woman would notice that kind of thing, wouldn't she? He thinks the press might have picked up on it and spun the story in their articles, so he reads all the articles he has copies of. Nothing is mentioned about her feet. His next thought is to ring Eric Petty to ask if, whilst eating at the diner, he has ever discussed his find with anyone. Although he doubts Eric would admit it, knowing full well he shouldn't have been talking about it. *Besides*, thinks Dean, *where would it lead you if Beth hadn't found out the victim was barefoot by any of these means?* Is he open to the possibility she may have been present at the scene at some point? Either before, during or after?

His instinct kicks in then and although he doubts this line of thinking will lead anywhere, he starts a new sheet of notes. He puts Beth's name in the centre and circles it. He instantly feels guilty and wonders how she would react if she ever knew he was doing this. He follows his instinct regardless and starts making notes around her name: arrived in town a few weeks before the suicide, lives at the diner where the stepladder was taken from, knew the victim had bare feet, works as a counsellor and knows a lot about suicide, plus she was with him when Rocky found the library card.

He stops, surprised at how many links there are. Trying to think why Beth may have been at the suicide scene, he considers whether the victim was a client of hers. Maybe she had been trying to help her, and when she tracked her down in the woods she found her lifeless body hanging there, too late to help. The thought of her potentially withholding information from him makes him doubt the possibility. He knows her as straight talking, plus she's had plenty of opportunity to confess that she was there. Just the fact they've slept together makes him think that Beth knows she could have trusted him if she told him this. Even if she was at the scene at some point, he thinks he knows her well enough to have confidence that she would have been there for the right reasons, not the wrong ones. Thinking he's being stupid to even consider this, he puts his pen down. His thoughts are so muddled since Linda's death, it's hard to concentrate and stay focussed on anything. Right now, he just wants to go home and sleep for a few days, but it's not an option. He needs to clear his head. He leaves the interview room to go and make himself a coffee.

As he stands waiting for the coffee machine to warm up, Sheila walks in with an empty mug. She seems to have a lot of meetings at the station lately. Dean suspects she's actually checking up on him.

'Hey, how are you?' she asks. 'You look exhausted.'

Any awkwardness between them is long gone since they stopped sleeping together.

'I'm good, but, yeah, a little tired. You?'

'Busy. Plus, I've still got Jane Doe downstairs in the freezer. Any chance she'll be claimed any time soon?'

'That's what I'm trying to figure out. Miller's back tomorrow so I'm in lockdown in the interview room, trying to solve it.'

She pours them both a coffee. 'Do you need any help? Maybe running me through where you're at with it might trigger something?'

Dean isn't sure he wants to run his theory about Beth past anyone at this stage as it sounds ridiculous. He takes a sip of his coffee and decides he has nothing to lose. It would be good to get a female perspective, seeing as the victim is female. He spends five minutes explaining everything he knows as fact, which is very little, and everything he knows about Beth, which is again very little. Even though he leaves out the part about them sleeping together, Sheila's immediately suspicious of Beth.

'And no one knows someone who can give you some sort

of background on Beth? She has no friends or family here at all?'

'No, she gave me the impression she's estranged from her wider family and she has no siblings or parents. I've only ever seen her sitting alone at the diner or in the Tavern with her colleagues, mainly Pete.'

Dean stops. He thinks about Pete and the prison, which reminds him of Shania's recent death. Shania was definitely a client of Beth's, and she killed herself, despite counselling.

'I know that look,' says Sheila. 'Have we stimulated a new lead in your head?'

Dean doesn't reply, he just walks out, back to the interview room. He's too jittery to sit down so he stands up as he adds Shania to his notes about Beth. Trying desperately to think fast and see what the answer is, he leans his head against the wall and closes his eyes. He doesn't want to believe Beth could have been at the scene as it means she's been lying to him about something serious. He thinks about Pete and wonders if he knows anything about Shania's mental state after her counselling sessions. Also, remembering what Derek told him about how Emily found Beth's conversation with her upsetting, he grabs his car keys and strides out of the station to his car. Captain Brown pulls up before he can leave. He opens his back door and Rocky jumps out and runs over to Dean, jumping all over him.

'Hey, boy!'

'This dog is eating me out of house and home so you're on daddy day care duty from now on,' says Brown. 'I just want to be the cool uncle who visits every now and then.'

Dean laughs. 'Okay, I'll drop him home on my way out.'

'Where are you off to?' asks Brown.

'I'm going to the prison. I want to ask the guards a few questions about their recent suicide. Just to see if there are any similarities between theirs and mine.'

Brown raises his eyebrows. 'Do you still think you can get this girl identified before Miller returns tomorrow?'

Dean thinks it's too early to be telling Brown he has a new theory. 'Probably not, but I want to know I tried everything.'

'Good. Okay, don't let me stop you.'

Dean puts Rocky in the back of his car and then drives home to drop him off.

When he unlocks his front door, something seems out of place to him. Rocky also spends longer than usual sniffing the entrance and hallway. Dean tries to listen to see if someone's in his house, but Rocky's sniffing is too loud. He walks into the kitchen when Beth jumps out from behind the door.

'Surprise!'

'Shit!' He suddenly realises he has his gun in his hand.

She doesn't even flinch when she sees it but Rocky's going crazy, barking and jumping at her.

'What the hell are you doing here?' he asks, shaken. He re-holsters his gun.

'I'm so sorry! I didn't mean to scare you. I just wanted to make you a nice lunch. Look!' She points to his dining table, which is covered with pastries and juices.

'How did you even get in here?'

'I asked your neighbour if she had a spare key. I've met her before in the diner so she knows I'm not a burglar or anything. I just came on the off chance that I could do something nice for you since you're prone to skipping lunch and working too hard. I was just about to call you and ask you to join me.'

Linda insisted their neighbour had a spare key for emergency situations. He had forgotten all about it. This definitely wasn't an emergency situation but he can't really blame her for giving Beth the key. He puts Rocky outside to shut him up.

Beth comes towards him and puts her arms around his neck, gently kissing his lips. 'Have I been a bad girl?'

He can't help but soften and laugh at this. She looks gorgeous in her smart work clothes. He feels conflicted that he's trying to dig up some background on her whilst wanting to have sex with her at the same time. He knows from experience that women are just as capable of being criminals as men are, but his gut tells him Beth's not that type of woman and being with her again now makes him realise how stupid his theory is. This woman is not a liar. Still, the cop in him knows it won't hurt to find out more about her and, if she's not willing to trust him with her background, he has a duty to find out for himself. That means doing a bit of detective work on her. *At least then I can rule her out of any involvement in the Jane Doe case*, he thinks. *But that can wait.*

'Nice pastries but I'd rather have you on that kitchen table.' He smiles.

She laughs and pushes the pastries to one side as she climbs onto it. Not quite believing his luck, he goes to her.

After a rushed lunch of sex and pastries, he sees her out and locks Rocky in the house. Something is eating away at him but he doesn't know what. Like when he thinks he's left the oven on and has a desperate urge to go all the way home to check. He's getting that a lot lately.

'Do I get the spare key back or is that yours now?' he asks.

'That's up to you,' she says, looking up at him with mock innocence. He kisses her outside his house in full view of his neighbours, knowing he'll be judged for getting involved with someone so soon after Linda's death.

'Keep it. But next time I want to find you completely naked.'

She laughs. Dean looks around and realises her car isn't here. If it had been there, he would have known she was already in his house.

'Did you walk here?'

'No, my car is parked a block over.'

This raises his suspicions again. Maybe it's the temporary secondment to detective that's sending his instinct haywire.

'I could've given you a lift back to work, I'm heading to the prison myself.'

'Really? What for?'

Did he see concern in her face or was she just curious? 'I've got to follow up on your patient's suicide. I won't be there long; I just have some questions for the guards.'

She kisses him again. He's in danger of dragging her back into the house but she pulls away before he can. 'Okay, well I might bump into you at work then. Maybe I'll show you my office.'

He smiles as he watches her walk away from his house. He can't think like a cop with her around. Shaking his head at the effect she has on him, he gets in his car and drives to the prison, spotting her a few cars behind him most of the way.

When he arrives at the prison he sees Steve's cruiser already parked up. Dean knows he's here to tie up loose ends from the inmate's suicide, so he hopes Steve won't mind that he's turned up to ask questions about the same case. His only interest is in clearing Beth from his own suspicion so that he can concentrate on more likely leads. After getting through security, he heads straight to the staffroom in an attempt to find Pete. He doesn't wait for Beth to pull up behind him because he doesn't want them to arrive together and start rumours. No matter how true those rumours are. Although he's not intending to ask the guards much about Beth directly, he still wants to know if there could be any similarities between the inmate's suicide and his Jane Doe. He finds Toad eating lunch in the kitchen.

'If you're looking for Steve, he's downstairs with Scottie, talking security,' says Toad.

'Okay, I'll go and find him in a bit. Is Pete working today?'

'Yeah, he's due up here shortly,' says Toad. 'But I'd stay away from him if I were you. You're not his favourite person right now.'

Dean's confused. 'Why?'

'He found out this morning that he was being given the run around from your woman.'

'What do you mean?' He doesn't understand.

'The counsellor. She told him you two are an item. Pete thought he was in with a chance. To me it sounds like she led him on.'

Toad's giving him attitude, clearly siding with his buddy, Pete. This angers Dean. 'Listen, who I'm seeing is none of your business. It's not like Pete would've really had a chance with her, she's way out of his league.'

He hears the staffroom door swing shut and turns to find Pete and Steve standing behind him.

'Oh, that's real nice,' says Pete. 'She's out of my league but not out of yours, right?'

Dean feels terrible. 'Pete, I didn't mean that. I just don't like the idea of everyone talking shit about me so I overreacted. I'm sorry.'

Steve looks uncomfortable. He walks over to the seats and sits next to Toad.

Pete doesn't care about his apology. 'You know you're an asshole for what you did to Linda. You're a cheating scumbag.'

Dean didn't know his affair with Sheila was common knowledge and wonders just how long his friends have been talking about him behind his back. 'Don't get involved, Pete. You don't know the facts,' he says, angrily.

'I think you both need to calm down,' says Steve. 'Pete? Linda's off limits. I mean, come on man, she's dead!'

'I know all the facts actually,' he continues. 'Your fuck buddy told me everything this morning. I bet you were glad when Linda died? So you were free to move Beth in? You didn't have the balls to tell Linda you were cheating on her so whoever ran her off the road did you a favour!'

Dean lunges at Pete, punching his jaw as hard as he can,

the impact sending a sharp pain all the way up his arm. Toad and Steve jump in to try to separate them. It takes a while as they're both so wound up, but Steve manages to pull them apart. He holds Pete back while Toad holds Dean back.

Dean shakes himself free and tries to catch his breath. 'How dare you? Do you even realise what you're saying? You're making it sound like I had Linda killed, for Christ's sake!'

Steve lets go of Pete and steps between them. 'Pete, what the fuck? Why do you think he would be glad for his wife to die? That's messed up!'

Pete practically spits it out. 'Because he was fucking around with both Sheila and Beth while he was still married. You think that sounds like a happily married man, Steve? Because I don't! Your brother would never have done that. John would be ashamed of you if he were still alive!'

Dean's shaking his head in disbelief at Pete's change of character; to bring up both Linda and John like this is devastating. He turns to Steve for back up but Steve's looking at him in a way he doesn't like. He feels like he should say something to stand up for himself but he's too angry. He storms out of the room instead and leaves the prison. He's so angry at Pete that he drives way too fast, not even with any location in mind. He's never had a disagreement with any of them before, never mind a real fight. He doesn't understand how they can misjudge him so badly when they know him better than that. He feels like he's been punched in the stomach. Eventually he pulls over at a gas station, which is advertising liquor outside. He goes in and buys a bottle of Jack Daniel's. Taking it back to his car he sits in the driver's seat and just stares at it.

He can't understand why Pete's making him out to be an asshole. Yes, he cheated on Linda with Sheila, but it was his messed-up way of dealing with John's death, and he hadn't started seeing Beth until after Linda died. They don't even know that Linda was cheating on him first. *And how does*

Pete know about Sheila and Beth anyway? The look on Steve's face said it all. Does he really think Dean was involved in Linda's death? He feels like he's been caught red-handed at something he didn't do. There's no way he wanted Linda dead.

He's not worried about Steve investigating because he's got nothing to hide and he needs his own answers about the crash, so the more Steve finds out, the better. But Pete's making him out to be something he's not. Or is he? He doesn't even know any more. This year is going from bad to worse. His cell phone rings repeatedly beside him. It's Steve. He doesn't answer it. Instead he drives out to the tree where they found Jane Doe. He sits in his car, holding the bottle of Jack Daniel's whilst thinking about how little he's grieved for Linda and the baby.

Chapter Twenty-Four

It doesn't take long for Beth to hear about the fight in the staffroom, and she's relieved. When Dean found her at his house earlier she had just finished snooping and planting some car keys, just in case things don't go her way. Dean had been so out of sorts when he found her there that she's worried he's starting to get suspicious. She doesn't know what he's thinking and the fact he didn't greet her with open arms straight away tells her he's too clever for his own good. He's a better cop than she was originally allowing for and now she has to throw him off the scent.

Distracting him with sex won't work for much longer, she thinks. She hopes that planting the seed of doubt in Pete's head over Dean's recent change of character will work in her favour eventually, just in case Dean finds out too much about her. When she moved here she was planning on the local police being far more incompetent than they are, because at this rate she'll have to flee the state sooner than she would have liked.

By the time she's been told about the fight in the staffroom, Dean has already left and Pete has been sent home for the afternoon. Apparently, Sue doesn't stand for 'schoolboy antics'. Dean's colleague, Steve, is still around when Beth walks into the staffroom, and she overhears Toad telling anyone who'll listen what happened. He has an audience but he goes silent when he spots her. At first, he doesn't say anything at all, but as everyone except him and Steve scatter at the sight of her, he speaks up.

'You're making quite an impression on people.'

'Really?' She smiles. 'That's nice.'

'I didn't say it was a good impression,' he continues. 'You've split up a marriage and now you're coming between old friends.'

She ignores him as she makes her tea.

'Your new boyfriend will probably be suspended from his job for hitting Pete.'

She turns around and tries to resist saying what she really wants to. After all, she needs Toad and Steve to like her. 'I'm sorry but I'm not the person who was married. I'm single and trying to make friends in a new country. I didn't know Dean was a serial philanderer. You can't help who you fall for. I feel duped by him too, he told me his marriage was already over when we started seeing each other. It was only after his wife died that I found out the truth. He certainly didn't seem that upset when she died,' she lies.

Steve takes umbrage at this. 'Listen, I was the one who had to drive him to the hospital to see her right before she died and let me tell you something, he was as upset as when his brother died a few months ago.'

'Well, he told me they'd had a nasty fight the night of the accident, but he can't remember what they said because he was so drunk. I got the impression that he'd gone after her in his car.' She stops, knowing full well her lying is planting a seed in Steve's head.

'Wait. What? He drove after her? While he was drunk?'

Beth turns away. Feigning innocence she says, 'Oh sorry, maybe I've said too much. I might have misunderstood him. He was pretty drunk so he wasn't making much sense, to be honest.'

'When was he telling you this?' asks Steve.

'The night of her accident, over the phone. I thought I was getting what you would call a "booty call" but he was just rambling. I've probably spoken out of place. Please ignore what I've said, I'm sure I've got it all wrong. He's normally such a good guy so I don't think he would drink and drive.' Steve and Toad share a look. She thinks she's done enough damage for now. 'Anyway, I don't feel comfortable talking about him behind his back so I'm going to leave.'

As she walks out Steve says, 'He's not answering my calls and I doubt he's back at the station so when you see him, tell him he needs to ring me. Urgently.'

She leaves, knowing she needs to lay low for a while and not antagonise anyone else. Everything's escalating much quicker than she'd anticipated. She thinks getting involved with a local cop maybe wasn't the wisest thing to do after all.

Chapter Twenty-Five

Dean didn't open the bourbon in the end. After sitting in the woods for a half hour, freezing his ass off, he knew he had to go and face the music back at the station so he reluctantly drove back to work. He doesn't think Pete will press charges, they have too much history together, but he wouldn't blame him if he did. He hesitantly walks into the station, avoiding eye contact with everyone. To his relief, no one is waiting for him and Steve isn't at his desk.

He sits down and starts shredding his personal notes about both the suicide and Tammy's potential murder. Whilst sitting in his car he came to the realisation that he's been deluding himself to think he could become a detective. He's nowhere near the league of Jones, or even Miller if he's really honest. Miller may be an overweight asshole but he has solved murder cases before. Dean knows he's reached a dead end and not only that, he doesn't care about these cases any more. He feels bad for Emily that he wasn't able to help her but maybe Miller can finish what he started. After shredding everything, he feels he doesn't want to talk to anyone so he clocks out an hour early, avoiding Captain Brown on his way out.

As he approaches the diner he pulls into the parking lot and sits wondering what to do about Beth. If the whole town is gossiping about him being a filthy cheat, the only way he can stop it is by not seeing her any more. She said she might not stick around for long anyway so it's not like it was going anywhere. It's a shame. He'll miss spending time with her and he thinks he could've fallen for her in the right circumstances. He sighs. Sometimes he hates this town and today, as he sits looking in at people eating in the diner, he considers making a fresh start, moving somewhere new. Somewhere Linda never existed, where he didn't cheat on her and where no one knew his brother. He could try a change of career seeing as being a cop hasn't worked out that well for him. He thinks of popping in to pick up some take-out but he doesn't want the familiarity. He knows Rachel and Frankie will want to chat but he's not in the mood. He drives out of the diner's parking lot and heads home to Rocky, and his new bottle of bourbon.

That evening, within a few hours of being home, there's a knock at the door. He's not drunk enough to ignore it yet so he goes to answer it. Beth is standing shivering outside in the fierce sleet.

'I heard what happened. Can I come in?'

He doesn't have the heart to turn her away so he moves aside for her to enter. Rocky's too asleep to greet her but he wags his tail in recognition. Beth steps over him and sits on the couch, removing her thick coat. Dean, who has changed into pyjama bottoms and a T-shirt, sits next to her.

'Drink?' he asks, indicating the bourbon and downing the rest of his drink.

'I'd love one. I'll get it.'

He watches her walk to the kitchen and knows he wants her to stay the night. He can't stay away from her. *Doesn't matter now anyway, I'm not working on the cases any more and I'll probably be suspended for hitting Pete*, he thinks. *May as well enjoy my unpaid time off.*

'Now don't tell anyone I said this, because it's not very professional of me,' she says, 'but I've heard that alcohol is the best solution to any problem.' She sits next to him, close enough for her knee to rub against his thigh.

'I'm not going to be good company, I'm afraid. I've had a shit day.'

'So I heard. I have to say, there's something romantic about men fighting over me.' She downs her first shot.

Despite everything, he laughs and feels his shoulders relax. He doesn't care that he might have just walked out on his career. It wasn't going so well anyway. He feels like he needs some more time off. Time off to forget everything. Looking at her, he thinks she can help him with that, in the short term anyway.

'You're gorgeous. You know that, right?'

'Of course!' She laughs. She pours them both another drink, without ice this time. 'Cheers to us both being gorgeous and to everyone being jealous of us!'

They down their shots and Dean pulls her close to him, kissing her hard. He can taste the sweet bourbon on her tongue. It tastes great. The booze has really hit him now but even if he wasn't drunk he still thinks this is how he would choose to spend the rest of today, hell, the rest of the week. They undress each other and Dean leads her upstairs.

Chapter Twenty-Six

Three days later, Beth emerges from Dean's house at six o'clock in the morning.

'If you get into trouble for being off work sick, just blame me. They'll be happy to lay the blame at my feet. They probably think I've abducted and murdered you,' says Dean as he watches her put her coat on. She's wearing the same clothes as Tuesday night, but that's okay because she's been naked for the days in between. She hadn't expected to enjoy using a cop so much. After three days of drinking, having sex and moaning about everything from their work colleagues to the unfairness of life, Beth needs to get back to her day job. She's happy for Dean's life to spiral out of control as it helps keep her safe from suspicion, but she needs to make sure she's an upstanding citizen of Maple Valley in the eyes of the other residents. That's why she's leaving his house under the cover of darkness, before anyone can see where she's been.

'I can honestly say I've had a thoroughly enjoyable few days with you. Thanks for my first Thanksgiving experience.'

He laughs. 'Yes, I can't believe we missed all the holiday hoo-hah. That's not really how Thanksgivings are meant to go. Although I'm very thankful for mine this year.' He kisses her. 'Seriously though, I hope my moaning about work didn't bore you too much?'

'Well, you had me moaning too remember, just in a different way,' she says.

He pulls her to him again as she tries to get out the front door. 'Are you sure you don't want to come back to bed?'

'I'd love to but I can't! I need to get back to work and you need to brush your teeth and drink some water. You have serious vodka breath! I'll let you know if everyone's still talking about your bust up.'

He lets her go. 'I can't wait. I suppose I should face the music too at some point.'

Beth knows his colleagues have been phoning him and his Captain even dropped by the house yesterday, but Dean refused to talk to any of them. 'Are you really going to quit the force?'

He hugs himself to keep warm from the cold damp air outside. 'I don't know. That decision might be out of my hands now anyway.'

'Okay, well I really do have to go.'

He kisses her goodbye and she walks away, knowing she has him eating out of the palm of her hand.

After showering and changing, Beth heads to the prison, arriving on time at eight o'clock. An email tells her Sue wants her, so she heads straight there.

'Hi, Sue, is it okay to come in?'

'Yes, of course. I just wanted to check in on you; how are you feeling now?'

Beth sits down. 'Much better today, thanks. I don't know what I ate that caused my stomach upset but at least it didn't last too long.'

Sue eyes her up. 'You do look a bit gaunt, actually.'

She has to suppress a laugh. She's lost weight on the sex and alcohol diet.

'So, tell me; what's your plan of action to stop what happened to Shania happening to anyone else?'

Beth's annoyed at being so closely monitored. 'I think I'll just take it slow with the ladies on my list at the moment. Not rush them into any great revelations, just baby steps for now. The problem is that different people react differently to counselling. Shania was clearly in denial about the pain and suffering she caused her poor children. Counselling gave her an epiphany that she wasn't ready to cope with.'

Sue looks somewhat reassured. 'Yes, well, these women

have committed some awful crimes so we can't tread too softly. The whole point of prison is to rehabilitate them so they're not repeat offenders. I'm sure this was just a tragic one-off that went wrong. But I still need your report on that final session you had with Shania, please.'

'No problem,' agrees Beth. 'I'll do it today. Now if you don't mind, I've got a client in an hour and I really need to prepare as I've not met her before.'

'Okay, that's fine. Thanks for coming to see me.'

On the way back to her office Beth heads to the staffroom to make a hot drink. She bumps into Toad who's on his way out.

'Oh, hi.'

'Hey, how are you? I hear you've been off sick,' he says.

'News travels fast around here, doesn't it?'

He stops her from entering the staffroom. 'The Warden has told us all to keep an eye on you.'

'What?' she says, shocked that Sue might be on to her.

'In case you aggravate any more inmates, I guess. Anyway, I don't suppose you've been with lover boy lately? Only, I hear his world is about to come crumbling down so you might want to get out before he takes you with him.'

'What do you mean?' she asks, still reeling.

'You'll soon find out. Just take my advice and avoid him like the plague.'

As Toad leaves her, she goes back to her office and closes the door. Her breathing is becoming panicked so she grabs her inhaler out of her bag and takes much more of it than she should, followed by two painkillers in case this gives her a headache.

Beth knows she can leave town with a moment's notice. She always carries her fake passport with her, with enough cash to flee the country. She wouldn't even need to go back to that awful apartment for anything as she doesn't own anything valuable or sentimental. As her breathing calms down, she tries to rationalise what Toad said about Dean being in trouble. If they accuse him of killing his wife, that won't reflect badly on her. If anything, she would be seen by the police, and the whole town, as a murderer's potential next victim so she knows she's covered on that front.

After Dean had told her on the phone that night that his wife was giving him a night's reprieve to think about the state of their marriage, it was obvious where the wife would stay overnight. There's only one proper hotel in this godforsaken town. Finding her on the road had been easy as she knew what car she drove. Even stealing a car from outside the mall had been easy. This town's residents are so naïve that some of them don't lock their cars. When she spotted a rental car sticker on one of them she figured it was likely to be unlocked, so she walked straight up to it, opened the door and just got in as if it were hers. She pulled the sun visor down and the keys dropped into her lap. Perhaps someone had left the car there to be collected, or they were inside the mall doing some shopping; either way, small town mentality was making things easy for her.

Once she pulled out of the car park, she knew she would kill his wife. She didn't need Dean getting back with her and playing happy families over a kid he didn't want. Where would that leave Beth? It's not like she wanted to marry him or anything but she needs him on her side. It would be even better if he's mourning someone and not thinking straight. That means he wouldn't be in a fit state of mind to solve any cases. Beth decides that if Dean's arrested for murder she'll give it a few weeks and then leave town and start afresh somewhere new. Again.

As for Sue getting the guards to 'keep an eye on her', Toad's probably just winding her up because of his loyalty to Pete. She gets to work on the report about Shania's last session, to appease Sue.

Chapter Twenty-Seven

On Saturday morning, the day after Beth leaves him to return to work, Dean's cleaning the house and trying to decide what to do about his job. He's starting to realise not answering his phone or the front door wasn't a good idea. He has to face Captain Brown at some point and delaying it is making it feel much harder. He hopes the fact that he's grieving will be considered when he finally faces the music. Or maybe he's used that excuse too many times already. When he hears a knock at the door he assumes it will be Brown or Steve and so he quickly lets Rocky out into the garden to avoid them being jumped all over. Slowly, he goes to open the front door, nervous at how this is going to play out. He still can't decide whether to quit the police force or not. He can barely contain his surprise at seeing Detective Miller standing on his porch.

'What are you doing here?' he says, before realising how rude it sounds.

'I'm doing well, thanks for asking. Can I come in?'

Dean's embarrassed to have Miller come into his home. He feels put out at the surprise and wonders why it's not one of his friends here instead.

'The lounge is on the left.'

He notices Miller has lost some weight but looks older rather than better for it.

'Can I get a glass of water?' asks Miller.

'Sorry, yeah, sure. Hang on a minute and I'll make us some coffees.'

'No, water's fine.'

Dean's confused. Miller's always hated him so why would he turn up here? He can only assume he wants his notes from the investigations. He pours some water and returns to the lounge.

'Why do you look so nervous? Sit down would you?' says Miller as he sips his water.

Dean sits but doesn't say anything.

'So I heard about your wife. My condolences.'

'Thanks. I appreciate it.' He notices Miller looking at everything in his lounge. There's nothing left of Linda's on display. What Chrissie didn't take away with her is now consigned to the spare room. Dean has plans to give it to goodwill. He's annoyed that Miller's probably judging him for having removed all traces of her.

'How have you been coping without her?' asks Miller.

This makes Dean laugh out loud. 'Are you kidding me? Are you trying to console me or something? Come on, Miller. Why are you really here? Your forced chit chat is freaking me out.'

'Why? You got something to hide?' Miller puts his glass down and to Dean he looks nervous. His hands are shaking slightly.

'What kind of question is that? Tell me why you're here instead of Captain Brown.' Dean's pissed off now.

'You want to know why I'm here?' Miller asks. 'Well, you're not going to like it. I'm here to arrest you for the murder of your wife, you piece of shit.'

Dean jumps up and tries to resist punching him.

Miller gets out his handcuffs. 'Are you going to come with or without the cuffs? It'll make you look even more guilty to your neighbours with them, but I'd get a kick out of it.'

Dean can't resist any longer. He punches Miller as hard as he can across the head, pain instantly spreading up his wrist. He didn't realise until he hit Pete recently that it physically hurts to hit people. Rocky's barking outside, trying to get in the back door. Miller's surprisingly resilient for someone of his size; he quickly recovers and spins Dean around and slams him against the wall, winding him. He pulls Dean's arms behind his back and cuffs him tight.

'I'm glad you did that. It gives me an extra charge against you.'

When Miller walks Dean into the police station, still cuffed, it draws a crowd. He tries to steer him straight to the holding cells but Marty and Jenny confront him, loudly.

'Woah, what's going on? Miller, what the fuck are you doing?' asks Marty.

'Uncuff him, you asshole.' Jenny runs to Captain Brown's office as Dean stares at the ground, completely humiliated.

'He assaulted me so he's staying cuffed.'

'He should be given a medal then, not handcuffed,' says Marty.

Steve was in Brown's office and they both come charging over to see what Miller has done.

'Uncuff him immediately,' shouts Brown. 'And get in my office, RIGHT NOW. Everyone else, get back to work.'

Miller throws the keys at Jenny who gently uncuffs Dean.

'Are you okay?' she asks.

He doesn't look at her or respond, he just follows Steve, Miller and Brown into the office.

'Close the door, you moron,' Brown says to Miller.

Miller slams it hard.

'Enough with the attitude. What the hell were you thinking bringing him in like that? Who told you that you could bring him in at all?'

'Come on, we all agreed he murdered his wife!' spits Miller.

Dean's heart sinks. 'What? You think I would hurt Linda?' He looks at Brown when he says this. From Dean's very first day in this department, he has always respected Brown. The thought that he would think the worst of him makes Dean's legs shake. He collapses into a chair. 'Does Jones think this too?'

'Listen to me, Matheson,' says Brown. 'No one outside of this room knows anything about what we've discussed over the last few days. Although Miller's stupid stunt has probably wrecked that now.'

Steve speaks up. 'We just have some unanswered questions and we've been waiting for you to get in touch so that we can ask them to you face-to-face. But you wouldn't return our calls.'

Dean almost shouts. 'I'm grieving for my wife, for Christ's sake! How can that look suspicious to my friends?'

'Because you've been shacked up with that British woman, that's why. I've been outside your house every night this week. She stayed for three nights in a row. Helping you grieve, was she?' Miller says, sarcastically.

Steve just manages to react in time to Dean jumping up. He grabs Dean's arm before it gives Miller a second black eye.

'You piece of shit! This is what you wanted all along, wasn't it? To get me fired?' Dean's feelings overcome him and he collapses back down into the chair and barely holds it together. He's lost everything.

'That's the final straw! Miller, go home. You're suspended without pay,' roars Brown as he stands up from behind his desk.

'What? He hit me! And I'm the one suspended? You better watch it, Brown. I'm in the union.'

Captain Brown doesn't like threats. 'I have two witnesses here who, as well as myself, will be happy to tell the union about your unprofessional conduct. Put your badge and gun on my desk and then get out of my office before I decide to fire you instead.'

Miller throws his things onto Brown's desk. 'Maybe you should be thinking about how your friend Matheson here was also the last person alone with Tammy Gordon.' He slams the door shut behind him. Steve and Brown shake their heads in disgust.

Dean tries to pull himself together by taking some deep breaths. He can't believe this is happening. 'Am I going to be accused of being a serial killer next? Thanks for getting rid of him, Captain.'

Brown sits back down. 'Don't thank me yet. We have to interview you officially, to rule you out as a suspect.'

Dean doesn't understand. 'Why a suspect? I thought Linda lost control of her car?'

'She did,' says Steve. 'Because she was forced off the road by someone.'

'What?' Dean can't believe what he's hearing.

'That's what CSI have told us and it's hard to refute when you see their evidence. They even told us what make of car it was, a Ford, and yesterday we found what we think was the actual vehicle. It was burnt out behind a gas station and reported by the store owner. Now we need to find out who was driving it. We're hoping it was an accidental hit and run by a drunk driver and not a personal vendetta.'

Despite everything, Dean goes into detective mode. 'Any prints on it? Licence plate? Any CCTV around there?'

Brown shakes his head. 'No. There were no keys in the ignition and the car wasn't jump started so once we find the keys, we might have the perp. Because of that I need to search your house.'

'Fine, go right ahead. But why the hell am I a suspect?'

'You know how it is,' says Steve. 'The husband or wife always need to be ruled out first and, well, you don't have a great alibi for that night. You were drinking home alone.'

'Plus,' says Brown, 'the whole diner saw you having a heated argument with Linda before she drove away. You're probably the last person to see her before the crash.'

Dean puts his head down. It does look bad when you look at it like that. But that argument was over before she left the parking lot. He knows it will do no good to explain that though.

'Search my house. I didn't kill my wife.'

Chapter Twenty-Eight

As Steve lets himself into Dean's house that afternoon, Captain Brown follows him in. Steve doesn't believe Dean would have run Linda off the road, but he knows this is the best way to rule him out as a suspect. He's willing to bet Miller starts spouting his theory to anyone that will listen now he's suspended. They've let Dean wait in the diner while they get this over with; it's not like he's going to skip town. The first thing they hear when they enter his house is Rocky barking in the back garden, so Brown goes to let him in.

'What are you doing out there?'

Rocky jumps higher than Steve would have thought possible for a dog of his weight. His tongue licks Brown's face with every jump. Brown kneels down to stop the bouncing as he gives Rocky some attention.

'Okay,' says Steve. 'So if you were trying to hide some evidence would you really hide it in your house?'

'No,' agrees Brown. 'I'd throw it in the river or mail it out of state or something. But if I was drunk and angry and pumped up on adrenaline, I might forget to do that on my way home from killing someone. The car key would probably still be in my coat pocket.'

Steve looks at him for a second. 'It sounds like you're seriously considering Dean might be capable of this.'

Brown gets up as Rocky loses interest in him. 'Steve, we're cops. We have to consider every possible angle, no matter how much we like someone. Cops aren't immune from losing their shit. I've seen documentaries proving cops are actually more likely to lose their shit than someone from any other profession, because of all the craziness we get called out to. It's not like we get psychological help after a call out to the worst domestic violence cases, or the abused child cases. I'm just surprised it doesn't happen more often.'

Steve shakes his head. 'If Dean's guilty of this then I'll never trust another human being in my life.'

Brown walks past him, into the living room. 'Come on, let's get this over with. You search upstairs, I'll search down here, starting with coat pockets.'

Steve slowly walks to the stairs and has to squeeze past Rocky who's blocking his way, hopeful of some attention.

'Not now, big dog.'

He heads upstairs and starts in the bathroom because it's the first door on the left. Steve's been to Dean and Linda's house many times, but rarely upstairs as he always used the downstairs bathroom. It feels strange being here without them. As he opens the bathroom cabinet, he feels like a voyeur and it doesn't sit well with him. Does he really need to know what medications he's on? He sees the usual supply of headache pills, stomach pills and plasters. Plus, a shaver, toothbrush and toothpaste, mouthwash and floss. He's about to close the cabinet door when he notices there's a second layer behind the first. He moves the tall mouthwash box and sees a small bottle of vodka, half empty. *Maybe it's for cleaning wounds*, he thinks.

He moves on to what looks like the spare room. It's already small but it's also filled with boxes and garbage bags. Steve can tell these are Linda's belongings and he immediately wants to leave the room. He can't go rooting through her things, it wouldn't be right. Instead, he shouts down to Brown from the top of the stairs.

'Found anything, Captain?'

He hears Brown approach the bottom of the stairs. 'Not yet. You?'

'Nothing in the bathroom. It looks like all Linda's stuff is in the spare room. Please tell me I don't need to go nosing through it?'

Brown starts up the stairs. 'You know we have to be thorough. But I'll help you.'

They both enter the spare room and have to close the door to stop Rocky coming in. There's barely enough room for them as it is. Rocky sits outside and they can hear him sniffing the gap under the door.

Steve opens a box of Linda's clothes. He picks out each item and checks any pockets. When he's done, he puts them neatly back in the box and moves onto the next. Behind him Brown is checking the bags. Steve notices a small handbag under some jeans and picks it up. Inside is some rolled up tissue, which must've been Linda's. He feels around in the small zipped pockets and his fingers find a leather key ring. Attached to that is a key. Steve looks in and sees that it's a rental car key ring. His heart sinks and he tries to think what to do. He looks behind him. Brown hasn't noticed anything yet and Steve has a split second to make a choice: tell Brown of his discovery or pocket the key and pretend he hasn't found anything. He could go straight to Dean and demand answers, but then what would he do with those answers? Would he go so far as to help Dean get away with murder? He thinks about how badly Dean reacted to John's suicide. That must have tipped him over the edge. That's the only reason Steve can think of that makes Dean less of a monster for killing his wife. Steve knows what he has to do.

'Captain? I found something.'

Brown spins around and looks at the car key in Steve's hand. 'Holy shit.'

Chapter Twenty-Nine

On Sunday morning, just before her session with her next patient, Beth receives an unexpected phone call and all she can do is listen. Afterwards, she switches off her mobile phone and has to sit down at her desk. She's shocked. Toad knocks on the door.

'I've got Judy waiting out here for you.'

'Sorry,' she says. 'I've got to go to the police station. They want to interview me.'

Toad looks surprised. 'What about?'

Beth doesn't know whether to tell him or not, but thinks it's probably good if word spreads quickly.

'They think Dean killed his wife.' For sympathy, she forces herself to cry. 'Oh my God, I've been dating a murderer.'

'Hang on a minute.' Toad leaves, presumably escorting Judy back to her cell as Beth can hear Judy's angry protests.

While he's gone, her mind races. Why do they want to speak to her? Surely Dean hasn't put two and two together. Have his colleagues searched for the car key in his house? Is it time to leave town? Maybe she shouldn't have told Toad as she could have gotten a head start. Quicker than she would have expected, he gets back.

'Are you telling me they seriously think Dean killed Linda? Do you think he's capable?' he asks, sitting on one of her comfy chairs.

'You know him better than me. I should have listened to Pete. Oh my God, I'm shaking.'

Toad walks over to her and gives her an awkward hug. She can smell his sweaty armpits. *That's the problem with polyester uniforms*, she thinks.

'Do you need someone to drive you there?'

'No thanks, I'll be fine. I better get going. Please

don't tell anyone about this just yet. It could all be a big misunderstanding.'

Toad doesn't seem so sure to her. She grabs her bag and leaves her office.

The dispatch woman is giving her dirty looks. Maybe she needs to be brought down a peg or two.

'What did you say your name was?' Beth asks her.

'Jenny. I've worked with Dean for four years so I know he isn't a murderer. You better be careful what you say around here.'

'Are you harassing me?' asks Beth.

Jenny shouts over to one of the cops. 'Steve? She's here.'

If she wasn't trying to play the victim she'd put Jenny in her place.

'Hi,' says Dean's colleague. She recognises him from the night Shania died. 'Thanks for coming. Would you follow me?'

She follows him silently to what are obviously interview rooms. On the way over here she considered skipping town but she doesn't want to leave yet if she doesn't have to. On the phone they said they had some questions about Dean, not her. If they wanted to arrest her they would've collected her themselves.

'Please, take a seat. I just have some questions for you.'

She sits on the hard, plastic chair in this small, windowless room. This isn't the first police interview room she's ever been in, but it is the first American one she's been in.

'I'm sorry, Sergeant Dalkin—'

'Call me Steve.'

They always say that. '*Please; use my first name so that you trust me better*.'

'Steve, I'm sorry but I'm really shaken up over what I was told on the phone. Are you seriously implying I have been dating a murderer?'

She can tell from his reluctance to speak that he's conflicted over arresting his friend. She just has to hope her acting skills are stronger than this man's friendship with Dean.

'He was brought in yesterday evening, but he's not yet been charged. Obviously, we want to make sure we're not holding the wrong person, which is why I've called you in.'

'But I barely know the man. What can I tell you that you don't already know about him?'

'I'm under the impression that you've spent a lot of time with him recently so you're best placed to give me an insight into his recent state of mind. Also, he phoned you the night his wife died. I need you to give a statement about what was said during that conversation.'

She relaxes a little. This is definitely about Dean, not her. 'Well, I can't remember whether he phoned me or I phoned him but we were just talking about the argument he had with his wife; what was her name again?'

'Linda,' he says.

'Yes. Look, it was no secret that he thought his wife was a bit of a bitch. He told me they had an argument that night because she'd turned up at the diner and told him there, in front of everyone, that she was pregnant with his baby. But she also told him that she'd been having an affair with someone, so I think he thought the baby wasn't his and she was trying to trick him. He seemed very bitter on the phone. I should've put two and two together and realised he was angry enough to go after his wife. In my professional experience, I see many cases of men not being able to live with the fact their wives cheated on them. It makes them feel inadequate, less masculine. Dean was very drunk on the phone. If I knew he was going to drive I would have called the police.'

Steve's listening to her without making notes. She's not sure he believes her but she's not intimidated by him.

'I need you to write down everything you remember from that phone call. Then I'll need you to sign it and, if it comes to it, give evidence in court.'

She feels like he's waiting for her to realise the severity of the situation, so that she doesn't make any false claims, but she's well ahead of him. She can lie under oath without any problem at all. Being completely alone in this world means she has to look after herself. They don't know it but she's actually helping the police clean up this town. She's eliminated two bad mothers already: Shania and that drug addict who owned Rocky. Their kids will grow up to be better people now. Beth can't abide bad mothers. They're the root of all evil. Dean's wife, Linda, was just someone who got in the way. She doesn't remember the details of that night. It was only when she got home afterwards that she realised what she'd done. She must've blacked out or something. That's happened more than once over the years. Probably the result of all the medication her mother used to feed her as a kid, at least that's what her doctor at the hospital would have concluded. Beth's thoughts turn to the woman in the woods, Sarah. She knows there's no way they'll ever find out her identity.

Chapter Thirty

Dean's trying to sleep because that's all he can do right now. He's hoping he won't wake up until all this is resolved. The more he thinks about how he's ended up in this cell, the more confused he becomes. He doesn't know why there was a rental car key in Linda's handbag. It wasn't even the bag she had on her when she crashed. Steve's confirmed it was the key to the car that they think ran her off the road, but it doesn't make any sense. He's finding it so hard to concentrate on anything right now. It's freezing in the holding cell and he doesn't have a sweater. He hears footsteps approaching and sits up.

'Hi.'

Dean looks up and is shocked to see Jones here. He can feel shame spread as heat through his reddening cheeks. There's no way he wants Jones to see him like this. He crosses his arms to try and warm up but he feels both hot and cold at the same time, like he's coming down with something. He's so mentally exhausted from the last few months that it wouldn't surprise him if he's ill.

'I've brought you a coffee. I forgot to request decaff though, I'm afraid.' Jones passes it through the cell door.

He hesitates in getting up to reach for it. His discomfort at Jones seeing him like this must be obvious, but he knows Jones is too good a friend to acknowledge it.

'I probably shouldn't tell you this,' says Jones, 'but Steve just spent an hour with Beth Smith. Unfortunately, he won't let me read her statement because I'm no longer on the payroll. But don't worry, I'll find a way of reading it eventually.'

Dean looks up as his confused brain slowly puts together the pieces he's been missing since his arrest. 'She was in my house without me.'

Jones leans in. 'What?'

'Beth. I got home from work at lunch on Tuesday, I think,

and she was already in my house. She got the key from my neighbour and had lunch all set out for me. Jones, she's the only person who has been in my house alone since Linda died. She could have planted it.'

'But why would she plant a key to make you look guilty? I thought you two were sleeping together?'

Dean tries to hide his embarrassment. 'We were but ...' He trails off, realising how stupid he sounds. He doesn't even know what he's saying any more. Jones is right; why would she have anything to do with it? She never even met Linda so she wouldn't know what she looked like. Beth's been nothing but good to him.

'I can ask Steve to do a background check on her if you like, to rule her out?'

Dean can tell pity when he hears it. 'No, it's fine. I just don't get it. I honestly don't get why that key was in my house. Maybe I did go after her, once I was drunk. Alcoholics use that as their defence all the time, don't they? They have memory lapses because of the booze. Maybe that happened to me. Shit, I've become a walking cliché.'

Jones grabs his arm through the cell. 'Listen to me, Dean. You had nothing to do with this. I know I don't have much sway around here any more but I'm going to find out who did this so that you can get out of here and back to work. The whole team is on your side so you just sit tight. We're going to figure this out.'

Dean lets his head hang. 'Thanks.'

'I've got to ask: what were you doing sleeping with Sheila and this Beth woman when you were married to Linda? It's just not like you.'

Dean shakes his head. 'You don't know what's it's been like since John died. Linda was so cold towards me. I guess I was just looking for a distraction. It worked at first, until I fessed up. But Jones, I only found out recently she had been sleeping with someone else for the last two years!'

Jones tuts and looks down. 'That's rough, I'm sorry. It sounds like your marriage was over a long time ago.'

'Exactly. And then Beth was new in town and the attraction was just overwhelming. I tried to ignore it but I guess ... I don't know. It didn't start until Linda moved out. This isn't just a fling for me though, I think I'm genuinely falling for her.' He shakes his head and sighs. 'My emotions are so fucked up right now I don't know what I'm feeling, to be honest.'

'What do you know about her?'

'Not much,' admits Dean. 'She's pretty cagey on the family history front. I figured she comes from a broken home and doesn't like to revisit the topic, which is fair enough. She's a counsellor at the prison.'

'You don't say?' says Jones.

'I know that look. What are you thinking?'

'Didn't an inmate die there recently?'

'Yeah, one of Beth's clients. But she was nowhere near the prison at the time and it was an obvious suicide.'

'Okay.' Jones changes the subject. 'Brown tells me they haven't charged you with anything yet because you're one of us and they want more time to figure this out. That's good for you because the press won't get hold of anything. But you need to be ready to lawyer up quick, just in case. In the meantime, I'm going to see about getting you home while we figure this mess out.'

Dean feels hope rising in his chest. 'You think they'd let me go home?'

Jones smiles for the first time. 'Well, someone's got to take care of that damn dog of yours.'

Dean hadn't thought of Rocky once during his ordeal. The thought of Rocky and going home brings a massive relief to him and his shoulders relax a little. Jones leaves him to go and speak to Brown. He lies back on the hard bed and feels some fight return to him. He needs to figure out why he's in this situation.

Chapter Thirty-One

Within two hours Jones is driving Dean home through the snow. Captain Brown has given Jones strict instructions to hide him, which is why they're driving under the cover of darkness at seven o'clock in the evening, but they must also keep their mouths shut and not tell anyone anything. Dean has no intention of talking to anyone, he just wants to see Rocky and have a bath. As they enter his house, Jones fights Rocky off.

'Hey, Rocky! Long time, no see. You better look after my buddy here, okay?'

Rocky responds by forcing his whole body weight against Jones' legs, almost knocking him over. Then, as Jones bends down to stroke him, Rocky gives him a face full of dog breath and tongue.

For the first time today, Dean laughs. 'Come on, Rocky, leave him alone.' He grabs Rocky's collar and leads him to the stairs. 'Sit!'

'You'll never get that dog to obey instructions,' Jones says, laughing.

'I hope you're wrong because I'm going to train him to become a police dog.'

Jones shakes his head. 'I'll believe it when I see it. By the way, I wasn't sure whether to tell you this or not, but I've asked Brown to let me look into Linda's death, officially, and he's agreed. Now I'm temporarily back on the payroll that means I'll have access to all the reports and crime scene photos so that I can try and get this solved fast. I didn't want Miller to get his grubby mitts on the case, as he's biased. Is that okay with you?'

Dean feels his chest swell with gratitude. He nods. 'Yeah, that would be great. Thanks.'

'Right, I'm going to head home for a good night's sleep. I

feel like tomorrow's the first day of a new school term.' He laughs. 'I might even get a haircut.'

Rocky tries to make one more lunge for Jones but he manages to get out the front door before the dog reaches him. After he's gone, Dean heads to the kitchen to make himself a hot drink.

'Did Auntie Sheila feed you dinner earlier, Rocky?' Steve told him as he was leaving the station that Sheila had been feeding the dog for him during his short incarceration. It feels good to have the support of his friends. Rocky runs circles around him at the sound of the word 'dinner'. Dean has been teaching him certain words, like dinner, walkies, squirrel, and Rocky has been surprisingly quick to learn. He puts out the pasta bowl used for Rocky's kibble and fills it up. Most of it lands on Rocky's head as he doesn't wait for Dean to stop pouring before he starts eating.

The house feels cold and empty, even with Rocky chomping away. He has no appetite himself and he's trying to resist the urge to drink bourbon or vodka. He chooses a decaffeinated green tea instead and stirs the teabag around his mug. He wants to be completely clear-headed, not only so he can think things through clearly, but also so that he can't be accused of being a drunk should he be breathalysed in the near future. He's not sure how to spend this evening seeing as he has to lay low. He can't risk running into anyone he knows because the first thing they'll ask him is why he's not been around the last two days, quickly followed by 'Why do you look like shit?' Hopefully Miller hasn't told the whole town what happened yet. Brown made it pretty clear to Miller that he wouldn't be returning to work if anything got out, so Dean hopes he won't risk it.

With his mug in one hand, Dean switches the heating on and lets Rocky into the garden. He leaves the back door ajar in case it's too cold for him outside now it's snowing, and then wanders around the house. When he gets to the top of the stairs he thinks about Linda. He's managed to put most of her things in the spare bedroom but he hasn't sorted through them yet. Reluctantly, he enters the room and puts his drink on the table. He's tried hard to think of a reason as to why Linda would have a rental car key in her bag, but he doesn't get it. If this were anyone else he'd think they were being framed by someone, but Dean knows almost everyone in this town and doesn't think he has any enemies, well apart from Miller. He's even friendly with the felons, once they're released. It makes life easier. He also doesn't know of anyone who would want Linda dead. He's still convinced her car crash was an accident by some out of towner or tourist driving through. Probably a drunk driver. He refuses to believe it was personal.

He starts sifting through some boxes half-heartedly and can tell which ones Steve and Brown went through as they didn't do a good job of folding the clothes after checking them. He'd like to bin it all instead of giving it to charity, but at the moment he can't do anything with it. It's potentially evidence. Just thinking that word makes him shudder. If he gets arrested for Linda's death, his friends will bag all this up and take it away to be checked for DNA. His DNA is all over it already but it could prove useful if they find someone else's DNA on it.

He doesn't know if he can go through a lengthy court battle and have his reputation ruined. The only thing that brings him any relief is the thought that Jones is now on the case. He should be able to figure out what's going on. He'd do a better job than Miller anyway.

Accidentally, as there's hardly any room in here, he pushes over a stack of boxes, revealing a small oak chest sticking out from underneath a pile of clothes. He's never seen this before. It looks like the kind of thing a woman would keep her nicest trinkets in. It has a small metal clasp, which he hesitates to open. This feels to him like a foreign object; something that doesn't belong to Linda or in their house. Surely, he would have seen it before now? He pushes the clasp open with his thumb and slowly opens the lid. It's stuffed with old Valentine's cards and some letters. Dean sits on the floor.

Against his better judgement, as he's not sure he's ready for another emotional roller coaster, he starts reading each card and letter, one at a time. Some of these cards are years old and he remembers sending them to Linda in the post so that she'd receive them while he was at work. He had no idea she'd kept them all. He doesn't remember keeping any of hers. Once again, he feels like he was a bad husband.

When he gets to the last one it's still in its envelope. He recognises the handwriting but it's not his or Linda's. His heart starts beating harder and he can suddenly hear the blood pumping in his head. His face is warming up. He knows whose writing it is but it doesn't make any sense, unless it's a birthday card, or even maybe a Christmas card to them both. But then why does it have a small heart drawn next to Linda's name?

He opens the unsealed envelope and confirms it's a Valentines card. It looks expensive, not like the tacky supermarket ones he bought for Linda. His hands are shaking as he opens it.

Linda,
You're the only woman I've ever loved. Once our baby is born we'll find a way to be together, and not just behind closed doors. Please don't worry.
All my love, J.

Dean feels like he's been hit over the head with a baseball bat. He winces as the implication of what he's reading hits him. This is his brother's writing. He screws up the card and rushes downstairs, almost tripping over, to get his cell phone. He finds the name he wants and calls it. On the fourth ring, Linda's sister answers the phone.

'Did you know?' he barks. He's met by silence. 'How long did you know? My own *brother*? And I'm the one treated like shit by you two! You're disgusting.'

'Dean, calm down! How did you find out?' asks Chrissie.

'So, you're not even going to deny it?'

'Look, it wasn't me who had an affair with your brother! For the whole first year I told her to either stop it or pick between you. She wouldn't listen to me.'

'You could've told me yourself!' he suggests, bitterly.

'It wasn't my place to get involved.'

'But you got involved in my business all the time!'

'She was in love with him, Dean. She said they were going to move in together. She was waiting for him to tell you everything but he kept backing out; said he couldn't find the words. He wouldn't let her tell you, he said it had to come from him. They were happy to begin with but the lies made it seem tainted after a while, until she fell pregnant. Linda was the happiest I'd ever known her when she went for that first scan. The baby was perfect.' He hears her struggling to hold back tears. 'But then, when she lost the baby, John changed. He couldn't bear to be with her. He said they lost the baby as punishment for going behind your back.'

Dean has to gulp back tears now. 'Is that why he became depressed?'

Chrissie sighs, possibly feeling bad for him at last. 'I think so. Linda said he stopped returning her calls and messages and stopped leaving his house. He wouldn't even let her in when she visited him.'

'I couldn't understand why he spiralled downhill so fast,' says Dean, his voice thick with emotion. 'I thought he'd had a sudden mental health problem or started taking drugs.'

'It was because he'd been lying to you for so long. He couldn't bear the guilt.'

Dean cuts her off and lets his cell phone fall to the floor. He collapses onto the couch and covers his face.

'If he'd told me he wanted to be with her I would've let him,' he whispers to nobody. 'It wasn't worth dying over.' He breaks down and sobs for John, for Linda and for himself. Rocky comes in from outside and finds him broken on the couch. He nuzzles his face into Dean's and licks off the tears.

Chapter Thirty-Two

First thing on Monday morning, Steve is sitting with Marty and Detective Jones in the interview room, which feels weird to him seeing as Jones has been retired for some time. He feels re-energised now they have someone more proactive and experienced than Miller in charge. He and Marty try to relay to Jones as much information as they can about the recent homicides and suicides the town has seen.

'I can't believe how much has happened since I left,' says Jones.

'It's almost like someone was waiting for you to retire,' jokes Marty. 'They probably thought they could get away with murder with Miller in charge.'

'And so far, they're right,' says Steve. 'So, what did you find from the background check on Beth Smith?'

Jones pulls out a sheet of paper. 'I got one of the guys to look into her overnight but they found absolutely nothing, she's completely clean. In the US, at least. She's even paying the right level of taxes.'

'What have you got against her?' asks Marty.

Jones turns his piece of paper over to show his notes. 'Number one: she was counselling the inmate who killed herself. Number two: she's new in town, arriving just weeks before all this began. And number three: she was sleeping with Dean. I keep wondering whether she could be a bunny boiler; jealous of Dean's wife. Jealous enough to get her out of the picture. The only thing is, she didn't know him long enough for that level of possessiveness.'

Steve sits forward. 'You know, Pete and Toad have said she's been causing trouble at the prison. She's been insinuating that Dean was dishonest with her about his wife, and said she feels like she's been sleeping with a murderer.'

Marty shakes his head.

Steve continues, 'I think she's just annoyed that all this is going to wreck her reputation as a psychiatrist. I mean, it doesn't look good for her. Her very first patient at the prison kills herself and her lover is – in her words – a murderer. If I were an outsider who didn't know Dean, I wouldn't trust her professional opinion much. From what I hear from the guards, Sue Wells is about ready to fire her.'

Jones sips his coffee and nods. 'Yeah, I hear what you're saying. She's probably clean, it's just that my gut tells me she has something to do with all of this, no matter how small. I can't ignore the love triangle aspect of it. I'm going to see what I can dig up in the UK. She might have a prior record over there, or maybe some family will be able to tell me something about her.'

'Good idea,' says Steve. 'Now, moving on to Tammy Gordon. Marty? Do we know where Skylar Hutton was when Tammy died? Dean said only Beau showed up to the kids' appointment at the hospital.'

'I'll give you three guesses.'

Steve rolls his eyes. 'With her supplier?'

'Yep, she was with Shaun Flannery. Although, I don't know if he would testify to that in court, what with the business they're in. But I believe him. He only lives twenty minutes from the hospital so it looks like she dropped her boyfriend and the kids off there first, stocked up on drugs while they were with the doc, and then met them at the hospital for lunch before driving them home. She's on CCTV at the hospital coffee shop buying drinks before they left.'

Steve's shoulders slump. 'So we still have no leads whatsoever on who killed Tammy.'

'Is the inmate's suicide being treated as suspicious by the Coroner?' asks Jones.

'No, that's already been closed as a suicide. No one's contesting it. Her kids are living with a cousin but the cousin wanted nothing to do with arranging a funeral for Shania. As far as we're concerned that case is closed.'

Jones puts a line through Shania's name in his notepad. 'So what about this woman in the woods? Has that been closed yet?'

'No because Miller took it over from Dean,' says Marty. 'Now Miller's not here, I guess that falls to you.'

'Actually, Marty.' Steve smiles. 'Brown says we're meant to help out with this one. He's asked me to run the story again on social media. That means you need to speak to everyone who's phoned or tweeted us about her and try to find out what might be significant.'

Marty collapses back into his chair. 'Why do I always get the nut jobs?'

Steve laughs. 'You know what they say; like attracts like!'

'Thanks. I love you too.'

Jones finishes his coffee, stands up and organises his paperwork. 'Okay, I'm going to start with a UK background check of Ms Smith. Once I can rule her out as a suspect I'll start looking into Linda's crash from a different perspective. Someone get a copy of the CSI report to me ASAP?'

'Will do,' says Steve.

Marty collects the mugs. 'I'm going to need some strong coffee to get me through these callbacks.'

Steve laughs and shuffles his papers together. They head back to their desks to start work on identifying Jane Doe.

Chapter Thirty-Three

Dean finally opens his eyes just after lunchtime on Monday. His instinct immediately tells him he's done something stupid. He looks to his left and sees Beth asleep next to him in the bed.

'Oh shit,' he whispers.

He knows inviting Beth to his house was probably the worst thing he could do right now, and he can't even remember calling her. He remembers fragments of his phone call with Chrissie instead; the reason John killed himself, mainly. Then he remembers searching his cupboards for liquor, but he didn't have any. That must've been when he phoned Beth. He starts to remember. She was dubious at first, trying to act normal. It didn't take long for him to convince her he wasn't inviting her around to kill her. She was the one who brought the Jack Daniel's with her. They'd started drinking immediately. As he hadn't eaten any dinner, Dean assumes he must've passed out pretty soon after. He doesn't think they even had sex. She moves next to him, slowly waking up.

'Oh shit,' she says.

That makes him laugh. 'My thoughts exactly!'

She smiles and rubs her eyes. 'My mouth is so dry.'

Dean pulls the covers back and is grateful to see he has boxer shorts on. He pulls a T-shirt on. 'I'll go and make us some coffee. You stay there.'

He almost trips on Rocky when he opens the bedroom door.

'Did we shut him out all night?' asks Beth.

'Must've done. Sorry, Rocky. Come on, let's get you some food.'

Downstairs, he feeds Rocky first and then lets him out into the garden. After putting the kettle on he looks for his cell phone, which is on the worktop next to the empty bottle of bourbon and glasses. He has two missed calls from this morning, one from Steve and one from Jones. With a feeling of dread, he calls Steve back.

'Sorry I missed your call. I overslept. Is everything all right?'

'Yes,' says Steve. 'We were just checking you haven't skipped the country.'

'Of course not.' For Dean, it's too soon to joke about his current situation. 'What's the plan of action for figuring this mess out?'

'We're working on it. Jones ran a background check on your lady friend but it came back clear.'

Although Dean's relieved to hear Beth's not hiding anything, he didn't expect Jones to check into her. 'Why did he do that?'

'He just wanted to rule her out. You've got to admit that it seems a bit weird all this stuff started happening right around the time she moved to town.'

Dean knows if he were as good as Jones, he'd do the same thing.

'Still, don't forget you can't contact her, or anyone else right now. We're hoping to have this wrapped up soon now that Jones is on the case, otherwise that vein in Brown's temple – you know the one that looks like a worm under his skin – well, that's about to explode any day now. He's even got Marty and me looking into Jane Doe, that's how desperate he is. Marty's drawn the short straw for the callbacks again.'

Dean wonders whether he should confess he has Beth in his bed right now but thinks better of it.

'Okay, well I'll leave you to it. If you need any help just give me a call.'

'Understood. Be good.'

Dean cringes at that comment. The kettle boils so he makes their drinks and lets Rocky back in, who immediately runs up the stairs ahead of him. Beth is sitting up checking her cell phone. He wonders who calls or messages her. He doesn't remember her ever taking a call while he's been with her. When Rocky jumps on the bed, she laughs. Dean puts the coffees on his bedside table and climbs back into bed, next to Rocky.

'Here you go. Careful, it's hot.'

'Thanks. Who were you talking to?'

That reminds Dean he's left his cell phone downstairs. 'Just work. They just wanted to clarify something.'

'I know you didn't want to talk about this last night but I've got to ask, seeing as I'm in bed with you; what on earth is going on?'

He inwardly cringes, not sure what to say.

'I mean, obviously, I was called in to answer questions about our telephone conversation from that night your wife died, but I know they're barking up the wrong tree by looking into what you were doing that night. I've seen you with Emily; you wouldn't hurt a fly.'

He relaxes a little. 'Thanks. It means a lot. Hopefully this will be figured out soon and I'll be back at work. They're just checking into a few things and I guess I'm the lead suspect because of the argument I had with her in Frankie's. Plus, I'm the husband. It does look bad to the outside world, but Brown isn't taking it that seriously, thank God. He knows me too well. Now that my old mentor's out of retirement specifically to solve Linda's case, I'm pretty confident I'll be cleared within the next day or two. Jones is the best detective we've ever had, with a one hundred per cent success rate. He has amazing instincts.'

Beth looks a little annoyed. 'I thought Linda's crash was an accident? Why do they suddenly think it was anything else? What could possibly have led them to believe that? Do they have some evidence of something to suggest otherwise?' she asks, clearly wanting full details.

He's desperate to change the subject so he kisses her. He doesn't want to think about anything right now and the longer he can delay processing what he found out yesterday about John, the better. She seems to want to pull away at first but his insistence pays off. He pushes Rocky off the bed with his foot and gives Beth his full attention.

Chapter Thirty-Four

By Monday afternoon, Jones has had no luck trying to dig up any information about Beth Smith in the UK. The police over there need more information from him: her full name (*'Is it Elizabeth or Beth? Does she have a middle name? Smith is a common surname, you know.'*), date of birth, her National Insurance number, or even some DNA. He can't really go digging too deep for that level of personal detail unless she's a suspect, which, officially, she's not but Jones is convinced there's something not right about the timing of her arrival in town. As he catches up with Steve and Captain Brown, he tests his theory.

'I didn't want to tell Dean too much, in case his new girlfriend turns out to be above board and I end up being best man at their wedding, but I have a bad feeling about her.'

'Have either of you met her?' asks Steve.

They both shake their heads.

'She seems okay, but she's not easy to talk to. Whether that's because she's a psychiatrist, I don't know. She's very standoffish. I felt like she was looking down her nose at me when I was taking her statement. Pete and Dean got into a fight over her recently so she's not popular at the prison either. It sounds like she's been leading Pete on, whilst sleeping with Dean. Also, she told me that Dean was angry the night Linda was killed, implying he might've gone after her whilst drunk.'

'Yes, I read her statement,' says Jones. 'I think she's a troublemaker. But why would a professional psychiatrist get caught up in something so ridiculous as a love triangle between two working class men? If anything, shouldn't she be calming situations down? And the fact that one of her patients killed themselves within hours of a counselling session rings alarm bells for me.'

'I can see your instinct is kicking in and, I'll be honest, we've missed that around here,' says Brown. 'But don't let your friendship with Matheson cloud your judgement, either of you, because he's still the main suspect for Linda's death, no matter how we feel about it. Whatever we do needs to be completely above board because if any of this goes to court, we can't be seen as showing favouritism to a member of staff. Especially if it turns out he's guilty.'

Jones thinks about this for a minute. He's always been nothing but professional, but this is the first time in his career that one of his investigations has involved a friend. 'Captain?' he says. 'I want to bring her in for questioning.'

Both Brown and Steve raise their eyebrows.

'Not to charge her with anything, but to check further into her alibi for the night of Linda's death. And to question her about how much she knows about the other deaths. I don't know how much Dean has told her about them, hopefully nothing, but I want to bring her in under the illusion that we need her professional opinion about what kind of person we should be looking for. She may even have an opinion on why our Jane Doe hanged herself. If I can just talk to her myself, without Dean present, I can get a feeling for what she's really like. I just have to put to rest this nagging feeling I have about her.'

Captain Brown agrees. 'Okay, fine. Most psychiatrists are flattered to be asked for their professional opinions about cases so, if she declines, we'll know you're onto something.'

'I have her cell phone number. When are you thinking of calling her?' asks Steve.

'I'll wait until the morning. Early. You know me, I like to catch people while they're still half asleep. It's harder for them to lie.'

Steve smiles. 'It's good to have you back.'

Chapter Thirty-Five

Beth tries to find out more from Dean but he's avoiding the subject. She's alarmed he's so confident his colleagues are going to clear him, and so soon. She thought planting the car keys would at least get him arrested, which would lead to news of his arrest spreading across the media. Everyone knows that once a husband is publicly suspected of their wife's murder, it's hard to recover from that. That would have put her completely in the clear, which would mean she could have stayed at her job at the prison. The prison is full of potential for her. Potential to get rid of as many evil women as possible. It's a compulsion for her to do this. To put right the wrong that so many children experience.

With Sarah dead, there's no one in the US who knows Beth's real identity, so this would've been a good town to work in for a while longer, but if Dean gets cleared within the next few days things could go wrong for her. She should've known a small town like this wouldn't abide religiously by the law. It seems if you're a cop you're pretty much untouchable, whereas anyone else in Dean's situation would've been arrested and charged by now. She's annoyed she hadn't considered this might happen; that they'd all stick together. She's also annoyed that she's never heard Dean mention this Detective Jones before. If he really does have a one hundred per cent success rate, she's glad she moved here after he retired.

To try to put her mind at ease she considers how much he could really solve now he's presumably old and irrelevant. Surely, he wouldn't have the same authority and sway as he once had, making it more difficult to do his job this time around. Feeling fidgety, she climbs out of Dean's bed.

'I'll go and make us some drinks,' she says.

Dean's watching the early afternoon local news on the bedroom television, presumably checking he's not starring on it.

'Are you sure? I'm sorry I can't go out to fetch you a cappuccino. Hopefully, I won't have to lay low too much longer.'

'No, it's fine. I need to stretch my legs, it won't take me a minute. Tea or coffee?'

'Tea. I'll turn this off when you get back.' He smiles.

Inwardly, she grimaces. The attraction is over for her. He's annoying now she's finished with him. She forces a laugh and heads downstairs. Once the kettle is on, she notices Dean's mobile phone on the worktop. The notification light is flashing. She picks it up and has a look. He doesn't have it pin locked. '*Some cop*,' she thinks. There's a new text message from Steve.

'*Forgot to mention; Jones ran her background check in the US (like I said; clear) but he's checking her UK record too. Enjoy daytime TV while we do all the hard work.*'

Beth lets out a stifled grunt and has to stop herself from throwing the phone across the kitchen. 'How dare they?' she mumbles. 'How dare they do a background check on me when I'm not even a suspect?' She starts pacing the kitchen as the kettle boils loudly, water bubbling away behind the glass container. She's trying to think what she should do, but her thoughts are clouded by panic. She starts a reply text to Steve. '*Don't bother with the UK check, I've done one already, that came up clear too.*' She hesitates to press 'send' because it might prompt a call from Steve. She deletes it and slams the phone down on the worktop.

Rocky starts barking from outside. She notices it's started to rain hard and she can hear the wind rattling the windows. She opens the door and Rocky runs through it and over to Beth in excitement. He wants attention but he's soaking wet and smelly, and Beth is wound up so she pushes him away, hard. Rocky thinks she's playing so he comes running back immediately, expecting the same rough and tumble wrestling he has with Dean, but she's infuriated with him jumping up at her and getting her wet. She thumps him hard across his jaw.

'Stupid dog!' she shouts, just as the kettle finishes boiling.

Rocky yelps and runs away. She has to resist the urge to run after him with a knife. She hasn't felt this angry since she held Tammy Gordon down with the force of her whole body, waiting for the overdose to kick in. That stupid bitch fought hard for her worthless life, and for what? So that she could treat her only daughter like shit? That kid will never be normal thanks to that monster.

'Everything okay?' shouts Dean from the top of the stairs.

Beth has to calm herself down or there's going to be a dead cop and a dead dog in this house if she doesn't pull it together immediately. That really wouldn't help her situation.

'Coming!' she shouts, silently trying to slow her breathing.

Realising she wants to stop moving from pillar to post like a hobo, and valuing the good set-up she has in this town, she decides she needs to become Dean's next 'victim'. That way, she can give evidence against him when she accuses him of attempted murder, and what better witness than her? Last time she was involved in a court case, she was the defendant and she lost. But that case was too personal to her and she was too ill to know what was going on. Her judgement was clouded. This time she'll give the acting performance of her life. Her mind starts working overtime, trying to hatch a plan. She knows it would be easier to just kill him and run, but she's sick of running. And, unlike with felons, the law takes it seriously when you murder a cop. She pours the hot water into their cups as she thinks. When she heads upstairs with their drinks, Rocky's nowhere to be seen.

By the time Beth gets back to the bedroom, she has a plan. When she first arrived in town she had investigated the whole area, making sure she knew all the exits and hiding places. She had found a small run-down log cabin deep in Maple Valley woods, off the beaten track and inconspicuous. She had to plan ahead in case she ever needed to disappear for a while and there was nothing at the cabin apart from some old furniture and log storage, but there was a key to the front door under a log on the porch. She pocketed it, just in case.

Then, once Sarah tracked her down, Beth had to use the cabin to store Sarah's belongings after her death: her handbag, suitcase, a few clothes, hardly any make-up. Plus, her black ankle boots. Sarah had surprised Beth by turning up in America, and at her flat, without asking first. She had followed Beth's movements without her knowing.

'I wanted to make sure you were well enough to be travelling and I knew you wouldn't let me come with you,' she had told her when Beth reluctantly let her into her flat.

'You need someone to look after you, just until you're a hundred per cent re-acclimatised to living in society again. Starting afresh in a new country could set you back because of the stress of the move.'

Beth was fuming. She didn't need Sarah watching her every move and babying her like her mother used to. She wanted to be left alone, to live her own life as she wanted to for the first time. As Sarah had just arrived from her flight, Beth made her a small meal to give herself time to decide what to do. She liked Sarah, but she had overstepped a boundary and having her here was making Beth anxious. She knew asking her to leave wasn't going to work, so she had to get rid of her. She tricked Sarah into going for a walk in the woods. She told her it would be a good way for them to catch up.

'I'm not really dressed for a walk in the woods as I didn't realise how cold it would be in New Hampshire at this time of year. I didn't have much time to plan my trip, to be honest. Plus, it's a bit late to go out now, it's the middle of the night!' She had laughed. 'I just want to go to sleep. I don't mind taking the couch, if that's okay with you?'

Beth had insisted on the walk by saying it helps to reduce her anxiety before she sleeps. She lent Sarah one of her own long thick coats and some trainers and socks, and then drove them to Maple Valley woods. Because of the jet lag, the hour and the drink laced with sleeping pills that Beth had given her, Sarah fell asleep during the drive. When she next came to, she had a makeshift noose around her neck and Beth was about to pull the rope, which was wrapped around a thick branch. Sarah had struggled immediately and pleaded for her life. Beth hadn't said a word. She doesn't remember pulling the rope and tying it. The next thing she remembers is taking her socks and trainers off of Sarah's feet. It annoyed her that she had to remove them from Sarah's hanging body. It looked odd for a woman to hang herself without any shoes at this time of year, but they contained Beth's DNA, so she couldn't leave them there. She still curses herself for not taking Sarah's shoes with her in the car, but she hadn't been thinking straight. This was all unplanned and spontaneous. That's why she also left the stepladder there. She had been careful to wear gloves, so she wasn't worried about the ladder giving her away but she wishes she had been given some time to plan it properly. Beth had burned Sarah's belongings a few days later, leaving no evidence that she was ever in Maple Valley and making it much harder for the police to identify the body.

'How about we get out of here for a refreshing walk in the woods?' she suggests.

Dean leans forward and kisses her on the lips. 'How about you get back in bed?'

She pushes him away with a fake laugh. 'I don't want to waste the rest of my day off work and we've been in bed all day so far!' She looks at the bedside clock. 'It's almost three o'clock already! Come on, Rocky will want a walk by now.' She knows mentioning Rocky will tug at his heartstrings, because he's weak. She won't allow herself to feel that way for anyone, never mind a stupid animal.

'Where is Rocky?' asks Dean, suddenly remembering him.

'He's downstairs, sitting by the front door. Waiting to be taken out.'

'But it's raining out there, can you hear that? And Steve would go mad if he knew I'd left the house.'

Beth stands up and starts getting dressed. 'I'll take him for a walk on my own then.'

As she expected, he's too chivalrous to let her go alone when it's his dog that needs walking. He gets out of bed and starts pulling his jeans on. 'Okay, okay, I'll come.'

She heads downstairs ahead of him, to find the dog. He's hiding behind the sofa in the living room, somehow wedged into a small gap, so she tries to coax him out before Dean notices something's wrong.

'Come on, Rocky. Walkies!'

He starts wagging his tail but he doesn't move. There's no way she could physically move him herself, he's huge. She can hear Dean brushing his teeth upstairs as she pops to the kitchen to get a dog treat. Just the sound of the cupboard door opening is enough to bring Rocky running to her. He knows exactly which cupboard his food is stored in and it makes a barely audible creak as it opens, just enough for a dog to hear it. Despite her feelings towards dogs, she can't help but laugh at him. She's feeling calmer now she has a plan and she's feeding him treats when Dean walks into the kitchen.

'It's no wonder I have to walk him so often if you're slipping him that many treats.'

'I can't help it,' she says. 'He's adorable.'

Dean collects his keys and coat and looks for his cell phone. She freezes momentarily as he picks it up from the worktop and gives it a quick glance. The notification light isn't flashing so he doesn't pay it any attention and just slips it into his coat pocket. She needs to make sure she gets that off him as soon as possible in case Detective Jones manages to find anything out about her. If he rings Dean, it's all over for her. Without knowing her real name she knows Jones won't get far very quickly, but she needs to move fast regardless. If she can get Dean arrested before Jones finds out anything about her, building a case against Dean will take priority and she'll be forgotten.

Chapter Thirty-Six

Jones has just returned from viewing Jane Doe for the first time when he hears Marty shout, 'Bingo!' from his desk. Everyone looks up and laughs. Marty isn't known for being an introvert, so this isn't entirely out of character for him.

'You gotta come and see this!' he exclaims.

Steve and Jones head over to his desk as Captain Brown emerges from his office and follows them.

'What have you found?' asks Jones.

'I'm on one of the UK missing person websites and—'

Brown cuts in, 'Why a UK site?'

'Because I've spent hours on the US sites and not come up with anything and, you know what it's like, when you follow link after link you usually end up with cat videos, and I did, but then I followed a link to this UK site and I thought, "What the hell?" I started scouring the missing women and I'm glad I did because look what I found.' He moves away from his PC so everyone can see his screen.

Steve gasps. 'Oh my God, that's her! Let me call Sheila up here.' He moves to his desk and phones her.

'Are you saying this is the woman in the woods?' asks Brown.

'I think you're right,' says Jones. He can see similarities between the photo and the woman he just visited in the morgue. He immediately wonders what another British woman would be doing in their small town and thinks of Beth again. He's glad he has permission to interview her tomorrow and knows he'll be kept awake tonight, thinking of questions and angles at which to approach her.

Within minutes, Sheila comes rushing through the front desk, towards them.

'Sheila, who's this?' asks Marty.

She bends towards his screen and immediately exclaims, 'Oh, thank God, that's her! That's our Jane. I'm so glad you've identified her. So, she's been reported missing?'

'Yes, in the UK. It was her distinguishable features that helped me find her. It narrowed down my search because whoever logged her as missing mentioned the pattern of freckles on her shoulders, which brought up just a few results. As I scrolled down the list, she jumped out at me because, well, she's beautiful.'

'She is,' agrees Sheila. 'Or was.'

They all fall silent for a minute. The initial excitement of identifying her turns to sadness that they're looking at a photo of her alive and smiling. A photo taken by a loved one. One of them is going to have to contact her family and break the bad news.

'So, her name's Sarah. Sarah Glover, and she's twenty-five,' reads Sheila.

'Write the organisation's contact number down for me. I'll give them a call,' says Jones. 'I'll need that reference number too, the one next to her photo.'

Marty hands him a piece of paper and Jones goes to Dean's desk, which he's using in Dean's absence. He checks his watch; it's just after seven o'clock. He works out what time it is in the UK; midnight. He still tries calling them but he's put through to a recorded answer message asking him to leave his details. He leaves his name, contact details and the reference number and asks for a callback as soon as possible.

'That's all we can do for tonight,' he says to the others. He washes his mug out in the kitchen. Then, as he gets his belongings together, intending to head home for the night, he receives an international phone call.

'Detective Jones? This is Aaron Wheeler from the missing person's organisation in London. I just listened to your message and wanted to call you back as soon as possible.'

'That's great, thanks. You're working late.'

'Yeah, well, I'm a volunteer and I work best overnight seeing as I'm an insomniac. I get excited when I get credible contacts about one of our missing people. I'm an amateur detective myself and a huge Sherlock Holmes fan!'

Jones can't help but laugh. 'If only he were real. We have a few cases here he could help us solve.'

'Ha! I bet. So, I've got the website open now on the reference number you quoted; Sarah Glover. Is that right?'

'Yes. I'm afraid it's not good news for her family though. She was found dead over here in New Hampshire. It looks like suicide.'

'Oh no, that's awful.'

Aaron sounds genuinely upset by this. He must have to deal with as much bad news as they do.

'Obviously we're just going by the photo on the website. She looks the same, same age and the same freckles mentioned in the write-up. But we'd either have to get the family out here to ID her or we could organise some DNA testing, with the family's agreement.'

'I understand. I'm just getting her family's contact details for you. Do you have a secure police email address I can send the details to? Due to our data protection laws, I can't release contact details over the phone.'

'Understood.' Jones gives him Steve's email address seeing as his own email account was closed down when he retired. Aaron stays on the line as he sends the information, to check they receive it. Steve gives Jones the thumbs up when it comes through.

'Thanks for your help, Aaron. Appreciate it.'

'No problem. Wait until my steampunk book club hear about me taking a call from a US detective in the middle of the night! My social media profile is going to rocket after this!'

Jones shakes his head as he says goodbye.

As it's almost eight o'clock he considers waiting until the morning to call Sarah's family, but he wants to speak to Beth in the morning and he would like to know more about Sarah before he does so. He notices Captain Brown leaving for the evening.

'Captain? I've got the contact details for Jane Doe's family. Can I use your office to call them?'

He doesn't want to make the call in front of everyone. The noise levels in the office can be distracting.

'No problem. Here.' He gives Jones his key. 'Lock up after. Good luck.'

Jones shuts the door behind him, sits at Brown's desk and looks at the details Steve printed out for him. This is something he hasn't missed since he retired. He dials the international code, followed by Sarah's mother's telephone number. It rings for a long time and he's about to hang up when a woman finally answers.

'Hello?'

'Hi. I'm really sorry to call you so late but my name is Detective Jones and I'm calling from the Maple Valley Police Department in New Hampshire. Are you Laura Glover?'

'Yes. Oh my God. I know what you're going to say. I knew she followed her out there.'

Jones is confused. 'Sorry, Mrs Glover. I'm not sure what you're referring to? I have some news about Sarah Glover, your daughter?'

'She's dead, isn't she?'

She seems strangely calm to Jones. 'I'm afraid to say that we have a deceased woman here who looks like the photo of Sarah on the missing persons' website. She also has the same distinguishable features. I'm sorry.'

He hears sobbing for the next few minutes and knows all he can do is listen. When she starts trying to ask 'how', he tells her. 'We believe she committed suicide as she was found hanged in the woods.'

'No! Never!' shouts Laura. 'Sarah would never kill herself! This was done by that woman!'

Jones sits bolt upright as he starts making notes. 'Who do you mean? You think Sarah was murdered?'

'Of course she was! She shouldn't have gone over there. I knew she'd be dead by now. Everyone in that family ends up dead.'

'Which family?'

'Hers! The crazy one; Lizzie. She killed her mother so what's to stop her killing my girl?'

'Lizzie, is that Beth Smith by any chance?'

'What? No, Lizzie Glover. Her father is my husband. He divorced her mother and then we met and had Sarah together. Lizzie is Sarah's half-sister.'

Jones deflates a little. Although Beth almost shares this woman's first name, the surname is different so he can't go jumping to conclusions that she's Lizzie Glover. Also, most parents of suicide victims refuse to believe their child would ever consider suicide. It must be difficult to realise they didn't know what their child was going through and how desperate they were. He reminds himself he's listening to the ramblings of a distraught mother in the middle of the night. He needs to end this conversation for now and call her back tomorrow, when the news has sunk in and she has some family around her for support.

'I wouldn't put it past her to change her name. She was in a secure hospital for killing her mother, so of course she's going to want to flee the country and start again somewhere new once she was released. I just wish Sarah hadn't gone after her. She thought she could help Lizzie, but that woman is beyond help.'

Jones can't ignore this new information. 'Do you know the name of Lizzie's parole officer or doctor at the mental health unit?' He needs to find out more about Lizzie Glover, just in case.

'Just a minute.' She leaves him waiting for a few minutes and he can hear her opening and closing drawers until she returns. 'Doctor Khan.'

Jones takes Doctor Khan's phone number from her. 'I'm sorry I've had to break this news to you about Sarah and, of course, we'll need to get her formally identified as soon as possible, but I'll be in touch about all of that at a later time. For now, do you have anyone with you tonight?'

'My husband, Sarah's father, is away with work so I'm not going to tell him until he gets home in a few days. He'll be devastated but at least he can have a few more days' reprieve from the truth. I'll phone my sister. I know she'll come straight round. I'm sorry if I sound like a lunatic. I've been so desperately worried about her. I can tell you everything you need to know tomorrow. I just can't think straight right now. She was our baby.' He hears her trying to hold back tears.

'Of course, that's not a problem.' He's about to end the call when he asks, 'This Lizzie, what does she look like?'

'She has blonde hair and blue eyes, like Sarah. She's always been a bit overweight too, but I haven't seen her since her release.'

'Okay, thanks. Sorry again for waking you, and for the bad news. We'll speak soon.'

She hangs up and Jones immediately leaves Brown's office and rushes up to Steve.

'What does Beth Smith look like?'

Steve looks taken aback by the urgency in his voice. 'Er, she's got browny-reddish hair, brown eyes and she's attractive.'

Jones deflates as he sits down. 'Overweight?'

'No, slim. You can see why she's caused a stir with Pete and Dean, put it that way. Why?'

Jones looks at his notes. 'I just had a hunch but it looks like it's probably wrong.'

Before Steve gets a chance to quiz him on how the family reacted, Jones picks up his coat, ready to head home.

'You're on the night shift, aren't you?' he asks Steve.

'Sure am.'

'Would you give this doctor a call?' He passes Steve the

contact name and number of Lizzie's doctor from the secure hospital. 'I know he won't be at work this late but leave a message if you can and ask him to ring me as soon as he gets in, no matter what time it is. Tell him it's about Lizzie Glover and it's urgent. I want her photo and record either emailed or faxed to me.'

'Sure thing.'

'See you bright and early tomorrow,' says Jones as he leaves.

When he gets in his car at just after eight o'clock his mind is working overtime, wondering if Lizzie and Beth could be the same person. After all, it wouldn't take much to dye your hair and lose some weight. But the eye colours are different. Contact lenses, perhaps? Maybe he's overthinking things. It's been a while since he's worked such a long day and he's so desperate to get these deaths solved. He's convinced they're all linked somehow and he needs to do this for Dean. He decides to pay him a visit with an update on his way home.

After knocking on Dean's door twice and getting no response, Jones curses him under his breath and hopes he's just out walking Rocky under the cover of darkness and not skipping town. He doesn't want to wait around in this cold weather, so he gets back in his car and texts him an update.

Jane Doe is called Sarah Glover. British! Mother suspects she was murdered by her half-sister, Lizzie Glover. Some similarities between her and Beth. I don't know where you are right now but stay away from Beth until I can put the pieces together. And get your ass back home like we told you. Call me.

He drives away from Dean's house slowly, in case he spots them returning from their walk.

Chapter Thirty-Seven

Dean is exhausted. After Beth picked up some take-out food from the diner for later on, while he waited in her car, they drove to a part of the woods that Dean hasn't been to before. They spend almost an hour walking with Rocky. It felt good to get some fresh air, even if it is freezing cold and raining on and off. It's taken his mind off all the drama, which he's grateful for. As darkness closes in around them he realises he doesn't know where they are any more, and even Rocky's looking tired.

'I think it's time we headed back to the car now, although I'm not sure I remember where we parked,' he says.

Beth's charging ahead, in front of both him and Rocky. 'No, look! There's a cabin through those trees ahead. We can take a break there before we head back.'

Dean can't see a cabin. She must have really good eyesight. He follows her for a while longer until they reach it. It's not lit up at all. Beth suddenly seems animated and cheerful.

'Come on, let's go in and rest for a while. I have dinner in my bag. It'll be like a picnic!'

'Er, newsflash: picnics are meant for summer. Plus, I'm a cop, in case you hadn't noticed; we're not allowed to break and enter, just like everyone else.'

She skips up the wooden steps and fiddles with the door. It quickly opens. He's not sure whether he just imagined it but it looked like she put something in her pocket.

'Look, it's open!' She goes straight in, quickly followed by Rocky.

His face is so numb from the cold that he just wants to get into some shelter for a few minutes. Plus, he's starving, so he follows her in. It's so dark inside he can't even tell where she is, but he can hear her opening and closing drawers.

'Excellent!'

Somehow, she has found candles and matches, and she begins lighting them and spreading them through the room. It's pretty empty apart from a couch, a bed and a sink. He can also see an internal door, which presumably leads to a bathroom.

'I really don't think we should be in here,' he says. But Rocky has already sprawled across the couch and Beth's opening the sandwiches she bought from the diner.

'They're obviously pretty cold by now but I got you meatball marinara, is that okay?'

His mouth starts salivating as he sits beside her on the bed and grabs the sandwich from her. 'Give me that!'

She laughs as she opens her own sandwich; chicken salad. They sit in silence as they eat; the only sounds are the rustling of the wrappers, Rocky's heavy breathing and the sleet hitting the cabin. Dean saves Rocky some of the meatballs and hand feeds him. The cabin isn't as cold as outside but it's not exactly warm.

'Come on, now we've eaten we should head back. I'm freezing.'

Beth scrunches the wrappers up, throws them on the floor and pulls him onto the bed as she straddles him.

'I know a way to warm up.'

She starts kissing him hard. He hadn't expected her to find a place like this a turn on. He flips her onto the bed and kisses her.

'This bed could be full of insects, you do realise?' he says.

'It takes more than insects to scare me. Tie me up, Dean.'

Dean's taken aback for a minute. She's never asked him to do anything kinky before.

'Really?' he asks, unsure.

'Yes. Let's pretend we're alone in the woods.'

'Well, we are alone in the woods,' he interrupts.

'Yes, but let's pretend we're strangers who have just

stumbled in here and can't control ourselves. I want to be tied up and I want to be hurt.'

Dean has no intention of hurting her but the way she's talking is turning him on.

'There's some rope over there.' She points to under the sink.

He can only just make it out in the candlelight but there is indeed a bale of thin rope.

'I hope you know how to tie a knot,' she teases.

He laughs as he retrieves the rope and uses it to tie her wrists to the wooden bedstead. This might just be the strangest request he's ever had.

Dean looks at his watch in the dark and just manages to make out the time; it's almost ten o'clock. They must have napped for a while. Beth's naked beside him in the bed, but even their body heat can't keep them warm for long in this cabin. He can make out Rocky's shape on the couch as he gets up to use the bathroom. Beth doesn't wake, so he retrieves his phone from his coat pocket and takes it with him. As he flushes the toilet with one hand, he holds his phone with the other and notices he has a text from Jones, received an hour ago.

Jane Doe is called Sarah Glover. British! Mother suspects she was murdered by her half-sister; Lizzie Glover. Some similarities between her and Beth. I don't know where you are right now but stay away from Beth until I can put the pieces together. And get your ass back home like we told you. Call me.

He freezes in the bathroom. He doesn't know what to make of this but he can't call Jones back while he's with her. His cell phone signal is in and out of service range because they're so deep into the woods. He tries to think fast; does this mean Beth's involved in Sarah's suicide? He thinks about how she knew the woman had bare feet.

'Shit.'

He puts his phone on silent in case Jones manages to call

him out here. Beth would be suspicious if he didn't answer his phone but he can't answer it without her overhearing whatever Jones says to him, whether good or bad. He considers checking Beth's jeans pocket on the floor for a key. He could swear he saw her put something in her pocket after opening the door to the cabin. But that would mean she knew this cabin was here. Why would she want him out here? His police instincts kick in fast; she must have something to hide. She's brought him here for a reason and he doesn't think that reason is good. His adrenaline kicks in and his heart starts hammering in his chest. He creeps out of the bathroom and feels for her jeans on the floor. When he finds them, he feels something long and metal in her pocket; clearly a key. He tries not to overreact, and instead tries to think logically. There's nothing she could do to him out here, she doesn't have a weapon. He thinks about his gun; it's at home. Brown never took it off him because he wasn't charged with anything.

Suspecting the worst like this is making him feel stupid. He's spent plenty of time with her already and nothing bad has happened. So what if she knows about this place and pretended she didn't? Maybe it's her retreat from working at the prison. It's not like the diner apartment is a quiet place to live. And would she really have sex with him if she was about to do him harm? He'd like to think he was good enough to warrant a final session before she killed him, but that would be highly unlikely. Still, he needs to get out of here.

'Dean?'

She's awake.

'Come and keep me warm, it's freezing.'

In case she's planning something, he decides to play it cool to get out of here in one piece. Once home he can call Jones and ask him what the hell is going on. He goes to her and kisses her gently. 'Come on, sleepy. We need to get back before we freeze to death.'

Chapter Thirty-Eight

Beth made sure she told the diner staff that her sandwiches were for her to take to work the next day, so they don't go telling the police that she was buying sandwiches for her and Dean to enjoy together. She can't have the police thinking she went with Dean to the woods voluntarily. She needs to keep him here at least overnight if she wants to be able to accuse him of kidnapping. She also wants people at work to notice she's not turned up in the morning, and she could do with some bruising to her arms. She made sure that during sex she rubbed her wrists raw against the rope Dean tied around her wrists, but he wasn't as rough with her as she needed. She wanted to be bruised and bloody down there for when the hospital performs a rape kit on her. It's the only way his police buddies will believe he kidnapped her and the sex was against her will. She's looking forward to tearing her clothes apart and messing up her hair and make-up. By the time she's done, no one will believe a word he says in his defence.

'We can't leave now, it's too dark outside. Let's enjoy one night here. Rocky's already settled.' She sits up in the bed. 'Where have you been?'

'Just to the bathroom. I'm too cold to stay here. Let's get back to my place and I'll make us some soup and run us a hot bath.'

She tries to contain her irritation by closing her mouth. She lies back down and pretends to sleep. She can hear him pulling his clothes on before he sits on the bed.

'Wakey, wakey!' he says as he strokes her arm.

She has to control her anger right now. She could quite happily break his arm. If he's not going to play ball, she needs to take control of the situation sooner than she planned.

'Okay, okay. Let me get dressed and use the bathroom first.'

227

Gathering all her clothes on the way to the bathroom, she slams the wooden door behind her. She can hear him shuffling around and talking to Rocky as she gets dressed. As she pulls her coat on, she feels the heaviness of his gun in her inside pocket. She's not afraid to use it if she really has to, but her first option is sleeping pills. She's going to have to drug him until she's ready to leave. She quickly dresses and retrieves the pills out of her handbag. Silently, she crushes four of them in her hand and then returns to the main room.

'Right, I'm dressed. Let's have a quick drink before we leave, I'm thirsty.' She retrieves his bottle of water first and quickly dissolves the crushed sleeping pills into it while he gathers the rubbish they've left. The candles have all burned down, making it easier to hide what she's doing.

'Here you go.'

Having not drunk anything since before they arrived, Beth watches Dean drink over half of his water in one go.

Chapter Thirty-Nine

Jones arrives at Beth's apartment at seven o'clock the next morning. He wants to speak to her before she leaves for work and while she's not expecting a visit. He was awake until the early hours going over in his head all the questions he wants to ask her, and what the best approach would be. He wasn't sure whether to mention the name Lizzie Glover to her and see if she reacts. Or he could play it cool and pretend he's there for her professional expertise, while he figures out a first impression of her. In the end, just to get some sleep, he decided to go with the latter but he also plans to lift something from her apartment if possible, so he can get her DNA checked against Sarah Glover's. It's not above board but he'd only check it if he had solid suspicions about her after speaking to her, and if he doesn't hear back from the British doctor anytime soon. He knows time is against Dean. If anyone finds out he's suspected of murdering Linda, the department will have to arrest him. If he can avoid that by checking out Beth's DNA first, then he will. It doesn't sit well with him but it's got to be done.

He knocks on her door and rubs his tired eyes as he waits. He can't hear any movement inside so he knocks again. And waits. Nothing. He looks around the parking lot but he doesn't know what car she drives, so he heads downstairs to the diner for a coffee and a chat.

'Detective Jones!' exclaims Frankie from the kitchen doorway. 'Good to see you! We've missed you. I know you gave up the force but you didn't have to give up Frankie's!'

Jones laughs. 'Good to see you too, Frankie. And you, Rachel.'

'How's Barbara?' asks Rachel.

'She's good but probably glad I'm back at work for a

while. Think I was driving her crazy sitting round the house all day watching crime shows and shouting at the TV. It's unbelievable how many liberties those shows take with the truth.'

She laughs. 'Once a cop, always a cop! What can I get for you?'

'Just a coffee please, flat white.'

'I heard you were back at work,' says Frankie. 'How come? And where's Dean? I hardly see him any more. He's more absent than when Linda made him go on a health kick, God rest her soul.'

Jones knows he can't say much. 'I'm just helping Captain Brown out with a staffing problem, it won't be for long. I'm sure you'll see Dean soon.' Jones didn't get a text or call back from Dean last night and he's trying not to let it worry him. Dean's a grown man who can look after himself, but it would be nice if he'd put his mind at rest. If he doesn't hear from him by lunchtime, Jones will phone him. 'I wanted to ask about your tenant, actually.'

'Beth? Great tenant and great customer. She never has anyone upstairs and she eats in here a lot. It's a win-win for me!'

'Do you know what time she leaves for work? I just tried to catch her but she must be gone already.'

Rachel hands him his coffee. 'She has breakfast here at about this time, five days out of seven I would say. Then she leaves for work straight after.'

Jones looks around him but the diner isn't busy yet. 'She's not in here now I take it?'

'No,' says Rachel.

'Okay, no problem. It was good to see you both.'

He notices Frankie and Rachel share an intrigued look. He leaves with his coffee and heads to work.

Steve's on his way home from the night shift when Jones

arrives at the station. As they pass each other in the parking lot, Steve asks him for an update.

'How did it go with the family of Sarah Glover last night?'

Jones sighs. 'It was rough. I spoke to her mother and she's convinced that her daughter was murdered by her half-sister.'

Steve raises his eyebrows. 'Really?'

'Yeah. And I have a horrible feeling the half-sister she mentioned could be Dean's new woman.'

Steve looks incredulous. 'Do you need me to stay, to help you with it?'

'No, that's okay. You must be exhausted. Just keep your eyes and ears open if anyone mentions her or Dean. I tried calling at his house last night but he wasn't in. I'm assuming he was walking Rocky.'

'If you need me to come in earlier than usual, just say. I'll leave my cell phone on while I sleep.'

'Thanks, I appreciate it. Hopefully, I've just been watching too many outlandish cop shows.'

Steve laughs but Jones sees the same concern in his eyes that he has. Just then, Steve's radio crackles to life. It's Jenny in dispatch.

'Steve if you haven't left yet, get back in here ASAP. We have a report of a kidnapping and rape. We need you.'

They look at each other for barely a second and then run into the station.

'The caller identified herself as Beth Smith. She said she's been kidnapped and raped by Officer Matheson,' Jenny's voice is shaking slightly. 'She said she thought he was going to kill her and she only just managed to get away. She sounded absolutely hysterical,' she says to the crowd gathered around her desk.

Jones asks, 'Where is she now?'

'In the woods, hiding. She called from her cell phone.'

Captain Brown springs into action, barking orders. 'We

are driving to the woods immediately in two separate cars.' He points to Jones, Marty and Steve. 'Jenny, do we know whereabouts in the woods?'

'She said she doesn't recognise it because she's so panicked. But, Captain?' she hesitates. 'Before you leave, I think you should know that she said Dean confessed to killing Linda. He told her it was because Linda was pregnant with another man's baby.'

Jones and Brown don't let that faze them, unlike the others who all gasp and look around at each other.

'We'll see about that,' says Jones as he storms out of the station.

Chapter Forty

The sleeping pills kicked in within thirty minutes, rendering Dean useless as they were walking away from the cabin. He said he felt dizzy so Beth led him to the bed and told him to lie down for a few minutes. He's been asleep ever since, snoring loudly, which made Rocky join him on the bed for a while.

Meanwhile, Beth has had time to check her getaway bag, filled with cash, a fake passport, fake qualification certificates, all her medications plus her knew acquisition: Dean's gun. She can't be found with that on her. Plus, it will look more incriminating if Dean can't tell his colleagues where his gun is when they ask. It will look like he's hiding evidence. She found a basement entrance at the back of the cabin, which is almost overgrown with weeds and shrubs. Nobody would know it was there.

Just before leaving the cabin she tore up her jeans and top, rubbed mud all over herself and disposed of the sandwich wrappers and any other signs they'd been in the cabin. She doesn't want the police to find this place as she may need it over the next forty-eight hours. As she brought Dean here in the dark, she doesn't think he'd be able to find it very quickly and besides, he'll be rotting in prison pretty soon. She also bruised and scratched her inner thighs and intimate area with Dean's nails while he was out cold. She needs her DNA to be under his fingernails. She scratched him on his face to make it look like she was resisting. She smeared his blood on her face and between them, they look pretty fucked up. That was the part Rocky objected to and he's been barking at her and licking Dean's scratches ever since.

She knows how to get rid of the dog. She grabs his collar and tries to pull him out of the cabin, but he won't go. He won't leave Dean's side. He's so heavy she has to use all her force to push him along the wooden floor to the outside. Once away from Dean he gets up and tries to walk back in the front door, but she slams it shut and screams at the dog, 'You stupid animal! Do what I tell you for once in your life!'

Rocky immediately backs away from her yelling. She uses his submissiveness to pull him by the collar around to the back of the cabin, but it's still not easy. She opens the basement door, which is in the ground, and pushes him hard. He doesn't realise there's no immediate floor and he falls hard down the steps. She hears him yelp with pain. She knows that by the time someone finds this cabin, Rocky will be starved to death and she'll be long gone.

Beth has to wait for the police in the freezing cold, barely dressed. She dragged Dean far enough away from the cabin so that the police won't find it and then, after covering the tracks his body left in the snow, she punched him hard in the head, hopefully leaving a bruise big enough to confirm that's how she knocked him out during her 'escape' from him. He looked like he was going to wake at one point but instead he curled into a foetal position and carried on sleeping as if he was in his bed at home. She feels a satisfaction that she always carries the strongest dose of sleeping pills with her wherever she goes. They're leftover from her stay in hospital a few years ago so they're good ones. They've saved her in many situations before. After that, she ran as fast as she could to the area where she thinks the police will park. Less than ten minutes after she called the station on her mobile phone, she hears their sirens as they approach. A few minutes later, she hears them running through the woods. Her body starts shaking as she works herself up into a frenzy.

'I'm over here! Help me! He's coming!' She screams and stumbles towards the first one to arrive. 'He's going to kill me!'

Steve grabs her and she collapses. She used to have violent fits when she was younger, her mother taught her how to do it on command for the doctors. She does that now in Steve's arms and within a couple of minutes she's blacked out.

Chapter Forty-One

When Dean wakes, his head feels heavy, like he's got the worst hangover of his life. His mouth is unbearably dry, his eyes are stuck together painfully with sleep and he feels like he's lying on a hard surface. He takes a few minutes to clear his eyes and rub his face and then slowly sits up. He has no idea what day or time it is, or even where he is.

Slowly, the room comes into view. He's in the same holding cell he was in when Miller brought him in. 'What the hell?' he mutters. When he stands up, his head pounds behind his left eye with pain that almost makes him sit down again. He approaches the cell bars and croaks, 'Jones? Steve? Anybody?' He knows they'll be watching him on the CCTV so he sits back down to avoid the pounding in his head. Trying desperately to remember how he got here, he closes his eyes and puts his head in his hands. But nothing comes back to him.

Within a few minutes of waking, he hears doors slamming and Jones appears with a coffee. Dean doesn't know what he's more pleased about, Jones or the coffee.

'Here you go.' Jones passes it to him.

Dean drinks the whole thing in one go and asks for some water.

'In a minute. We need to talk.'

'You can say that again,' snaps Dean. 'I feel like I've got the worst hangover of my life.'

'So you've been drinking again?' asks Jones.

'What? No! I don't think so.' He notices Jones' disappointment. 'What's going on? Why am I here? And why are you looking at me like a disappointed father, for God's sake?'

'You really don't remember anything from this morning or last night?'

'Listen, I don't even know what day it is right now so you better fill me in on everything, fast.' Dean can't hide his frustration. He feels like he's the only one not in on a bad joke and it's already gone too far.

'Hey, less of the attitude. I'm doing my job. It's Tuesday lunchtime and you're about to be arrested for kidnap, rape and murder.'

Dean couldn't look more incredulous if he was aiming for an Oscar nomination. 'What?'

'Does that trigger any memories for you?'

He stands up, grimacing when the headache kicks in again. 'Jones, what are you talking about? Seriously, this is me, man. Talk to me!'

Jones' face says it all; they actually think he's guilty.

'Beth Smith has accused you of kidnapping and raping her. She said you were going to kill her out there in the woods. And, to be honest, Matheson, at the moment her story is looking more credible than yours. Your hangover and amnesia aren't helping.' Before Dean can respond, Jones finishes with a parting shot, 'Maybe you need a few more hours down here to pull your shit together. Until then, I've got work to do.'

Jones storms out, leaving Dean feeling like he's hallucinating. He doesn't understand why Beth would accuse him of anything. He still can't remember what actually happened, or even being in the woods. Then he wonders where Rocky is. The pounding in his head feels so unbearable he has no option but to lie back down and try to sleep, hoping that things will make more sense next time he wakes up.

Chapter Forty-Two

Jones is so disappointed that Dean would get himself into this kind of situation that he can barely keep it together at work. He hated seeing him looking like just another criminal down there in the cells, which is why he had to leave. A couple of hours later he's preparing for his interview with Beth. She's been at the hospital most of the day but the doctor has released her after completing a rape kit and cleaning up her wounds. Steve stayed with her at the hospital and is driving her here for the interview. They need to take her statement as soon as possible, while the details are fresh.

Jones still has his doubts about her, but the hospital confirmed her bruising looks like someone forced themselves on her, although there's no semen to use as evidence. That's not surprising seeing as Dean's a cop, he would know better than anyone that he has to cover his tracks. Beth was also clearly tied up at some point; Jones noticed her wrists were raw with burn marks. When they first found her, hysterical and shaking hard, he knew the situation was serious. No one could fake that reaction. She was genuinely terrified that she hadn't hit Dean hard enough to get away and that he was right behind her.

Jones shakes his head as he thinks about the implications of what she said. If Dean really did kidnap and rape her, it's believable that he's capable of running Linda off the road. He can't believe he didn't know Dean was capable of this. But every time he thinks like that, a fire within him defiantly reminds him of his doubts about Beth Smith and the whole Sarah Glover situation. *'I'll know once and for all who she really is after I've taken her statement,'* he thinks. He looks at his watch; just after four o'clock. They'll be here soon.

When Steve leads Beth through the station, Jones notices that all eyes are on her. He knows no one here will want to believe what she's accused Dean of, but as Brown reminded him again a few minutes ago, they have to be objective and impartial. Cops are human like everyone else, and therefore capable of the same things as everyone else they bring through the station doors. With a loud sigh, Jones gets up from his desk and signals to Steve that they're going into interview room one.

As Jones and Beth sit down at the table, Steve asks her if she'd like a female officer present.

'No. I just want to get this over with so I can go home and shower.'

Jones can't help feeling sorry for her, which is unexpected. From what the others had told him, he had the impression she was feisty and confident. But he doesn't get that impression from her now. She looks like a broken bird; small, thin and scared, almost like she's trying to make herself invisible. He's seen this look before with domestic abuse victims, and with kids like Emily. They don't make eye contact until you have their trust, and they don't want people to see their wounds, because they believe they brought it on themselves.

'Steve, could you get us some drinks? Ms Smith, what would you like?'

She immediately looks grateful. 'I haven't eaten or drunk anything since yesterday. I couldn't force anything down at the hospital, I was too nervous. I'd love a cup of tea, please.'

'We have sandwiches too, if you like?'

She looks shy, like she's too embarrassed to ask, so Jones answers for her. 'Get us both a sandwich, thanks.'

'While he's gone, I just need to inform you this interview is being recorded, so that we don't misinterpret anything. In order to build a case against the accused we need the full facts from you. That means every single detail of what happened from start to finish. I'll ask you the same questions in different ways, to try to remind you of anything you may leave out in the first telling of your statement. So, don't think I'm not listening properly if I repeat myself, I just need to be absolutely clear about what happened and in what order. Do you understand?'

She's looking at the cameras above her as she nods her head. Steve returns with food.

'Go ahead and eat your sandwich while I ask the questions.'

She tears it open and takes a massive bite of the first half of the sandwich. Watching her, he's finding it hard to cling on to the hope that she's not telling the truth about what Dean did.

'If I ask you something that you don't understand, just ask me to clarify, okay?'

She nods, mouth full.

'I'll just wait for Sergeant Dalkin to return with the drinks.' As he says this, Steve opens the door and sets the drinks down on the table, picking up one for himself. He takes a seat next to Jones. He's here to observe. If they had another detective at the station, they'd be in here with Jones helping with the interview. But Miller is still suspended, Dean is the accused and Brown is busy explaining to the D.A.'s office the mess they're in.

'Okay, I need you to tell me what happened. Take your time.'

She swallows hard, sets the second half of the sandwich down and nods. To Jones she looks like she just lost her appetite. After drinking almost the whole cup of tea, she looks Jones in the eye for the first time.

'Yesterday was my day off. I work at the women's prison as a counsellor.'

Jones already knows this but he always lets people tell their story in their own words. He's learnt over the years that it's easier for people to incriminate themselves if they think he knows nothing about them.

'The night before, I received a phone call from Dean,' she spits his name out as if it hurts to say it, 'asking me to go to his house for a drink. But after everything that he's been accused of lately, I'd already decided to take a step back and not see him any more. I don't need that kind of drama in my life, I get enough from the women I work with.'

Jones nods as she talks, making notes but trying to read her expressions.

'I turned him down and had an early night.'

'What time did you turn in?'

'About ten. I was tired from work and just wanted to do some reading before I slept. Anyway, at about ten-thirty, I hear a dog barking outside and it sounds just like Rocky. I went to have a look and Dean was standing outside the door to my flat, without knocking or phoning me first or anything! It was so bizarre that I opened the door and asked what he was doing. He said he was walking Rocky and asked if I wanted to come. I told him it was too late but as I was speaking he pushed his way into my flat and put something over my mouth. It smelt really strong of chemicals and it must've knocked me out because I woke up in his bed the next morning.' She starts crying.

Jones waits for her to pull it together but the tears turn to sobs as she pulls her knees up onto the chair and rests her face on them, clutching herself. After a few minutes, he asks her if she needs a break.

'No, I need to get this over with.' She dries her eyes with her sleeves.

He tries not to look at the rope burns on her wrists as he realises he forgot to bring tissues into the interview room. 'So, what happened after you woke up? Was Officer Matheson in the bedroom with you?'

She nods. 'Yes. He was next to me in the bed. We were both naked. He was sitting up, watching the TV and he said he'd made us coffees. I couldn't remember right away what had happened so I sat up, stunned, and tried to drink my coffee without spilling it. I was shaking so much. I asked him what happened the night before and he said we'd been drinking together. He laughed at how drunk I'd been. But I had a horrible feeling he was lying. It took a while for me to remember how he attacked me at my home. I went to the bathroom and could tell he must've raped me while I was unconscious. I had so many thoughts going through my head; am I crazy? Did I get drunk? Why don't I remember anything? It was then that I realised I needed to go along with it to get out of there alive.'

She starts crying again and drinks the rest of her tea to compose herself.

'What happened next?'

'I went back to the bedroom and started getting dressed. When he asked me what I was doing I said I had to be at work, but it was no good because somehow, he knew it was my day off. He said, "No one's going to miss you until at least tomorrow." That's when I started fearing for my life. He was so detached in the way he said it. Detective Jones, I've spent my career around some seriously sick people and they all have that mental detachment about them. I knew something terrible was about to happen.'

She starts sobbing again, this time rocking herself backwards and forwards slightly. Jones looks at Steve who simultaneously shakes his head and raises his eyebrows. Jones realises then that they both believe her.

Chapter Forty-Three

Jones doesn't come back to see Dean until nearly eight o'clock that evening and Dean's so wound up with anxiety that he immediately pounces at the bars.

'What the hell is going on, Jones? You can't keep me here like this without charging me with something! I want a lawyer, right now!'

Jones gives him a look of contempt. 'Oh don't worry, you're about to be charged. There's a lawyer on their way.'

Dean backs away from the bars. 'What?'

'I've just finished taking Beth Smith's statement. It took four hours.'

'What did she say?'

'She told us how you kidnapped her from her apartment, raped her while she was unconscious,' Jones says, pausing here and giving Dean a look of disgust, 'and then took her to the woods overnight where you played a sick cat and mouse game of chase your victim. During this you taunted her with tales of how you killed Linda. What about Tammy, Dean? Did you kill her too? You were the first person at the scene. Are you going to use coincidence as your defence on that one?'

Dean starts trembling all over and hears a ringing in his head as if his ears are objecting to what's he's listening to. He doesn't think he can take much more of this. 'Jones, listen to me. She's lying. You know me better than that!'

'Oh really? So where were you last night? Do you have an alibi I can check out?'

Dean still doesn't remember anything from the last twenty-four hours. He sits down on the hard bed in his cell, unable to find the words to fight these accusations.

As Jones turns to leave, Dean thinks of Rocky. 'Where's Rocky? He's always with me so why isn't he here now? Has anyone been by my house to check if he's there?'

Jones stops and answers over his shoulder. 'I don't know about the dog but the CSI team are at your house right now, searching for the truth.'

He leaves Dean alone again, presumably until a lawyer arrives so they can formally charge him. Dean knows he needs to start thinking straight to figure out what's happening to him. He can't believe Beth's accusing him of these things. But then if he doesn't remember what happened, could he have done them? Could he have been drinking so much that he got a little rough with her and she's calling it rape and kidnap? But why would she say he killed Linda?

It dawns on him that he's being stitched up by her. He thinks about the key found at his house, which she could have easily planted. But then why would she want to target him? He's not done anything to her apart from befriending her when she was new in town. He knows he needs to get his head together as quickly as possible in order to solve this riddle before he's formally interviewed and arrested. He starts pacing his cell to wake his body up and get some oxygen to his brain.

Chapter Forty-Four

Beth has to move fast. There's no time to reflect on what an outstanding performance she gave the police. After Sergeant Dalkin drops her at her apartment that evening, without saying one word to her in the car during the twenty-minute drive over, she watches him from her window until he pulls out of the diner's car park. Starving, she allows herself just a few minutes to wolf down whatever's in the fridge that doesn't need cooking: a cheese and bacon quiche. She knows it may be a while before she eats again. She pulls her holdall out from under the bed and starts filling it with some bottles of water, cereal bars, a few items of clothing and her books. She needs those. They've always been a comfort to her since she acquired them in hospital. She's read them numerous times already. She has the quickest shower in history to remove all traces of mud and blood and then uses the peroxide bleach she has had stashed away on her hair.

When she gets out to dry herself, she looks at her reflection in the mirror and gasps, at first thinking it's her mother looking back at her. Her mother was white-blonde, and Beth looks like the photos her mum showed her when everyone was younger. She stands there, transfixed. Tears form at the corners of her eyes, real ones this time.

'I miss you so much, Mum.'

The smell of the peroxide overwhelms her and makes her want to vomit, increasing her anxiety. She rushes around, dropping things as she goes and bumping into doors as she prepares to leave the apartment for good. She knows now that it's not going to be possible to stay in town and give evidence against Dean. Now she's met him she knows Detective Jones is way too sharp to drop his background check on her just because Dean's in custody. She needs to leave immediately.

She doesn't bother drying her hair, there's no time. Instead, she ties it up into a ponytail and stuffs it under a woollen hat. It's started snowing out so she needs to dress warmly. The more clothes she wears, the less she needs to carry. With everything she needs stuffed into her holdall, she goes to the window and checks outside. There's no sign of any police cars, so she leaves the flat as fast as possible and opens her car door. As she's closing it, she hears someone calling her name.

'Beth? How are you?'

It's Frankie taking the rubbish out.

'Shit.' She doesn't want him to notice her change of hair colour but it's almost pitch black away from the diner's lights and her hat is covering most of it. She starts the car and pulls away without acknowledging him or turning to face him. Thumping the steering wheel, she curses him under her breath. 'Stupid fat pig!' She hadn't wanted anyone to notice her leave. Still, she had told Detective Jones that she'll be moving to a hotel for a few nights as she didn't want to stay at the flat any more, so it won't trigger any alarm bells just yet.

Just before ten o'clock that night, Beth reaches the woods. She slowly drives her car into a ditch between two trees so it won't be easy to find, and then starts walking the rest of the way carrying her holdall. All she needs to do is to collect her getaway bag and then find a car somewhere that she can hot-wire. The best thing about having lived with the criminally insane for years was that she learnt a lot of new skills from them. As the snow picks up, so does the wind. The trees are creaking all around and the wind is howling after her. She feels like she's being slapped repeatedly in the face. Her visibility is reduced as she trudges along towards the cabin, not half as fast as she'd like.

Chapter Forty-Five

Jones collapses onto his desk chair, exhausted after such a long interview with Beth. When she left the station with Steve she seemed slightly less delicate and told them she just wanted to have a shower, change her clothes and go and stay in a hotel. Jones doesn't blame her for not wanting to be home alone, even though they have Dean in custody. He promised Captain Brown he'd update him immediately so he gets up from his chair. Before he makes it to Brown's office, his cell phone rings. He answers immediately when he notices the international code.

'This is Detective Jones.'

'Good evening, this is Doctor Khan from Ramsdale Secure Hospital in England, returning your call. I hope I'm not calling too late but it's four o'clock in the afternoon here and I've only just had a moment to listen to your message, which concerned me greatly.'

Jones is immediately intrigued. 'Thanks for calling me back. It's about Lizzie Glover; I believe you were her doctor?'

'Yes,' confirms Doctor Khan. 'She was with us for twelve years, after being convicted of killing her mother. I'm not surprised to hear from the police again, I'm just surprised it took so long.'

Jones sits down. He senses this is going to be a long phone call. He grabs his notepad and starts writing everything down.

'I have to be honest with you, I'm not sure Lizzie Glover is a person of interest to us just yet. We have a deceased woman here who hanged herself, and we believe her to be Sarah Glover, Lizzie's half-sister. I spoke to Sarah's mother last night who said she suspected Lizzie could've been involved in Sarah's death. At this stage, it's all just speculation. I guess I just wanted to know some background about Lizzie. Do you know her current whereabouts?'

Doctor Khan sighs down the phone. 'Unfortunately, no I don't. She was released with just a twelve-month supervision order. Once that monitoring stopped, I didn't receive any updates about her. She was a very sick person while she was with us, Detective. In fact, she was released against my wishes.'

'How come she was in a secure hospital instead of in prison?'

'She has a personality disorder which we think is the result of her upbringing. You see, her mother suffered from Munchausen's syndrome by proxy. Are you familiar with this?'

Jones has never heard of it. 'No, I'm afraid not.'

'Well, very briefly, it's a form of child abuse where a family member, usually the mother, fabricates illness in their child because they enjoy the attention it gets them from medical staff, family and friends. It's a cruel disorder for the child to have to live with and, as we know in Lizzie Glover's case, can cause life-long mental health problems. Unfortunately, once social services and health care professionals figured out her mother had this, Lizzie was too attached to her to believe them. She defended her vigorously and denied the lengths her mother went to to make her appear ill. I have witnessed Lizzie inducing fits, migraines, gastro problems and so on, upon herself. Her mother taught her all kinds of techniques, but mainly it was psychological manipulation that made Lizzie actually believe she was ill. Eventually, as she matured, she realised the magnitude of what her mother had done to her for seventeen years, and as a result she experienced a psychotic episode and killed her.'

Jones takes a deep breath in. 'Wow. If you weren't a doctor I'd find all that hard to believe; that someone can be so manipulated by someone else to believe they're ill when they're not. How did she kill her mother, out of interest?'

'She hanged her in the woods.'

Jones' stomach sinks. He immediately thinks of Sarah Glover. 'Shit. This is sounding familiar. Sarah Glover was found hanged in the woods.'

Dr Khan sighs. 'Oh. Do you need a photo of Lizzie to release to the media? Hopefully, someone knows where she is.'

'After what you've told me, I think I know where she is, but she's going under a different name: Beth Smith.'

'Smith was Lizzie's mother's maiden name.'

Jones jumps up and wants to immediately drive to Beth's apartment to arrest her, but he needs to be as sure as possible before Brown will let him. If she is Lizzie Glover, she could've killed Sarah and, she could've lied to them about Dean confessing to Linda's murder.

Steve's been listening in and is looking at him, confused.

'Just out of interest, Detective, how is your suspect supporting themselves financially?'

'She's a counsellor at the local women's prison.'

'I see. Well, Lizzie Glover spent the second half of her sentence reading psychology texts and quizzing her fellow patients on their conditions and upbringings. I thought she was trying to understand her mother's condition, perhaps trying to find a way to forgive her mother. But now I'm assuming it wasn't for good reasons.'

'How come she was released against your wishes?' asks Jones.

'She had almost served her time and she was showing remorse. Basically, she fooled the powers that be. She's very convincing when she wants to be, and highly intelligent.'

'Email me a photo of her right away. We need to act fast.'

Jones gives the doctor Captain Brown's email address, thanks him for his help and rushes to Brown's office. On his way he barks at Steve. 'Get Dean up here, now!'

Brown's on the phone, sweating, when Jones enters. It looks like he's still taking a verbal beating for the mess the department is currently in. Jones' face must say it all because Brown immediately brings the call to a close.

'I have an urgent situation I need to deal with and then I'll call you right back, sir.'

Chapter Forty-Six

Dean hears someone running down the stairs, banging doors. He immediately stands up in anticipation of a visit. He's angry they've let him stew down here for so long without giving him his right of reply via interview yet. But then he knows how Jones works and this is typical of his technique; make the perp sweat so they're ready to spill their guts by the time he interviews them.

Unexpectedly, Steve runs over to his cell and unlocks the door. 'Upstairs, now.'

Dean can see he's agitated. 'You can't even look me in the eye, can you? You all believe her!'

Steve pulls him by the arm and pushes him in front of him as they ascend the steps to get to Brown's office.

'I was supposed to have a lawyer by now,' says Dean. 'Or is no one interested in my side of the story?'

'Just get in there and shut up,' says Steve.

Dean doesn't know what to think. They haven't cuffed him and he can only see Jones and Brown in the office, no lawyer.

'This has gone on long enough! Someone needs to tell me what's happening!' He slams his fist on Brown's desk and Steve moves as if to restrain him. Jones steps forwards. 'It's okay, Steve. Leave it.'

Brown looks as confused as Steve, so it's up to Jones to fill them in. Dean notices Jones is trying not to look at him as he speaks.

'I have reliable information to suggest Beth Smith is a killer.'

In unison, they all say, 'What?'

Dean sits down immediately. His legs start to shake. Could this mean he's no longer being arrested?

'Captain, check your emails. Someone's sending you a

photo. There's a doctor in England who treated the half-sister of Sarah Glover, the hanging victim, for personality disorders. This sister, Lizzie, killed her mother and was in a secure hospital for twelve years.'

'Why did she kill her own mother?' asks Steve.

'Because her mother was mentally ill with a condition that makes a parent fake illness in their child. They thrive on the attention they receive for having a constantly sick kid, basically. Lizzie's mother was a severe case, totally messing her up. When Lizzie's blinkers came off and she finally saw what her mother had been doing to her, she didn't like what she saw.'

'Jeeze, I've heard it all now,' says Steve.

Dean doesn't know what to think. It sounds like they're talking about a stranger, not Beth.

'When we found out Jane Doe's identity, I spoke to her mother who was convinced Lizzie had killed her. Lizzie's doctor has just told me she killed her mother by hanging her, presumably making it look like suicide, I don't know, I didn't ask too many questions at this point. Anyway, to cut a long story short, I believe Beth Smith is Lizzie Glover and that she killed her half-sister and probably killed Linda, for reasons unknown at this stage. God knows how many other victims there have been.'

Brown keeps refreshing his email until he receives what he's looking for. 'It's here.' He double clicks on the attachment as they all gather behind him.

Dean gasps as the photo appears. This woman is chubby, with blonde hair and a blank look in her eyes. But it's Beth. He can tell. He sits back down and puts his head between his knees, trying to stop himself from passing out.

Steve puts a hand on his shoulder. 'You need some water?'

As he looks up and shakes his head, he notices the look between Jones and Brown and immediately knows they're thinking the same as him: Linda died because of this woman.

She planted those keys in his house. She must have wanted Linda out of the picture so she could distract him from doing his job properly. So, Linda and his unborn child died because he fell for Beth. And, because he's been grieving, all his instincts were clouded to the point of missing vital clues. He couldn't see trouble right in front of his eyes. He's on the verge of breaking down when Jones brings him back to reality.

'We need to go get her right now.'

'I agree,' says Brown. 'Do we know where she is?'

'I drove her back to her apartment at the diner, but didn't she tell us she was going to go stay in a hotel for a few nights?' asks Steve.

'She did, but hopefully she's not left her apartment yet,' says Jones. 'Steve, you're with me. Captain, can you organise backup, just in case? We don't know what lengths she's capable of going to to defend herself.'

'I'm on it.' Brown leaves the office and Dean hears him rounding people up.

'Dean?' For the first time, Jones looks him in the eye. 'I have a lot to apologise for, but it'll have to wait while I catch this bitch. In the meantime, you need to stay here, out of the way, so she can't accuse you of anything else when we send her ass to court.'

Dean knows he's right. He nods and watches them all leave the station like charging bulls.

Chapter Forty-Seven

By ten o'clock, Beth has reached the cabin but she's not well. The exposed parts of her body – face, neck and hands – are so numb she drops the cabin's key four times before managing to use it properly. Once inside, she dumps her bag and collapses down immediately on the bed. She's physically exhausted and her body's trembling as if she has low blood sugar. She rummages in her bag for some painkillers, caffeine pills and vitamins. She needs to stay awake for as long as possible so she takes four caffeine pills. As she's not eaten much today, they immediately kick in and add to the shakes she already has. Feeling light headed, she lies down just for a second, until she can think straight.

Outside, the wind is howling through the gaps in the cabin's walls. The snow has stopped but it's left a thick blanket on the ground which has made Beth's walking boots wet, seeping through to her socks. She tries to slow her breathing as she's still panting from the exertion of reaching the cabin quickly by foot. As her breathing slows, she listens to the wind and tries to think about what she needs to do next, but she hears barking in the distance. She remembers Rocky. He's down in the basement. She had completely forgotten about him. At first, she considers going to shoot him to shut him up, but they're in the middle of nowhere so she doesn't see the point. He can die barking for all she cares.

Chapter Forty-Eight

Dean has left Brown's office to speak with Jenny. He needs something to take his mind off what's about to happen, and she's happy to oblige him.

'I'm assuming you can't talk about whatever's going down, so how about I fill you in on the station gossip instead?' she offers.

This makes Dean smile. 'Sure. I could do with a laugh.'

'Miller's going to be back tomorrow, apparently. He complained to the union about Captain Brown suspending him, so him and his union official came in for a meeting. OMG, I've never heard the Captain shout so loud! As I was casually walking past the office, minding my own business, Miller looked like he was going to have another heart attack at the things the Captain was saying to him; calling him an embarrassment to the department and so on. But, unfortunately, it looks like Captain Brown had to back down in the end if we're getting Miller back, probably because of the union.'

Dean knows he should feel annoyed about Miller's return, but he doesn't feel anything.

'Also, I don't know if this is the right time to mention it, but Pete has been phoning to get updates on you.'

'Pete? Last time I saw him we hit each other.'

'Yeah, so I heard. He wanted me to pass on an apology for the fight, and he mentioned he said some awful things about John? Anyway, I couldn't really pass the message on while you were being held as a suspect downstairs, so I had to wait.'

Dean's touched that Pete would reach out. He makes a mental note to take him out for a beer once all this is over.

'He's convinced Sue Wells is going to sack that Beth woman because she's a crap counsellor, apparently. The inmates only have bad things to say about her, but I suppose we can't listen to criminals.'

Dean realises Jenny doesn't know what just happened in Brown's office. She's talking to him as if he's been cleared, but she doesn't know Beth's about to be arrested in his place.

'You believe I'm innocent, don't you?' he asks.

'Of course! I never doubted you, Dean.'

He unexpectedly wells up as Sheila walks into the station. She looks shocked to see him but she must notice he's emotional because instead of asking how he feels, she starts talking about a date she has.

'Hi, you two. So, give me your honest opinion. I'm about to go on a second date with this gorgeous man – we're not talking Officer Matheson hot – but still gorgeous, and he wants to take me away for the weekend. On only our second date. Is that too soon? Is he a psychopath?'

Dean can't help but laugh.

'That depends. Where does he want to take you?' asks Jenny, fully absorbed in this new topic within seconds.

'I don't know, some log cabin in the woods in Vermont. He says it'll be perfect because of the snow, and we can spend time drinking wine in front of the fire.'

Dean stops smiling and feels like he's remembering a dream all of a sudden. It was the mention of a log cabin. He can see one in his mind, with Beth opening the door.

'That just means he wants to spend the weekend having sex with you,' Jenny says, laughing. 'Which is fine if you're into him, but make sure you have cell phone coverage in case he's a serial killer!'

'Dean? Are you okay?' asks Sheila.

He's beginning to remember last night: eating sandwiches on the bed, tying up Beth while they had sex, but she was enjoying it. It was her idea. 'She said she wanted it rough,' he says as he thinks out loud.

Jenny and Sheila exchange a look.

'That's where she'll be, in the woods. Jenny, give me the keys for one of the spare cars.'

Jenny knows not to delay when she's asked something like this. She opens the key safe and retrieves a set of keys, immediately handing them to Dean with no questions asked.

Dean runs out of the station without saying anything else; his mind is in overdrive. He's responsible for this mess so he's determined to fix it. One of the police cars lights up when he presses the 'open' key, so he runs to that and speeds out of the parking lot.

Chapter Forty-Nine

When Jones and the team reach Beth's apartment, Jones heads up the stairs on his own, while the others remain close by, watching. After three knocks, there's no answer. She's either not in or she's hiding. Steve and Marty take their cue, run up the stairs and kick her door open. Steve enters first, gun ready to fire, but after a fast search of the small apartment, it's obvious she's not there. It's practically empty of all belongings too.

'Let me speak to Frankie for a second,' says Jones.

Inside the diner, everyone is talking in hushed tones. Although it's pitch black out, they noticed the arrival of three police cars with their blue lights flashing, followed by the sound of Beth's door being forced open.

'What's going on, Detective?' asks Frankie.

'Have you seen Beth Smith tonight?'

Rachel turns to Frankie. 'Didn't you say you saw her driving away a short while ago?'

'That's right. She completely ignored me. I figured maybe she didn't hear me over the wind, but she hesitated, like she was deciding whether to turn around and speak to me or not. I've gotta tell you, as her landlord and the person who feeds her every day, I was a little offended.'

'What time was that?' asks Jones.

Frankie looks to Rachel. 'What would you say, just after nine?'

Rachel nods. 'Yeah, I mean I think so. I wasn't really paying much attention when he told me.'

Frankie looks hurt. 'What do you mean? You don't listen to me?'

'Frankie, I was busy. You talk all day long, I've got to filter some of it out to stay sane.'

Jones doesn't have time for banter. 'Frankie, which direction did she drive in?'

'She turned right, and she was driving her red Ford.'

Jones turns to the customers. 'If anyone sees Beth Smith tonight or tomorrow, call us without delay. And, more importantly, stay away from her.'

The diners look intrigued and horrified at the same time, like they're watching a cop show on TV. Jones leaves the diner and runs back to the others.

'She left here just after nine in a red Ford and turned right.'

'That's the direction of Dean's house,' says Steve.

'Worth a try,' says Brown.

Chapter Fifty

Dean almost crashes in the snow more than once because he's driving too fast. When he finally gets the car as far into the woods as possible, way past the parking lot, the trees become too thick and he has to get out and walk the rest of the way. He didn't even put a jacket on before he left the station and it's freezing cold out here. He knows what exposure could do to him. Remembering each police car has a blanket in the back, he gets this out and wraps himself in it. He searches for a flashlight but whoever used the car last didn't leave one in the trunk like they should have.

As he looks around him, he doesn't know which direction the cabin is in. He finally remembers almost everything that happened with Beth, but it was dark like this when she led them here, so he doesn't know if he'll be able to find the cabin on his own. Also, tonight there are heavy snow clouds blocking the stars, so he has no sense of direction and no trickle of light to help him. He stands still, trying to come to an instinctive decision about which way to head. The wind is blowing fiercely right into his face, when out of the darkness, he hears what sounds like barking. But it's so faint, he can't tell if he's making it up. He stands completely still and stops breathing. There it is again.

'Rocky.' Until now, he hadn't allowed himself to think of where Rocky might be. He remembered he was with them in the cabin, but he didn't want to think about it too closely until they'd arrested Beth. Dean thinks he knows which direction the barking is coming from, so he runs as fast as he can through the snow.

Chapter Fifty-One

Beth pulls out some of her hair in anger and screams at the top of her voice. She had let herself doze off, despite the caffeine pills. Looking at her watch, she has lost thirty-five minutes. She tries telling herself to calm down. 'You cannot lose your shit. You need to get out of here. It could've been much longer if that dog wasn't barking. He's done you a favour.'

Her getaway bag is in the basement with the dog. After taking a lot of deep breaths, she shoulders the holdall and opens the cabin door. The wind almost rips the door from its hinges, and the snow has started again. She knows it's going to be hard work walking through this to the other side of the woods, where there's a small shopping mall. That's where she's hoping to find an unattended car she can hot-wire. Then, once she's far away from this shitty little town, she plans to treat herself to a drive-through dinner. She's planning to order the biggest meal of her life; as big as a death-row meal. She doesn't need to be skinny and sexy any more, she's through with that for a while. She smiles to herself as she thinks about how she intends to make up for lost time.

Where she has ripped her hair out, her scalp feels the cold as soon as she steps out of the cabin. She pulls her hat on, walks around to the back and finds the basement door. The dog starts barking even more loudly; he must be able to smell her. She swings the door open and peers down into the blackness, waiting for her eyes to adjust. As she does this, Rocky comes jumping up at her, hitting her square in the face and pushing her backwards with his weight. Beth screams in surprise and quickly gets up, rubbing her head where his massive skull caught her. She hadn't expected him to make it up the steps because she thought he'd broken a leg when she pushed him down there.

'Stupid dog!'

She looks around for him and can't believe it when she sees him taking a dump.

'Are you telling me you held it in all day so that you didn't shit inside?'

Rocky finishes his business and then runs over to her, jumping all over her, trying to lick her face. His tail is wagging so fast that it hurts when it hits her in the leg as he spins with excitement. He stops every few seconds to lick up some snow and she realises he must be thirsty for water.

What Beth feels looking at him both hurts and surprises her. She feels her eyes warm up as if she's about to cry and she's temporarily floored. She hates feeling like this about anyone, so she pushes him away every time he tries to jump at her. 'Get away! Stupid animal! No!' She can't help wondering whether, if she had been given a pet growing up, she might not have turned into the same person. But then she remembers her mother and knows instantly that she was destined to live a half life because of that woman. All because her mother loved attention more than she loved her daughter. She remembers how her mother hadn't put up a struggle as Beth placed the noose around her head.

'Lizzie? Mummy loves you. I'm so sorry for what I've done. I caused this, not you. You might be making me do this but you've helped me realise how sick I am. I'm so sorry.'

Lizzie knew that by this point her mother had accepted she was going to be killed by her daughter.

'I'm not a whole person because of you. You never let me live my real life. I'll never forgive you. But I still love you.'

'I know, my love,' said her mother. 'Look after yourself.'

Lizzie hadn't cried as she pushed the stepladder out from under her mother. She had watched her final, gasping breaths until the very last minute. Her mother didn't reach for her neck, something Lizzie assumed would be instinctive, but she understood why. There was nothing left for her mother to fight for. She had lost her first child to cot death and her second child to hatred. Lizzie wasn't lying when she said she still loved her. But she also hated her. She hated her mother for inflicting years of unnecessary pain. It was her selfish actions that meant Lizzie's life was ruined from the start.

Lizzie kneels down and feels inside the basement, under one of the steps, for the bag she hid earlier. She picks it up and slings it across her body. Now when she looks at Rocky, she sees her mother. She opens her bag and reaches for Dean's gun.

Chapter Fifty-Two

On the way to Dean's house, Jones radios the station to ask Dean to meet them there. They don't want to have to knock his door down.

'Sorry but he's not here. He ran off about a half hour ago,' explains Jenny.

'What? Where did he go?' Jones has a bad feeling about this.

'He didn't tell me but he took one of the spare cars and said something like, "That's where she'll be; in the woods." What's going on?'

'We're looking for Beth Smith, to bring her in for questioning. She's dangerous, Jenny. Make sure everyone at the station is alerted. We think she might be at Dean's house so we're heading there next.'

'The way Dean ran out of here I'd say he's going to the woods to find her.'

'Shit! Did he have his weapon on him?'

'No, sir. He didn't even have a coat on.'

Jones ends the call and barks at Captain Brown, who's driving. 'Don't stop at Dean's house, continue to the woods!'

'Understood. Why?'

'I have no idea but Dean headed there a half hour ago, so I guess we're about to find out.'

Chapter Fifty-Three

After just a few minutes of running, Dean's exhausted and is forced to walk the rest of the way. Ten minutes later, he can hear Rocky's barking much closer. Then he hears a woman scream. It's so blood-curdling that it makes him stop, but only for a second. He knows it's Beth, or Lizzie. He starts running again and spots the cabin within a few minutes.

The front door is slamming open and closed in the wind, and he can tell it's dark inside. No sign of any lights or lit candles. He hears Rocky barking so close that he's confused; it doesn't seem to be coming from inside the cabin. Then he hears Beth yelling something nearby, but he can't see her. It's only then that he realises he doesn't have his gun with him. 'Shit!' he mutters.

Not sure how to proceed, he drops the blanket and slowly creeps around the side of the cabin to try to get a view of them both so that he can formulate a plan. He worries that Rocky will smell him and run immediately towards him, giving away his position. As he peers around the corner, he sees Beth pointing a gun at Rocky. His heart skips a beat as he panics. That's his gun. How could he have been so stupid to leave it unattended at his house? Rocky notices him and jumps up from his cowering position but he doesn't move towards him. Dean can't help but wonder whether Rocky realises he can't let this woman know where he is. Then, Rocky runs off in the opposite direction instead, just as Beth shoots at him, missing him by a long way. With Rocky out of the way and Beth distracted watching after Rocky, Dean jumps out from behind the cabin and lunges at her. He manages to push her over with the full weight of his body, but she's so quick that she scrambles up faster than he's able to. She takes several steps backwards and points the gun at him while he's still down on the ground.

'Why aren't you in prison yet?' she pants. 'Wife killer! Rapist! Kidnapper!'

Dean's seeing a completely different side to her now. Beth is no longer here. He slowly sits up.

'Don't you dare get up. I might have missed the dog but you're an easier target,' she sneers.

Dean catches his breath and stays seated. The only way he's getting out of this alive is if Jones turns up with the cavalry. But Dean didn't tell them where he was going and they'll never find this cabin. He's completely alone.

'Lizzie? That's your real name, isn't it? We know about your sister.'

She doesn't even look bothered by this. He can see in her eyes she's way too far gone to keep up the pretence any longer. It looks to him like she's a completely different person now. Her face is set in a way he's not seen before. She almost looks feral to him.

'She wasn't my sister. Not really. She could've stayed out of this and still been alive but she kept meddling. Always following me, always checking on me, pretending to care. I told her not to follow me, she knew what the consequences would be.'

Dean's whole body is trembling, not just from being outside in the cold, but with fear for losing his life. She keeps the gun firmly pointed in his direction.

'So, you think you have a reason for killing your sister. Your mother fucked you up from an early age, so you think that's a reason to kill her. But what's your excuse for killing my wife, Lizzie? What possible reason could you have for killing Linda and my CHILD!' He screams this last word. He's worked himself up into an anger as the emotions come pouring out of him. 'You killed an innocent child, for God's sake!'

Unbelievably, she laughs. 'Hey, better them than me. You didn't want it anyway, you told me. I knew you wanted me to kill them when you phoned me after your argument. I'm not stupid, I know how to read between the lines.'

He should know by now not to expect remorse from criminals, but he shakes his head in disbelief all the same.

'I bet you didn't know I killed Tammy Gordon too? And Shania? Wow, she was the easiest out of the lot of them! I've never met anyone so easy to manipulate! Well, apart from you.'

Dean can't bear her gloating. 'I wasn't in my right mind. I was grieving. Surely you know what that feels like? Didn't you love your mother at all? Didn't you miss her after you killed her? You faked your qualifications, your illnesses, your feelings for me. You faked your whole life!'

This makes her mad. She screams at him over the wind. 'No! My MOTHER faked my whole life! My mother! I don't care that she lied to officials; I care that she lied to me! That woman didn't deserve to have kids in the first place!'

'Just like Tammy Gordon and Shania,' says Dean, finally understanding the link. 'Just like half the women at the prison.'

'Exactly,' she says.

'Wow. You were planning on working your way through all of them, weren't you?'

'Just enough to avoid suspicion before moving on to the next deadbeat town and the next deadbeat cop.'

Dean's glad they've managed to stop her killing anyone else. At least if she kills him it'll be clear who the real murderer is. He doesn't know what to do next. He doesn't know where Rocky's gone but he's not barking any more. All he can hope is that Rocky fetches some help, like the good police dog he could be. With a lot more training.

Lizzie's agitated, pacing back and forth. All Dean can do now is try to take her down and get the gun off her, but he knows that's going to take good timing.

'So, what now?' he asks.

'Shut up! I'm thinking.'

Dean waits for the right moment to pounce but she rounds on him unexpectedly. Pointing the gun at his head she says, 'The funny thing is, I've never killed a man before. I wonder if it will feel the same.'

Before he can move out of the way, Rocky appears from behind him and, with mouth wide open and teeth gleaming, he jumps at Lizzie's outstretched arm, biting hard. She screams in agony and as soon as Rocky's grip loosens, she turns and shoots at him. Rocky's cry is so high-pitched as the bullet hits him that Dean is too stunned to move. Lizzie's knocked over again by Rocky's weight landing on top of her so Dean pulls himself up and pushes Rocky away from her. Grabbing the gun from her hand, he turns her over onto her chest and digs his knee in her back whilst holding the gun to the back of her head. He can't bring himself to look at Rocky, who is wailing loudly. *'At least he's not silent,'* he thinks.

'You wouldn't dare shoot me. You're too weak.'

Dean digs his knee in harder, for Rocky. She's practically eating dirt she's pushed so far into the snowy soil. 'I wouldn't give you the satisfaction. There's a difference between weakness and doing what's right. You're going to be cellmates with those women you manipulated and, guess what? By then, they'll know what you did to their friend.'

Lizzie laughs. 'She was a convicted child abuser!'

'Yes, and she was serving her time, just like you did. You don't get to overrule the American judicial system and play God with people's lives, Lizzie. Most people would think you deserved to die for killing your mother.'

'Don't you dare mention my mother!' She struggles, trying to free herself.

Dean roughly pulls her arms behind her and pins them under his knee. Rocky's panting heavily now.

'Come on, Rocky. Stay with me, buddy!' He can't even comfort him with his hands because he has to hold onto

Lizzie and the gun. The bullet must've hit Rocky's chest as there's blood all down the front of him.

He slightly wags his tail when Dean speaks to him. He looks Dean in the eyes. Dean sees love in those eyes and can't stop himself from welling up as he watches Rocky suffer.

'After this we'll head to Uncle Frankie's for dinner, I promise. But you've gotta stay with me, buddy.' Tears freeze on his face as soon as they fall. Rocky whines and closes his eyes. Dean doesn't think he can handle losing anyone else. His body is shaking hard in the cold and he has no idea how he's going to get out of here.

As he contemplates forcing Lizzie to stand, Jones and the others miraculously appear out of the snow. Dean's beyond relieved, but he's too cold to say much. Marty and Steve move him off of Lizzie and drag her up.

'You'll regret this,' she says, looking at Dean as she's pulled away.

'No. You will,' says Marty.

Jones approaches Dean and covers his shoulders with a blanket. 'Are you okay?'

Dean can't speak. He takes the blanket and lays it over Rocky's fur, trying to keep him warm and comfortable for as long as possible.

Epilogue

The station is decorated with streamers and balloons for Dean's leaving party thanks to everyone chipping in. Frankie's provided a particularly unhealthy buffet spread and there's enough alcohol around the place to open a liquor store.

'So, we can't afford a new detective but we can afford all this?' says Captain Brown.

Someone switches on some bad music as Dean approaches them, looking embarrassed. He's surprised at the effort they've gone to, but he's touched too.

'Are you sure we can't persuade you to stay?' asks Jenny.

'Afraid not. This town holds too many bad memories for me right now. Plus, now the trial's over I'm free to go. I feel bad about how all this ended though. Is that crazy? Why do I feel sorry for her?'

'She has issues, Dean,' says Jones. 'It's right that she was sent to another secure hospital so don't feel bad about that. That woman is hell bent on revenge against you.'

'I hope she never gets released again,' says Jenny.

'Oh, don't worry,' says Jones. 'I'll be keeping an eye on her from afar.'

'I know what you mean though, Dean,' says Sheila. 'She was dealt some bad cards and she's one of the victims in all this too. It's not crazy to feel sorry for her, it just shows you're a good guy to feel that way after everything she's done to you.'

Dean needs time to process everything. He looks around at the liquor table. 'I thought I told you I'm hitting the road in a few minutes so I can't drink much? It's going to take me two days to drive to Vegas and I don't want to be pulled over by the cops.'

'That's okay, you don't need to get drunk. We'll do that for you,' says Marty.

Brown's not so sure. 'Officer Swan? You're on duty, so you'll be drinking lemonade.'

Marty winks as he says, 'Sure, Captain. This is lemonade.'

Everyone laughs.

'Where's Miller today? I thought he'd be at the head of the queue to wave me off,' says Dean.

'I've told him he's not welcome here today,' says Brown. 'I made him swap his day off and told him to get to the gym if he wants to keep his job.'

Dean notices out of the corner of his eye that Pete and Toad have arrived. He's pleased as he didn't think Pete would come. Pete approaches and asks if he can speak to Dean alone.

'Sure.'

They head out to the corridor.

'Look, man. I'm sorry for what went down. That woman was good at what she did; getting between us and pointing the finger of suspicion at you. We shouldn't have been fighting over her.'

Dean's already over it. 'It's fine, don't mention it. I'm just ready to put all this behind me.'

They have an awkward hug and re-join the others. Jones looks on the verge of tears, which Dean has never seen before.

Barbara hugs him for the fourth time. 'Are you really going? You're not ever coming back?'

'Of course I'll be back every now and then. This isn't the last you'll see of me. I just need a break, you know? There's been so much death here lately. The only way I can clear my head is to start afresh somewhere else. That might not be Vegas for long, but who knows?'

'Are you going to at least stay in the force?' asks Jones. 'Or was all my mentoring for nothing?'

Dean laughs. 'It wasn't for nothing. I'm not sure I want to be a cop any more though.' He had confided in Jones that he felt his attempts at playing detective were abysmal, so he's putting that dream on hold until he has more experience. 'But

I'm toying with the idea of being a private dick. You know; working undercover for people who don't know I'm terrible at solving crimes! I'd be my own boss and it would be fun.'

'Well, you're already a dick so you're halfway there!' says Marty.

As they all laugh, it's not just Sheila and Jenny with tears in their eyes. Jones hugs his wife to him as Dean starts saying his goodbyes to everyone. Eventually, those who aren't on duty follow him out to his rental car to wave him off. But before he gets in the car, he asks Brown to release Rocky from his office. They had to keep him in there when he started eating everything off the buffet table.

Within seconds, Rocky's running out of the station and towards the crowd.

'You'd never know he took a bullet to his shoulder,' says Brown in admiration. 'Are you sure you don't want me to look after him for you? You know, while you "find yourself"?'

Dean laughs as Rocky jumps into the car. He must've stopped by the buffet table on his way out as he has a mouth full of hot dogs.

'Absolutely not! All good private investigators need a dog for company.'

Dean gets into the car and finds that he can't look at his friends as he starts the engine. He desperately doesn't want to get emotional. 'Right, I guess that's it for now. Take care, everyone.'

'Enjoy Vegas!' shouts Steve.

'Let me know when we can visit, I need a tan!' jokes Marty.

They watch him as he pulls out of the parking lot, heading in the direction of his new life.

He didn't tell the others, but Dean has one more stop to make before he leaves town. He leaves Rocky in the car as he parks up in the cemetery and walks over to Linda's grave. He places some yellow roses on it before moving to John's grave, just a few yards away. Kneeling down, he touches the grey headstone.

'I miss you and I forgive you.' He looks over at Linda's grave. 'Both of you.'

After a few minutes of silence, Rocky barks from the car. Dean looks over and see's Rocky's head hanging out of the window and his tail bashing the car's interior.

'Okay, okay, I'm coming.'

As he gets back in the car and starts the engine, he ruffles Rocky's neck.

'Let's go, boy.'

Thank you!

Dear Reader,

Thank you for reading my first book from Ruby Fiction. *Who Cares If They Die* is the first in a series of crime novels featuring Dean Matheson and his lovable Rottweiler, Rocky. I've never written a canine character before and sometimes I have to stop myself writing more about Rocky than Dean because he demands so much attention! But Dean is the real main character and we will follow him on his attempts to become the homicide detective he deserves to be.

I really hope you enjoyed spending time in Maple Valley and if you did, please consider leaving a review, it would be much appreciated. Also, do get in touch with me (via Twitter, Goodreads or my Facebook Author page) to let me know what you'd like from the series going forward. If you want to know what Dean does next, the sequel to this book – *Where the Snow Bleeds* – is now available!

Thank you again.

Wendy

About the Author

Wendy is a former Coroner's Assistant turned crime writer who lives in the UK with her husband and 3 rescue cats.

Who Cares If They Die and *Where the Snow Bleeds* are the first two books in the Dean Matheson series, with more on the way. As well as her crime thriller series, Wendy has written a YA crime novel – *The Girl Who Died* – and she has several short stories published in UK and US anthologies. She has also been shortlisted and longlisted for various competitions, including the Mslexia Novel Competition.

For behind the scenes gossip and updates on her books (or photos of her cats), follow her on social media!

For more on Wendy visit:
Website: www.wendydranfield.co.uk
Twitter: @WendyDranfield
Facebook: Wendy Dranfield Author
YouTube: Wendy Dranfield Author

More Ruby Fiction

From Wendy Dranfield

Where the Snow Bleeds

"You want to know what I've learnt after living in Lone Creek all my life? I know the snow bleeds here …"

Former police officer Dean Matheson has been playing it safe since the case that cost him almost everything. But working as a PI doesn't quite cut it, that is until a British woman walks into his office with a job that Dean can't resist.

The woman's daughter, Hannah Walker, and her friend Jodie have gone missing whilst working at a ski resort in Colorado. It's clear there's something sinister about the girls' disappearance, but then why are the local police department being so unhelpful?

So begins Dean's journey to Lone Creek on the trail of the missing girls – and he'll soon find out that in Lone Creek, everyone has something to hide.

Visit www.rubyfiction.com for details.

Preview
Where the Snow Bleeds

by Wendy Dranfield

CHAPTER ONE

Las Vegas, Nevada

'Stop! Turn around or I'll shoot! I won't ask you again.'

Terry Andrews finally stops running. He's cornered at the end of the alleyway. He slowly turns around and grins.

'Come on! Are you seriously going to shoot me over a goddamn poodle?'

Dean Matheson smiles back at him. 'Try me.'

Rocky must smell defeat because he runs away from Dean's side and up to the poodle thief. Terry immediately tries backing away from the huge Rottweiler as Rocky starts barking menacingly, just as Dean taught him.

'Alright, alright! Take the stupid dog!' He throws the tiny poodle at Rocky in an attempt to block an attack and then runs away, fast.

They let him run. The fuzzy, prize-winning poodle seeks solace under Rocky's thick black and tan chest, as he licks her head. His tongue is so huge he almost pushes her over with each lick.

Dean holsters his gun and sighs. 'Is this what our life has come to, Rocky? Catching dog thieves?' Rocky wags his tail in response. He's having fun at least. 'Come on, you two,' he says, as he picks up the flowery-smelling poodle. He notices her toenails are painted pink. She's so nervous she trembles against his chest. 'Let's get you home to your crazy mother.'

When Dean arrives back at his small office behind the Vegas strip, it's empty apart from Marilyn Rose, his boss and fellow private investigator.

'How's your day been?' asks Marilyn. She doesn't look up from her computer screen.

'Pretty slow. All I've done is rescue dogs again today. Although having said that, Mrs Cooper was so grateful to get Lola back she gave me a hundred-dollar tip. There's certainly money in this game.'

Marilyn laughs. Which makes her cough, violently. Having been a chain smoker all her life, Dean knows she's reluctant to give up now.

'What are you watching?' he asks.

She turns her screen to face him. 'David Hunter getting arrested for killing his wife.'

Dean sits down. David Hunter is someone Marilyn clashed with a few months back. Running this business regularly puts her in difficult situations, but nothing will ever compare to her own life.

Not long after she took him on, she confided in Dean how she had suffered years of domestic violence at the hands of a husband she never wanted. She ended up killing him. She was able to claim self-defence because he was holding a gun to her head at the time, in a busy grocery store. She'd told Dean that she had always known that day would come eventually, so she always carried a knife on her. When her husband, Bob, found her in the bread aisle of the grocery store that day, after she'd told him she was leaving his lousy ass for good, he pulled his gun on her. Luckily for Marilyn, he was high on meth, which slowed his reactions, so when a customer distracted him by screaming, Marilyn reacted by pulling her knife and stabbing him straight through his heart without any hesitation.

'It went in like a knife through cake,' she'd said. 'Probably because he didn't have a heart there in the first place.'

Once she was cleared of any criminal offences ('Luckily the store had CCTV, otherwise I'd be in the pen right now!') she decided to live her life as the woman she was meant to be. She moved away from her small town in North Dakota to come here to Vegas, hoping she could make some money to support herself. She changed her name from Susan to Marilyn, after her favourite actress, Marilyn Monroe, and found love with a woman, Martha. She took shooting lessons and started this small PI business. Dean's currently her only employee and she treats him as her partner. She always says he's way more trustworthy than her previous staff.

Dean reads through the messages Marilyn's left on his desk. Three clients want updates on their missing pets. He throws the slips of paper back on his desk and runs his hand through his thick black hair.

'How do you do it, Marilyn? How do you deal with crap like this—' he gestures to his messages '—every day when there's so much real crime going on all around us? We're in sin city! My life should be much more exciting than this.'

This isn't the first time they've had this conversation. Dean has been sharing this Las Vegas office with her for a year now, ever since he left New Hampshire after the year-long trial of his wife's killer. He asks Marilyn the same question at least once a month.

'Listen to me, Dean. You're meant to be a cop, not a private eye,' she says. 'Get yourself back on the government payroll and go catch the bad guys. Leave it to me to find the stolen dogs, cheating husbands and the prostitutes who've rolled their clients. That's enough drama for me, but you? You're too good for this racket.'

He leans back in his chair as he listens to her. The problem is, he doesn't know whether he *is* too good for this racket. Not after everything that happened back home two years ago.

'You're handy to me for the legal stuff,' she continues. 'I mean, thanks to your law enforcement background I don't have to Google every goddamned law and regulation any more. But, just remember kiddo; no-one's irreplaceable. Go and do what you need to do. Sure, I'd miss gazing into your deep blue eyes and staring at your rapidly increasing biceps, but don't tell Martha that.' She winks at him.

'You'd never get with a man now, would you?' he asks, surprised.

'Hey, if you were a few years younger you'd be fighting me off.'

'You mean older, right?'

'Nope.'

Dean laughs, assuming she's joking. He knows she steers clear of men whenever possible, and with good reason. There are a lot of angry wife-beaters out there who would love to catch her off guard and take revenge for her daring to help their spouses escape. She's a petite woman who likes showing off her curves in skin-tight leopard-print dresses, even though Dean suspects she's in her early sixties, give or take a few years. The biggest thing about her is her Dolly Parton wig. He wasn't surprised to learn she carries the infamous knife in her left boot and a gun in her belt.

A shadow crosses their front window. A man with an unkempt appearance is staring in through the grimy glass. He bangs on the window, looking angry.

'You better watch yourself, lady!' he shouts. 'I haven't forgotten about you!'

Dean looks at Marilyn who rolls her eyes.

'Not him again.' She stands up, pulls her gun out of her belt and waves it at him. 'Piss off back to Stupid-Ville, you moron!'

When the man sees her walking towards him with her gun out, he runs.

Dean used to be shocked by this kind of behaviour, but not any more.

'Another fan?' he asks as she returns to her desk.

She picks up a cigarette. 'He's annoyed he doesn't have a wife to beat any more. Loser.'

Rocky looks up as Dean gets out of his chair to grab himself a drink; an iced tea from the fridge they keep beneath the messy, unattended reception desk. 'Want a Coke?'

'Always,' she says.

'You need to switch to the diet version you know. This stuff will rot your teeth.'

'No, it won't. They're all fake. Which means they're stronger than real ones and they don't stain. I treated myself one Christmas.'

Dean laughs. 'I should've known.'

As he closes the fridge, the bell over the front door jingles and they both immediately look up. A short white woman with dishevelled brown curly hair and bright red cheeks walks in, sweating. She leans heavily on the front door while she tries to catch her breath. Dean's heart sinks. He knows exactly what she's going to say before she says it.

'It's my Tinkerbell! She's been stolen! And the police don't care!' She starts wailing so dramatically that Rocky barks, as if he's telling her to shut up.

Dean leads her to a seat and asks, hopefully, 'Is Tinkerbell your daughter?'

'Yes! Yes, she is! She's *like* my daughter! She's my precious purebred Bichon Frise. I can't live without her and she definitely can't survive without me! We spend twenty-four hours a day together.'

Dean looks at Marilyn who's struggling to contain her laughter. Not at poor stolen Tinkerbell or her mother, just at Dean's bad run of cases.

'You finish up for the day,' she says to him. 'It's my turn to take on the dog thieves.'

He doesn't need to be told twice. Feeling like he's dodged a bullet he grabs his keys and heads for the door.

'Don't forget your appointment at the V-E-T.'

He looks at his watch. They were meant to be there five minutes ago.

'Shit. Thanks for reminding me.'

He's been noticing that Rocky has slowed down lately, compared to what he was like when he first rescued him. That was two years ago now, before Beth Smith's murder trial and their new life in Vegas. Back then Rocky was bouncy and fast, but Marilyn thought she saw him dragging his leg recently, so she suggested that Dean took him to see the vet. Somehow, Rocky must've known what they were talking about because he hid under their reception desk. Ever since then they'd had to spell the vet word.

'Come on, Rocky.'

Rocky's obviously suspicious, as he hesitates to get up, but eventually he accepts the chicken treat Dean's holding out. With the leash clipped to his collar they leave to walk to the nearby vet's surgery.

Rocky clearly smells the unfamiliar scent of strong disinfectant as soon as they enter the sparse reception area because he immediately tries to back out the door. But Dean's fast and manages to close it behind him before Rocky can escape. The cute brunette receptionist smiles sympathetically as they're called into a small examination room. The vet, a tall man called Greg, actually tries to lift Rocky onto his examination table. Dean can't believe it when he succeeds. 'That dog weighs more than me!' he marvels.

Greg has a deep, hearty laugh. 'I bet I could get you

on here too then. So, what's wrong with this magnificent beast?' He starts stroking and prodding Rocky.

Before Dean can explain, Greg hits a sensitive spot when he prods the dog's chest. Rocky winces and howls gently. Then he licks Greg's hand to let him know it's not his fault. Greg wasn't to know.

'That area's a bit tender,' says Dean. 'He took a bullet in his shoulder two years ago. They got it out at the time and it seems to have healed well but he doesn't like anyone to touch it.'

Greg looks shocked. 'You were shot! Who would do such a thing to you?' He turns to Dean. 'What are you, some kind of drug dealer? How could you let this happen to your dog?'

Dean's surprised. 'What? No! Of course not. I was a police officer at the time. Rocky took a bullet for me. He almost died.'

Greg smiles broadly and pats Rocky's large head. 'So, you're Rocky the Rockstar! What a good boy.' He retrieves a rawhide treat from the pocket of his white coat and gives it to the dog.

Dean wonders how Rocky isn't obese with all the treats he gets, although he has put on a bit of weight recently.

'Is that why you're here? Is it acting up?'

'I don't think so. He's just slowed down a lot recently. And we think he may be dragging his left leg occasionally. He just doesn't seem as fast as he was.'

Greg examines his hips while Rocky slobbers the rawhide. 'Well he's an old dog. What do you expect? We all slow down as we age.'

Dean's confused. 'Old? What do you mean? He's still young. I got him when he was five or six and that was only two years ago.'

'Do you know he was definitely five or six, or is that a guess?'

'Well, it's a guess but he was so healthy and fast. I knew him as a puppy, and I'm pretty sure he couldn't have been older than six when he came to live with me.'

Greg looks at Rocky's teeth and shines a light in his eyes and ears. 'I would age this dog as eight, maybe eight and a half, years old. Which would fit with what you're saying if you've had him for two years.'

'So that's still young then?'

Shaking his head, Greg explains, 'No. Rotties have a lifespan of about nine to ten years, maybe up to eleven years at a push, and only if they've led a sedentary life.'

Dean looks at Rocky. He's shocked. He's never owned a dog before so he had no idea they lived such short lives. His childhood cat lived to twenty-two. He just assumed Rocky would be with him for a long time yet.

'Don't look so devastated,' says Greg. 'If Rocky's nearer eight than nine you still have a good two years left of him. If you stop getting him shot, that is.'

Dean has to swallow his shock. This isn't what he expected to hear today.

'I'd say he has some ailments though. Maybe arthritis. I'll take some blood this time to rule out a few other things first. He'll probably need to come back for an X-ray, depending on the results.'

Rocky doesn't flinch while the blood is drawn. He finishes the rawhide and sits up, wagging his tail and ready for action. Greg picks him up like it's no effort at all and gently places him back on the floor while Rocky licks his ear.

'He's got a great temperament. And I'm glad to see you kept his tail.'

Dean's too stunned to say much. He thanks Greg, settles the bill with the receptionist and walks Rocky back to the office.

Marilyn's still busy with Tinkerbell's mother so she doesn't pay him any attention. Once Rocky's settled on his large blanket, Dean heads back out, alone. He needs a drink.

Available to purchase as an eBook on all platforms.
More details at www.rubyfiction.com

Stories that inspire emotions

Introducing Ruby Fiction

Ruby Fiction is an imprint of Choc Lit Publishing.
We're an independent publisher creating
a delicious selection of fiction.

See our selection here:
www.rubyfiction.com

Ruby Fiction brings you stories that inspire emotions.

We'd love to hear how you enjoyed *Who Cares if They Die*.
Please visit www.rubyfiction.com and give your feedback
or leave a review where you purchased this novel.

Ruby novels are selected by genuine readers like yourself.
We only publish stories our Tasting Panel want to see in
print. Our reviews and awards speak for themselves.

Could you be a Star Selector and join our Tasting Panel?
Would you like to play a role in choosing which novels
we decide to publish? Do you enjoy reading women's
fiction? Then you could be perfect for our Tasting Panel.

Visit here for more details ...
www.choc-lit.com/join-the-choc-lit-tasting-panel

Keep in touch:
Sign up for our monthly newsletter Spread for all the latest
news and offers: www.spread.choc-lit.com. Follow us on
Twitter: @RubyFiction and Facebook: RubyFiction.

Stories that inspire emotions!